# THE RAW MAN

George Makana Clark was raised in Rhodesia. He currently lives in Milwaukee, Wisconsin, with his wife and daughter.

GEORGE MAKANA CLARK

# The Raw Man

VINTAGE BOOKS
London

Published by Vintage 2013

2 4 6 8 10 9 7 5 3 1



First published in Great Britain in 2011 by Jonathan Cape

Vintage
Random House, 20 Vauxhall Bridge Road,
London SW1V 2SA

www.vintage-books.co.uk

Addresses for companies within The Random House Group Limited can be found at: www.randomhouse.co.uk/offices.htm

The Random House Group Limited Reg. No. 954009

A CIP catalogue record for this book is available from the British Library

ISBN 9780099548782

The Random House Group Limited supports the Forest Stewardship Council® (FSC®), the leading international forest-certification organisation. Our books carrying the FSC label are printed on FSC®-certified paper. FSC is the only forest-certification scheme supported by the leading environmental organisations, including Greenpeace. Our paper procurement policy can be found at www.randomhouse.co.uk/environment

Typeset in Adobe Garamond by Palimpsest Book Production Limited, Falkirk, Stirlingshire

Printed and bound by Clays Ltd, St Ives PLC

*Just for Rikki*

# *Prologue: The Owner of the Story*

April, 2011

I BUILT MY HOUSE FROM BORROWED MEMORY, EVERY detail as it was described by Gordon long ago in the complete darkness, three miles beneath the earth. The roof is not iron but rather wood carved to appear corrugated. The sills, clapboards, jambs, and eaves are hewn by hand, doors and shutters hung on dowels, boards fitted tongue and groove. I don't remember when I learned to work wood.

If you pass through each of the twelve interior doors, you'll find yourself back where you began. I live here alone with Gordon's story-ghost. It's naught: a draught to swirl the leaves on a windless day, to stir the chimes that hang from the verandah. Whenever it passes through me, I smell peaberry coffee. Hear a lullaby. Imagine a garden.

The story-ghost inhabits the study, surrounded by empty bookshelves, waiting for Gordon's daughter to return to the glen. She would be well into her thirties now, a blood reader like her father perhaps.

Three decades have passed since Gordon's spirit was harvested into the neverness of death. His grave lies in the shadow of the thorn tree where his umbilical cord was buried. The corpse whispered to me as I arranged it in a crouching position, and the earth shuddered and loosened as it received the owner of the story. I strewed thorns to discourage the hyenas, shaved my skull, beat the grave, though there was nothing to inherit, save these memories that swarm in my head like bees.

Stories want to circle back on themselves. Blame it on the Weaver of the Universe, the Teller of All Existence. Here's how Gordon died all those years ago. *Let it come. Let it go.*

It begins with a homeward journey. His legs carried him hundreds of miles over a drought-blasted landscape, his blood sluggish with poison. There was no food. We ate busika fruit blended with ash to keep it down, and our tongues turned black with hunger. I chased butterflies and stuffed them into my mouth.

When we came at last to the glen, Gordon sat down on the granite mountainside, his back against the trunk of the ancient mahogany tree where his daughter had been conceived. He watched the moon turn for the last time over the glen.

Gordon came down from the mountain with the dawn, but the land no longer recognised him. The long grass had swallowed Three Man Road. The ancient orchard that once surrounded the abandoned mission had been clear-cut and sawn into coffin wood. The river of his baptisms had run dry, and all the water drawers had gone on, bearing their creation stories into the next world.

The foundation of the bungalow was covered with blown sand, the garden a brake of witchweed. A tribe of baboons watched as Gordon scrabbled at the bleached earth, trying to excavate a bit of wind chime, the binder rings from a ledger book, a heart-shaped locket warped by heat, some evidence to support the narrative of his existence. His fingertips rubbed off against the hardpan, erasing his prints. He tried to rise but was not able.

I made a mercy cut at the base of Gordon's neck and a small fountain rose – venous pink, then arterial blue – the blood candescent in the sunlight.

This is what Gordon saw as he died, so says the story-ghost, if it can be believed:

*Water commences to flow from the jumble of crumbled concrete and exposed copper tubing that had once been the garden's fountain. The sky brightens over the mountain, softening the glen's horizon, and the world of the living falls away like mist. The bungalow and garden rise up before Gordon, untouched by fire and neglect. The canaries return, lighting in the flame trees where they warble their getting-ready-to-sleep song.*

*Gordon steps through the kitchen door to find Mahulda drinking her peaberry coffee. 'A song, a song!' he wheedles, his ginger hair aflame in the sun that streams in through the window.*

*'A song,' Mahulda agrees, because she loves this child better than her own eyes, and even in death she can refuse him nothing.*

*Outside, Timothy prunes and shapes the bougainvillea, while Mahulda sings the same lullaby that she sang to Gordon on the evening of his birth:* Oh what would you do if the cows ate the clover? *Timothy stands erect in his garden, his back unbroken, watches them through the window glass.* What would I do but to set it again? *His shears snip at the bougainvillea,* shick shick shick, *in time with the music.* And what would you do if the kettle boiled over? *The canaries fall silent, listening.* What would I do but to fill it again? *All the timepieces in the house sound the hour – first the stainless steel clock over the stove,* a rout da da doubt da da diddly da dum, *then the tidewatch that lies face up in its peachwood case in the study,* a rout da da doubt da da diddly da dum, *the brass chronometer that hangs beneath a glass dome on the night stand,* da diddly da dee da dee da dum, *the grandmother in its spruce cabinet,* da diddly da dee da diddly da dum, *their hands spinning backwards.*

## *The Earthworks of the Universe*

October, 1978

IT BEGINS WITH SILVER TANKS FILLED WITH LIQUID FIRE falling from the sky. This is the last thing Sergeant Gordon told us he could remember about the attack. The rest we imagine.

The white light of dawn penetrated Sergeant Gordon's eyelids and he woke with the smell of petrol and plastic and carbonised flesh in his nostrils. The river was dry and still, except for the current of scavenger birds that hobbled over its grey, cracked bed, picking the bones of Sergeant Gordon's comrades for sinew and marrow. The ground still burned in wide swaths, though there was nothing left for the fire to consume.

If a bomber pilot were to have looked down from a great height onto the northern frontier of Rhodesia in this, the nation's dying year, he would have seen the shadow of his warplane superimposed over many such patches of scorched and burning earth. Sergeant Gordon's legs folded when he tried to rise from the mud. His patrol had been knocked off the board during the night and he reckoned it would be midday before anyone realised and notified the mob from Combat Search and Rescue. It was the morning of his funeral.

The sound of an automobile engine floated in the dusty haze. Sergeant Gordon raised his head to see an ancient British Ford racing towards him. Thirst and concussion had warped his reality, and he imagined this to be the vehicle dispatched by God to fetch him to the afterlife.

Guerrilla soldiers with rocket launchers and AK-47s rode the running boards. Sergeant Gordon let his head drop, unable to bear its weight. The car slewed to a halt and several hands seized his arms and legs. There were words painted in red across the door: *The Sanctifying Fire.* The soldiers bound Sergeant Gordon to the bonnet like a game animal and drove north towards the Zambezi.

His skull struck steel as the car bounced over rugged terrain. As Sergeant Gordon closed his eyes to the wind, heat and bugs, he was a teenager again, riding in the back of a lorry, trying to dodge his national service by hitch-hiking out of the country. Or maybe I was the teenager, and Sergeant Gordon stole this fragment of memory and made it his own.

When they reached the river, the men untied their prisoner so he could drink from the shoals. More soldiers on the far bank heaved in unison on a rope that spanned its width, dragging a ferry across the current. As it drew nearer, Sergeant Gordon could see the craft was a platform of rough-hewn ebony lashed onto a bed of inflated lorry tyres. Bars of copper were stacked in the centre of the deck, causing the ferry to ride low in the water. Sergeant Gordon slumped against the automobile, his stomach knotted from drinking too fast. The cloth lining of the Ford's roof hung in tatters. The backseat had been removed to permit boxes of ammunition and landmines, open cartons of propaganda leaflets, and piles of uniforms.

A step van drove out from a stand of acacias and parked beside them. The sign on its side panel read:

Hawkings and Son
Copper Processing and Manufacturing, Ltd.
Heat Exchangers/Radiators/Tubing.

Two men in coveralls climbed down from the cab, one a younger version of the other. They stared out at the approaching ferry. 'The shipment was supposed to be ready to load,' the older one said.

'You see they are coming,' one of the soldiers answered.

Hawkings glanced at his watch. 'Meanwhile we're standing here with our asses hanging in the wind, waiting for the police.' The son looked at Sergeant Gordon without curiosity.

The ferry landed and the commander, a one-eyed man with an enormous, braided white beard, stepped off into the ankle-deep water. He wore twin holstered pistols and bandoleers. Two keys hung from his waist; one brass, the other steel. Fresh scar tissue lined his empty eye socket. 'Hurry, now now!' he barked, and his men formed a chain to load the copper bars into the van. When the transfer was complete, Hawkings counted out several bills into the bearded man's hand.

The old soldier frowned at the money. 'This is not what we agreed.'

'Take your bloody copper back then,' Hawkings said. The son drew a pistol from his waistband and placed it on the fender of the van.

The men looked to their leader. 'Next week when you come,' he said finally, 'you bring me the rest of my money.'

Hawkings climbed into the van. 'I don't even know if I'll be in business next week.'

The coppermongers drove off, the soldiers pushed the old Ford onto the deck, and the ferry began its return trip, listing beneath the weight of the car. Rhodesia shrank on the horizon of the river. Someone – a mission boy probably – called out, '*In Exitu Israel de Aegypto*' in a clear tenor. The others stamped on the ebony deck and sang the response as they heaved on the rope.

A lorry waited on the other side of the river, engine idling. The ferry lurched when it ran aground. The men pushed the car onto the bank, retied their captive to the bonnet, and climbed back onto the running boards. They followed the lorry along a road that was little more than a footpath, west-by-northwest into Zambia.

The rains came that afternoon and the ruts in the unsurfaced road filled with brown water that splashed over the grille into Sergeant Gordon's nose and mouth. This was a common story. Most of us came to the mine in a similar manner.

The moon rose and fell unseen behind a bank of storm clouds as the two vehicles sped through the torrent. Sergeant Gordon turned his face away from the sky to keep from drowning. Lightning struck the trees on either side of the road, close enough to charge the air and leave a metallic taste in his mouth. At some point during that jarring, deafening night, Sergeant Gordon looked at the soldier foremost on the running board. The guerrilla returned his stare, and together they broke into laughter, bawling over the roar of rain, wind and pistons.

When the ancient Ford finally came to a stop, Sergeant Gordon could see the outline of a mountainous slagheap. More soldiers fired rockets at a pile of mined ore nearby, shattering it into smaller pieces. Young women shovelled the rubble into ceramic smelters that were superheated over charcoal. Canvas tarps kept the rain from dousing the fires. Older women wore leather aprons and asbestos mittens as they fanned the charcoal with great goatskin bellows. An ancient diesel generator chugged noisily and blew black smoke, its engine threatening to die, then catching again as an old woman fiddled with the machine. The scene alternated between the dim illumination of the smelting fires and brilliant flashes of lightning.

The soldiers stripped Sergeant Gordon and squabbled over his boots, lighter and jacket. The commander stood before an outcrop of sandstone. Rainwater fell in streams from the braids in his beard. The solitary eye studied Sergeant Gordon for a long moment.

'Time for your funeral,' the commander said. He led Sergeant Gordon to the top of the outcrop. 'Beneath us is your burial place.' He helped his prisoner pile stones to mark the grave and together they beat a stick into the sandstone roof of the copper mine so that, when Sergeant Gordon died, his soul might escape back up into the world. Hundreds of cairns dotted the summit.

'Mwari, God of the Universe, please take this boy's spirit and leave his empty body to its suffering.' The guerrilla's white beard shone a dirty orange in the light from the smelting fires.

After the grave was beaten, the commander led Sergeant Gordon into a fissure in the sandstone where they stood before a gate of solid branded copper. He removed the two keys from his pistol belt, turned them both in the lock at once, and pushed the gate open in a screech of unoiled hinges. They stepped through the portal and the gate slammed behind, shutting out the surface world. Sergeant Gordon found himself in the mouth of a mineshaft. The walls curved into the ceiling and floor seamlessly, as if the shaft had been dug into the earth by some great burrowing insect. Humming lights strung from copper wires dimmed and brightened.

The commander led Sergeant Gordon around a red circle painted on the floor of the shaft. 'Landmines,' he explained. 'The East Germans brought us thousands. You don't want to walk here after the lights are put out.'

Pipes hissed air overhead. Copper dust muted all sound and light. A maze of galleries radiated from the shaft, following the ore, their cuprite walls dark and purplish. Each gallery they passed was marked with a chalk letter.

During the descent Sergeant Gordon's breathing grew more difficult, as though his lungs were labouring beneath the increasing weight of rock separating him from the earth's surface. The commander drew forth his pistols and looked at his captive meaningfully. 'I apologise. Prisoners go easy in the open air. It's only down here that they make trouble.' The belts of ammunition lay flat against his chest.

His training in the Rhodesian Security Forces had

prepared Sergeant Gordon to die. But not like this, deep beneath the earth in the suffocating gloom. He tried to keep his voice level. 'Can't you let me go?'

'Sadly, no. My men would lose respect for me. Then we'd both be working in this mine.'

An armed soldier passed. The commander returned his salute.

'You call yourself freedom fighters,' Sergeant Gordon said, his voice rising.

'This war is over. I'm a businessman.'

As they continued their descent, the one-eyed guerrilla talked about the house he would buy in one of the upmarket whites-only suburbs of Umtali, and the bride price he would pay for a young wife to replace the one he'd buried in the trust land. 'I used to call myself "Comrade Winter Palace" after the final battle of the Russian Revolution,' he said. 'We all took new names to protect our villages from reprisal. But with the war almost over, I am Winston Chaminuka.' He said the name slowly, as if he were still getting used to it. 'Winston, for Churchill. Chaminuka, for the Shona prophet who foretold the coming of the Europeans – and also their defeat. Now there's a name to vote for when we have free elections, hey?'

From time to time, children passed with baskets of ore tied to their backs. Winston Chaminuka fell silent. They skirted the red circles that marked the landmines, each step slower than the last, as if gravity had an inverse pull so deep below the surface.

Perhaps an hour passed before they stopped at the entrance to a gallery marked with the letter *Z*. Winston Chaminuka thumbed the safeties on his drawn pistols. His empty eye socket twitched. 'Gallery Zed. You work here.' The remaining eye peered nervously into the gloom, as if it expected a demon to come charging out. The commander checked his watch. There was a red star on its face, Soviet Army issue. 'Four hours go quickly. I must return to the surface before the lights go dark. Find the abbot. He'll sort you out. Stay well.' Winston Chaminuka backed up the shaft a few metres, turned, and scurried away, his step lighter now that he was returning to the surface.

Alone, Sergeant Gordon felt the full weight of the rock above. The walls vibrated. He entered Gallery Zed, his hair brushing the rock ceiling. Rough-cut logs braced the gallery at uneven intervals. He came to a stope dug into the wall at a sharp downward angle, its low ceiling supported by dark blue pillars of un-excavated azurite. Despite the intense underground heat, a group of naked, copper-dusted men stood around a bonfire of logs similar to the ones which buttressed the gallery. The stope emitted the off smell of an inexpertly butchered game animal, roasted flesh tainted by glandular secretions. Two of the copper men turned a large, twisted creature suspended on a spit over the flames.

Another who wore only a cowl and sandals addressed the assembly: 'Let this flesh sustain us until the day Christ tears down the gate of this abyss and delivers us from our abandonment.'

Sergeant Gordon drew close enough to see what animal they were roasting this deep inside the earth. It was a man.

* * *

When Sergeant Gordon was still a child, a servant caught him setting fire to a beetle. 'All the bad things you do,' she warned him, 'will come back on you.' The memory of this would return to Sergeant Gordon here, in this blasted place, three miles beneath the world.

His saliva turned to paste as he looked upon the copper men and their dinner. The speaker stepped forward. He'd once been stout. Slack skin now hung over his wiry muscles, the belly folds almost obscuring his uncircumcised penis. Perhaps as a joke, his captors had let him keep a cowl and sandals.

'I am the abbot.' He picked up a small shard of ore. 'Give me your hand, demon.' He carved these characters into Sergeant Gordon's forearm: *Z-10*. 'Down here, your name is Zed Stroke One Ought,' the abbot said, his voice raspy. 'Look upon your namesake and predecessor.'

He pointed to the man on the spit. 'You'll work his stope.' The roasting man's eyes were closed, his charred face reposed. 'No worries, he was dead before we started cooking him. God may have abandoned us, but we're not heathens.' The abbot narrowed his eyes and put his face close to Sergeant Gordon's. 'Tell us, demon, what have you done?'

'How's that?'

'You must've committed some hateful offence for God to send you here. Tell us and be done with it.' All new arrivals to Gallery Zed had confessed to the abbot, though with time, fatigue and misery we came to forget our trespasses in the surface world, and the punishment of our existence ceased to have meaning.

'Why should I?' Sergeant Gordon asked the abbot. 'What did you do to get sent here?'

The lights sputtered, grew bright. I stopped turning the spit. The others looked as if lightning might travel through the earth and strike Sergeant Gordon dead. Though few memories of surface life persisted, the monk had long ago convinced us that we deserved this place.

The abbot worked his jaw as he stared up at the rock ceiling. 'I always strove to live a blameless life. In my particular case, God made a mistake.'

On the earth's surface, the old woman switched off the generator, plunging the mine into darkness.

* * *

The lights flickered on four hours later, the bellows forced air from the surface, and we crowded around a tiny vent in the pipe and breathed.

We worked the stopes in two-man excavation teams. Sergeant Gordon's workmate introduced himself as Zed Stroke Ought Nine. As they struck the rock walls with their picks, Zed Stroke Ought Nine questioned Sergeant Gordon about his captors. 'Does a man with only one eye lead them still?' Sergeant Gordon nodded, already breathless from the work.

'I took that eye from him,' Ought Nine said with satisfaction, 'on the day when he challenged me for the leadership of my cadre. But someone hit me on the back of my head with a rifle, and so you see, comrade, here I am.'

Sergeant Gordon lowered his pick. 'You used to lead the freedom fighters?'

Ought Nine spat. 'Freedom fighters? Look at this place.'

'Their commander calls himself a businessman,' Sergeant Gordon said.

'You can call him a dead man if ever I get out of this hole. He was too afraid to kill me when he had the opportunity. Now he urinates in his trousers when he comes near Gallery Zed.' Ought Nine struck his pick against the rock wall with increased fury. 'When he and I trained together in Algeria, they taught us that property is theft. But I keep one possession.' Ought Nine stopped digging.

'Let me show you something you've never seen before, leastways not like this.'

Sergeant Gordon followed him to the entrance of Gallery Zed, where Ought Nine reached his hand into a recess in the rock. 'I held onto this, comrade, even as my men dragged me unconscious down into the copper mine.' He opened his hand to reveal a withered object the size of a date. It was Winston Chaminuka's eye.

Sergeant Gordon and Ought Nine returned to their stope and put their backs to their work, throwing their weight behind each swing. The picks sparked against ore and tiny shards stung their faces. Sergeant Gordon felt blisters rising on his palms, like all of us when we first arrived, his muscles sluggish with fatigue and pain. 'Welcome to the proletariat, comrade,' Ought Nine said, grinning. 'Your back will grow strong and your hands will become rough, but always the aching gets worse.'

'Be silent, demons!' The abbot had come round to check on their progress. 'Save your breath for digging.'

Ought Nine gripped his pick like a war club and the abbot retreated back up the stope. 'Don't listen to all his talk about God and punishment,' Ought Nine said when they were alone again. 'The church is a tool of the oppressor.'

The blisters on Sergeant Gordon's hands burst and the pick handle became sticky. The old woman shut down the generator and we lay down where we stood in the subterranean darkness. Sergeant Gordon stared at the starless rock sky, willing his lungs to breathe. There rose a low keening sound that grew into a scream, which begat other screams, and Sergeant Gordon joined his voice to ours.

According to Ought Nine, the copper mine was as old as Jesus Christ, deceiver of the proletariat. The former guerrilla leader had rediscovered the shaft accidentally when he set up headquarters in the sandstone fissure.

There were seventeen prisoners in Gallery Zed, eight pairs of labourers supervised by the abbot. We were captured members of the Rhodesian Security Forces, farmers, civil servants, fishermen, anyone the renegade guerrillas could press-gang. Obscured beneath a layer of copper dust, race and ancestry meant nothing. The ore was extracted under the same primitive conditions as when the mine had begun, the only way to make it pay after the collapse of the copper market. We stooped naked beneath the low ceilings of the rimose stopes, bent double in humility as we drove towards the centre of the earth at the rate of a half metre a day.

A day began with the starting of the diesel generator and ended four hours later when it was switched off. During these periods of light, an armed soldier roamed the main shaft with orders to shoot prisoners on sight.

Night fell instantly over the copper mine, four hours of perfect darkness.

One such night, Sergeant Gordon tried to feel his way through the labyrinth of galleries in hopes of reaching the surface. He marked the walls with a piece of sandstone so that if he failed to escape, he might find his way back to his stope. He blundered through the underground night, cracking his head on the low ceilings, walking face-first into the rock walls. Despite the ascending grade, it seemed as if he was travelling downwards into the blackness. It was here, he told us later, that he felt a dreadful presence in the darkness, and though he willed himself to move, he remained frozen in fear.

The lights came on with Sergeant Gordon's foot poised over a red circle of paint that marked the location of one of the surplus landmines. He followed his sandstone marks back to Gallery Zed before the guard came down. It took Sergeant Gordon only minutes to cover the same distance he had travelled in four hours of darkness. He promised himself he would try again, but his resolve failed when next the lights went out, leaving him to stare into blackness like one of the sightless fish that inhabit the ocean's bottom.

Asleep, Sergeant Gordon dreamed of his life on the surface. Awake, he imagined each detail and aspect of his past as he laboured in the copper-rich stopes. In time he could no longer separate waking and sleeping, imagining and dreaming.

The copper dust stained everything reddish brown. It

found its way into our eyes, blinding us, coating our sinuses and throats. We suffered from metal-fume sickness, endured waves of fever and chills.

Sergeant Gordon's saliva became thick, and though he spat forcefully, it only dribbled down his chin. His chest grew tight and he learned to take shallow breaths to avoid violent coughing fits.

Sometimes, when the lights came on, one of our number would fail to rise from his four-hour slumber and we would find the dead man curled up amid the spalls, defeated by the heat and dust. On such occasions, the abbot would order us to build a bonfire of wooden supports, and we would consume the fallen copper man.

We were given just enough sustenance to keep working, but not so much that we would have the energy to revolt. We ate corms and roots gathered by the smelting women, and sometimes rotted fish that the children collected along the banks of the poisoned stream running above the mine. The amount of food allowed us was directly proportional to the number of baskets of ore we sent up to the surface on the children's backs. The women drew our drinking water from the runoff. It was hot and tasted faintly of arsenic. We trapped and ate tunnel rats, chewed bark from the few remaining logs that braced the gallery, ate our dead.

When the rock was too hard and our picks and shovels could not extract enough ore to barter for food, the abbot directed us to remove the logs that supported the gallery, pile them against the stopes, and set fire to them. Then we poured water on the heated rock wall and it shattered with the sudden drop in temperature, enabling us to recover the copper. We pushed wheelbarrows of raw ore through the narrow galleries to the shaft where the children waited with their baskets. Nine pounds in ten were waste. The guerrillas had long stopped sending down logs to buttress the gallery and stopes. They needed all the timber to make charcoal for the smelters. As we progressed deeper into the earth, we stopped to make safe the ceilings, using our picks to pull down loose shards from the newly excavated stopes.

One day a concussion moved through Gallery Zed, followed by a choking cloud of dust. We dropped our picks and shovels and ran towards the collapsed stope where the abbot's bare feet protruded from the malachite rubble, his sandals kicked ten metres away.

'Leave him,' Ought Nine urged, but Sergeant Gordon grasped the abbot's legs and dragged him, sputtering and coughing, from the fallen rock ceiling.

Sergeant Gordon tracked the years by the rains which still found us deep in the ground. The rising water table forced us to sleep standing. The rains sometimes brought flashfloods and we braced ourselves against the rock pillars that supported the stopes, our cheeks pressed to the ceiling as we breathed from shallow air pockets and waited for the torrent to subside. Three seasons of rain had passed since Sergeant Gordon came to us, two thousand underground days, each four-hour period of light measured out in half metres.

One night, Ought Nine beat the abbot into unconsciousness with a shovel. Each blow rang dully through the gallery. When the lights came on again, Ought Nine appeared before us wearing the abbot's cowl and sandals, and we accepted him as our leader.

The copper had long ago found its way into the abbot's brain. At night he often ran blind through the gallery until he knocked himself unconscious against a wall. Stripped of his raiment, the abbot took his usurper's place at Sergeant Gordon's side. The two men began to converse in short bursts uttered between the falling of their picks. The abbot told Sergeant Gordon that, in life, he was the superior of a monastery in the order of Saint Augustine. 'I was father and teacher to the savages who fished and hunted hippos along the Zambezi,' the monk said. 'Most of them are dead now. I hope God treated their souls better than mine. What did you do in life, demon?'

Sergeant Gordon turned to his work without answering. Soon the lights went out and the two men lay down their picks and stretched out on the rock floor.

Several underground days and nights passed before

Sergeant Gordon picked up the thread of their conversation. 'I was a scout,' he said.

The abbot lowered his pick and stared. 'Scouts are the fruit of the bad garden. You sniff about the villages, hiding in the bush, watching. Sooner or later you see something: a bootprint that looks strange, three men walking together, trampled grass from dancing at a unity celebration, some fruit or vegetables left on the outskirts of the village, more sleeping places than people. Watch long enough and you'll find something. Were you the radio operator who called in the air strikes that burned all the villages?'

The lights went out, and Sergeant Gordon stared into the blackness. 'I was the man who gave the radio operator his orders,' he said finally.

A dozen half nights passed before the abbot spoke to Sergeant Gordon again. 'When I still walked God's earth,' he said, 'I celebrated 387 funerals. Bombed and burned to death, most of them. Entire villages levelled by your warplanes. Now I work and sleep shoulder to shoulder with the author of these wicked acts. There are no coincidences, demon. Only God's perverse will.'

When the lights came back on, we found the abbot straining against the ore ceiling as if through sheer will he might push his way to the surface. 'How have I offended you,' he shouted at the rock above, 'that you send me to bake in the earth's crust with these demons?'

Thereafter the abbot refused to work in the same stope

as Sergeant Gordon, and Ought Nine assigned me to work alongside the scout.

* * *

We carved out the stopes in steep downward angles, always following the copper. In the half-nights, unbound by time and light, Sergeant Gordon began to recite his story, weaving together the threads of his life. When the old woman switched off the generator, we gathered together, forfeiting sleep so we could breathe in the words. So long in the mine, our own stories were lost.

He told us of his childhood, when his world was still the kitchen and the garden. He recited the details of his birth, his baptism, the servants who raised him, all the events of his life leading to the day when he was captured by the guerrilla soldiers and bound to the bonnet of the old Ford. He recounted his funeral. The time he attempted to escape the mine. His conversations with the abbot and Ought Nine.

At first Sergeant Gordon ordered the events of his life chronologically, then in patterns according to theme or metaphor in an attempt to make some sense of it; adding and taking away, until the story became its own breathing, speaking entity. It spoke to us in the perfect darkness of the underground night, a disembodied voice.

*Listen,* it said.

'A story,' we called out.

*A mouth-filling story!* it answered.

'Bring it!' we said, and Sergeant Gordon's life emerged from the darkness as a mosaic of disjointed details and images: a bit of a nursery song his housekeeper once sang to him, the scent of peaberry coffee, the brilliance of a flame tree, the roaring in his ears as he grunted and strained over a girl's naked body and lost his virginity, the agony etched into the charred faces of bombed villagers. When Sergeant Gordon came to some shameful episode, we leaned towards his voice and asked him to repeat the offence so we could commit it to memory, make it ours. We'd forgotten our own misdeeds and sorely needed some justification for what had been done to us. If, as the abbot claimed, Christ had taken away the sins of the world, Sergeant Gordon, through his story, brought them back where they belonged.

Sometimes the story became a theatre of the dead. We heard drop tanks whistle through the air and we touched our faces as the combustion washed over us, surprised to find the skin still attached to our skulls. Other times we listened to the soft footfalls of Sergeant Gordon's patrol as their ghosts combed the copper mine, searching for evidence of guerrilla activity. One night I heard hundreds of murdered villagers running madly through the stopes, their fleshless soles slapping wetly against the rock floor.

'Maybe above ground they can pretend to separate the

dead from the living,' the abbot said when the story fell silent. 'But not here. We live shoulder to shoulder with them. To believe otherwise is just wishing.'

Sergeant Gordon no longer spoke as we worked our stope. The story consumed all his words. In the silence, images from my surface life would appear in bas-relief on the rock face. A woman's face, a child's. When I tried to break them apart, their shattered features would re-emerge under my pick until, breathless and arm-weary, I sank to my knees and stared into the fragile malachite of their eyes, almost remembering.

The copper dust found its way into Sergeant Gordon's blood, thinning it. His skin began to weep where the napalm had splashed his neck and shoulder. He was racked with nausea, vomiting, and diarrhoea. His kidneys began to fail. Sergeant Gordon was dying.

*He killed them,* his story said to us one night.

'Who?' I asked.

*Sergeant Gordon called down the airstrike on his own tracking team. They were following the banks of a river when the bombs fell. Even the water burned away.*

Acts like this were common on the surface. Perhaps I'd even committed some of my own. The lights popped and buzzed, casting their yellowish pall over the gallery, and we rose to take up our work.

* * *

Then came a day when the generator did not start again, leaving us in unending night. The dust and heat fell away as we listened to Sergeant Gordon's story, and the darkness split open to reveal a cross section of the universe. It appeared as an immense excavation, its outspreading corridors like an upside-down tree growing into the world – the main shaft constituted its trunk, the galleries its branches, each leaf a stope. I saw the filament of my own spirit joined with multitudes of others to create an intricate pattern of glittering veins. Some deposits ran alongside mine, over and under; others crossed briefly, then shot in different directions, compressed beneath an overburden of rock and alluvium. Sergeant Gordon's story revealed to us the worm that mines the world, separating the mineral from the gangue in a great smelting fire that consumes without end. In the mouth of that infinite, blasting furnace, I glimpsed its face.

I cannot say how long I lay there, gazing upon the earthworks of the universe, before I was shaken roughly awake.

'Rise up!' Sergeant Gordon's voice was directly over me.

'Leave me sleep,' I said.

'It's time to quit this place,' he said.

'What about the landmines?' I remained on the rock floor, unwilling to leave Gallery Zed and its comforting darkness.

'Move towards my voice,' Sergeant Gordon persisted.

My body rose of its own accord and I joined with the other miners from the gallery in a human chain. We followed, hand to shoulder, stepping in Sergeant Gordon's footsteps as he guided us out of the gallery and into the shaft that led to the surface. I sensed the presence of the dead. Sergeant Gordon had brought along the ghosts of those he'd murdered so they could be released from the endless underground night. He spoke to them as we moved through the darkness and the landmines, and they responded, though their susurrus did not reach me. Communications between the dead and the living are like mists that come together and disperse.

Each time I placed my weight on the floor of the shaft I expected an explosion. Still I pressed on, my courage rising with each step that brought us closer to the sky. We stopped at the entrances to the other galleries, where Sergeant Gordon banged on the air pipe until the work gangs emerged and joined their numbers to ours. When the last gallery emptied, each man called out his prison name in turn, the numbers echoing through the shaft, 459 copper men.

Something strange began to happen to the air when we resumed our passage. It no longer had the metallic smell of air forced through copper piping. We were breathing surface air! I began to weep uncontrollably. Behind me, the man whose hand grasped my shoulder began to cry also, and the man behind him, a wave of emotion travelling down the quarter-mile file until we were overcome by all we had endured in this place, and there was laughter at the prospect that our misery might soon end, and shouts of anger that our destinies should have brought us here, and the file came to a halt. I can't say how long we remained immobile in the shaft, overwhelmed. Ahead, the branded copper gate was open. Outside, the glow from the smelting fires.

It's beyond my ken how Sergeant Gordon brought us up from the copper mine. Maybe it was blind luck and desperation. Or a simple act of faith. Perhaps the land-mines never existed – easier to paint red spots on the rock floor than bury explosives in it, leaving our own fear to stand guard over us.

When Sergeant Gordon ushered us through the gate, the abbot refused to cross its threshold. 'I'll leave this hell when God begs forgiveness for having condemned a righteous man,' he said, and he withdrew down the shaft to await his apology.

We emerged covered in copper dust, blinking at the light. Our spines had bent beneath the low ceilings and wouldn't straighten. We filled our shrunken lungs, stretched our hands above us, laughed when we touched nothing.

The corrupted sunset cast a red pall over the denuded land. The forest had been fed into the fires that burned night and day under the smelters. Ochre clouds of sulphuric acid hung low in the sky. Flashfloods had carried away the unprotected topsoil, leaving only dust and waste rock. The stream stank of arsenic, fish and sewage. I washed my arms and hands in it, stared at the skin in wonder. I'd forgotten what race I was.

Winston Chaminuka and his renegade soldiers had departed long ago. Yet the women continued to stoke the smelting fires and pour the copper into moulds dug into the sand where it cooled into bars. Without the guerrillas to take it away they had stacked the pig copper like bricks until it formed a wall against the world. The old woman still tended the generator, though she had run out of diesel. I watched her check her wristwatch, rise and switch off the dead engine. The children still collected the corms and roots and dead fish to bring down to us. And we had continued to fill their baskets with ore. And the copper wall grew.

Ought Nine commanded the women to stop, but still they worked, unhearing. He ordered the men to douse the smelting fires, and even so the women had to be restrained from their labour. They rocked and swayed, their muscles willing them on.

In the twilight, in our idleness, we grew aware of our nakedness. The women made smocks from black plastic bags. Some of the men pulled on trouser fatigues they found in the derelict Ford or wrapped shirts and field jackets around their emaciated waists. Others clad themselves in leather smelting aprons. I wondered if I'd once known any of the women who stood before us. The one who tended the generator looked at me with dim recognition. Perhaps we'd been married in some long-ago life before we came to the mine. I lay down beside her to sleep in the incomplete darkness beneath the limitless ceiling of sky.

I rose the next morning and surveyed the desolate landscape. Ought Nine was gone, his footprints heading south. He would comb the upscale suburbs of Umtali, I reckoned, until he found Winston Chaminuka and took his other eye.

There was nothing there so we trekked south on ground hardened with drought, more than a thousand men, women and children, not counting all those ghosts, an army of copper people. On occasion we saw other people walking in the distance. Africa is a continent of walking people. Sergeant Gordon's breath rattled in his lungs and it smelled like the forced air that came from the ducts in Gallery Zed. He would soon rejoin his murdered patrol.

We passed ruined villages with empty kraals. We came to a deserted airfield littered with military documents. Amid the scatter of orders, files and records, Sergeant Gordon found a yellowing edition of the *Guardian*, dated April 19, 1980. The newspaper had been printed, so we would learn, a year earlier. We crowded Sergeant Gordon as he read aloud. Rhodesia and its minority government no longer existed. We were now citizens of the new nation of Zimbabwe.

* * *

Thirty years have passed since our resurrection. These days I sleep on the roof of my house on the sunrise side of a town in the eastern highlands where I get the light before anyone else in Zimbabwe. It has become a nation of doorstep Christians. They come into my yard and threaten me with God's wrath. 'Too late for that,' I say.

On the roof, beneath the brilliant night sky, this story still speaks to me. I inherited it from Sergeant Gordon, along with his offences. It is now I who order Sergeant Gordon's radioman to napalm the villages. I murder his patrol. I force myself on his girlfriend, set fire to the beetle he caught as a child. I order the bulldozing of homes and fields that is reported over my transistor radio, help carry out the massacre in a neighbouring country that is chronicled in this morning's newspaper. The sins multiply after sundown, grow louder with each telling, until the morning's hush when I rise from the shingles covered in dew and new sunlight. Without sin there's no meaning in the cairns, the hard labour, the lost years in the copper mine; and all our suffering is reduced to a bit of malice doled out by a wanton God.

I've heard the confessions of mankind and there's no limit to our trespass. Time now for me to leave this world and take up my pick and shovel in the next. The worm waits in the half-night; its terrible presence ever before us, behind us, around us, unseen.

# *Blood Reader*

September, 1978

AHEAD, FIVE PILLARS OF GREASY SMOKE ROSE TO support the gloaming. Below us, a blur of barren land strung with Christmas tree lights. A flare arced over the Zambezi River, reflecting on its surface. The Alouette made its descent and the Christmas tree lights became strings of small ground fires. Bongi dangled his legs out of the open door of the helicopter, ignoring me as he pretended to read *Being and Nothingness*, not even looking up when the pilot made a steep banking turn to throw a scare into us. Bongi held the cigarette between his middle and index fingers, palm covering his mouth, like Sartre does on the dust jacket.

We used to smoke Kingsgate cigarettes together, but Bongi switched to Madisons. By changing brands he hoped to distance himself from me and my blood reading. The ground rushed up at us. There were no waves of grass beneath the beating blades, only seared earth. Takeoffs and landings in this sector were touch and go, and the Alouette was already rising before our feet touched the ground. The concussive din of rotor, turbine, and blades faded away to a faint drone.

We'd been delivered, Bongi and I, into a kraal on the edge of a burning village. I checked my kit – two canteens, salt and glucose tablets, a carton of Kingsgates, an empty Coke can, a Zippo and a tin of butane. Smoke poured from the window of a hut that formed one side of the kraal. Charred goats littered the enclosure, their stomachs heaving as they released their grassy gases. Vampires had descended on the village, each jet armed with a fifty gallon drop tank filled with frantan, Rhodesian napalm. The smoke stank of jet fuel, polystyrene and burned animal fat.

Bongi stowed *Being and Nothingness* in his rucksack. The book had belonged to Weatherhead, the third member of our tracking team, newly deceased. I slung my rifle over my shoulder and stared across the river into Zambia where the enemy lay hidden in the hippo grass, their gaze as palpable as the shimmering heat.

A bulldozer rumbled towards the kraal. I reckoned the village had been singled out for destruction because its inhabitants provided meat and information to the terrs. Or they'd participated in an all-night unity celebration. Or someone was observed using the triple handshake that identified them as supporters of the guerrilla movement. A stick of police reservists had rounded up the surviving villagers and loaded them onto a bus that would take them to a keep where they would live out the war encircled by razor wire. The bulldozer peeled back the earth like a scab.

Nearby, two scouts were erecting an eight-sided tent. Bongi and I squatted on our haunches and waited for someone to come along and tell us what to do. Leaflets littered the ground. One read: *Your ancestral spirits are very angry with you. As a result, there will be great famine. Only the government can help.* The scouts carried something flat and heavy into the tent, its surface flashing the grey-blue of the twilight sky. It was a full-length dressing mirror.

I examined the ground in the failing light. The bulldozer had thrown up a lot of dust which would complicate things in the morning. Already it was settling over the spoor; mostly women's footprints, smallish with splayed toes. The rest of the prints were partials made by children, balls of feet and toes. They'd been running blind. One had trodden on a bowl. I glanced sideways into the bloodied shards – the periphery of the vision is better suited for this sort of thing – and an image superimposed itself on the stain: *It's daybreak, the villagers emerging from their houses. The air is laden with humidity and the breathless shriek of fighter jets. As the drop tanks fall from beneath the Vampires' wings the owner of the blood cannot help but stare upward to see what rains down on her from the sky. A searing splash, the melting away of flesh and consciousness, the exposure of bone and agony.*

Bongi's voice came from behind. 'Haven't you brought us enough bad luck with your blood reading?'

'Weatherhead made his own luck,' I answered.

An unbroken egg rolled through the scatter of fence sticks – not an egg after all, but a golf ball. A curious parade moved towards us across the wasteland; Major Sowers carrying a patch of artificial grass, followed by a soldier with a bag of golf clubs. A parrot hopped after them, swearing in Spanish. I recognised the major from his photo in *The Umtali Times.* The headline ran: *Actor Finds New Role Fighting Terrs.* According to the article he'd been at the Rep Theatre in Salisbury. 'You're standing on my fairway,' Sowers said, ignoring my salute. He was dressed all in red, boots to beret.

The caddy wore no rank. Like Bongi and me, he sported the tan beret of the scouts. He was greying at the temples, a bit old for this business. I read the name sewn above his breast pocket: *Foote.* Foote signalled to the bulldozer driver to switch off his engine. Major Sowers placed the artificial turf beneath the golf ball. Foote selected an iron and offered it, handle foremost. The major accepted the club and addressed the ball. I'd never been to the theatre, but there was a sort of staged ritual between these two that I imagined must exist among actors in a play that had run too long. Major Sowers sent the ball sailing towards a distant pennant that fluttered near the riverbank. Foote waved at the bulldozer and the machine roared back to life, fuming. '*Chupa mi pinga*,' the parrot said, laying down the low plot.

The major regarded Bongi and me, then turned to Foote. 'Are these the chaps who were tracking that Zorro character?'

'Comrade Zorro,' the caddy said. My heart jumped at this.

Sowers harrumphed. 'A ridiculous name.'

'The terr snipers fancy themselves action heroes,' Foote explained. 'Comrade Tarzan, Comrade James Bond, Comrade Batman, and what not.'

'Just so,' the major said, losing interest. He squinted into the twilight. 'Can't see a bloody thing.'

'I'll have the engineers pour petrol on the river.' Foote tossed the clubs at my feet and stamped away.

Sowers turned to me. 'You're the blood reader, then.' Bongi shuddered at this casual utterance of my birthgift. The major strode across the desolate fairway, his red clothes turned purple by the dusk, Bongi and the parrot falling in step. I shouldered the clubs and slogged after them. Behind, the bulldozer pushed the burnt goats into the pit.

Major Sowers looked back at us. 'There's only two of you. I ask for a tracking team, I expect to see four trackers.'

'We just lost a man,' I said, regretting my choice of

words. Bongi shot me a look as I lined up excuses: our team was already a man short; Weatherhead had been reading when he should have been paying attention; the man we were tracking possessed supernatural abilities; my blood reading had brought bad luck down on us. But Major Sowers didn't ask how Weatherhead was lost. Instead, he ordered Bongi to run ahead to the flag that marked the cup.

'Your man reliable?' he asked when the right flanker was out of earshot. I shrugged. The major mopped his brow. 'If you don't know, then you can't trust him. Foote'll have to go with you. Good man, Foote. Knows the basics of tracking. I'm sure we can scare up someone else to round out the foursome.'

'Who're we after?' I asked, afraid of the answer.

The major looked at me like I was simple. 'Foote'll brief you once you're underway.'

As if summoned by the third incantation of his name, the orderly appeared from the darkness. Bongi hunched beside the flag in the light of the burning river, waiting to be struck by a sniper's bullet or the major's golf ball. Major Sowers chipped onto the patch of hardpan that had been designated as the green and two-putted into the cup. '*Jau ma se poes*,' the parrot squawked, switching to Afrikaans.

Sowers kicked at the bird with his red boot. 'The bugger'll outlive me,' he grumbled. The parrot clacked its beak at him. 'Belonged to my father, and his father before, damn him. Bought it from a whorehouse in Cape Town.' Sowers handed me the putter. 'It's getting dark. Curtain time, Foote.' Sowers looked out across the burning river into the darkness. 'There's drama in combat,' he said, facing his unseen audience. 'The terrs know this. It's why they'll probably win.' The major marched off towards the octagonal tent that served as his dressing room, the parrot hopping after him, swearing.

'Silly old git,' Foote said to the major's back. With Sowers gone, the golf course ceased to exist.

'Why's he dressed in red?' I asked.

Foote looked across the river at the unseen enemy. 'Their spirit mediums can't abide blood – even the colour blows their coals.' He rummaged a flask from the golf bag and took a long pull. 'The sort of hocus pocus you come to expect out here.' He wiped his mouth with the back of his hand and offered me the flask. 'Ever hear of the Hippo Hunters of the Unspeakable River?'

'No,' I lied. Bongi shifted uneasily.

Foote watched me drink his scotch. 'The locals have nightmares about them,' he said. 'A dreadful mob, by all accounts. It'd be choice to have them on our side.'

Pinpoints of light shone from across the Zambezi. Strains of music floated above the far bank, finger pianos and voices. 'The terrs are truly switched on, young sergeant,' Foote said in a fair imitation of the major. 'They'll be at it all night. Hope you're a heavy sleeper. We'll be underway at daybreak while the tracks are still fresh.'

'Whose tracks?' I asked.

Foote narrowed his eyes. 'I hear your last mission was a proper balls-up,' he said. 'Last chance, sergeant. Don't bitch it.' He left Bongi and me alone beneath a yellowed toenail clipping of a moon. The fire on the river had gone out. I could no longer see the hippo snouts that dotted the far bank, though intermittent bellows confirmed their presence. We sat cross-legged, each with our own packet of cigarettes, empty Coke can, and Zippo. I flicked the lighter, taking in the smell of butane, savouring it. The trick to smoking at night is to keep the burning end inside an empty can. A sniper will shoot you in the mouth if you show him a lighted cigarette. A landmine exploded on the periphery of the village and we were flat on our stomachs, rifles in hand, sighting on nothing. A porcupine, probably, looking for bones to chew.

The ground was still hot from the napalm, so we returned to the kraal to bash up on the cool, turned earth. There were other patches of disturbed ground in the village, but I'd sleep better knowing it was only goats buried beneath me. I closed my eyes and dreamed the same dream I'd had three nights running: *It's a tracking mission, Bongi on my right flank, Weatherhead on my left, head in his book. With a three-man team, I act as both lead tracker and tracker control. We're after Comrade Zorro, a sniper credited with eleven kills. Bongi and I break training and walk close enough to speak.*

*'I hear Comrade Zorro summons the mist to hide his approach,' Bongi says.*

*'Before the war,' I say, 'Comrade Zorro made his living as a strangler who procured human organs for sorcerers.'*

*'Comrade Zorro's ancestors direct his aim.'*

*'A sorcerer curses all Comrade Zorro's bullets.'*

*We're like children, scaring each other into laughter. The spoor's old, time has eroded Comrade Zorro's footprints, so I don't bother telling Weatherhead to put away his book and pay attention. A mist rises from the river.* The dream ends with Weatherhead alive, Bongi still my friend, Comrade Zorro waiting in the mist.

There was a barracks story going round about a commando leader who conducted a sweep of a remote tributary of the Zambezi. His scouts found bare footprints along the banks, but no other trace of inhabitants. On the third night a patrol returned with a naked man smeared skull to toe with mud. The commando leader wrapped his fist in his belt and ordered the tent cleared. A sentry heard the soft thump of leather on ribs.

The interrogation was interrupted when shots rang out on the perimeter. Dozens of hippos had lumbered out of the river to stampede the camp. The bulls roared as the sentries' bullets struck their snouts and shoulders, but still they came on, pushing past the soldiers, their fear of man and the inland world overcome by whatever had chased them from the river. Scared witless, the scouts sighted their rifles on the impenetrable water. The frogs had fallen silent. Splinters of moonlight were strewn across the current. Yet the commando leader could discern countless points on the river's surface which reflected no light. The realisation came to him gradually, as he found his night vision, that each point was a face, its skin dulled with mud. The river itself seemed to exhale sharply – *Shoo!* – as a thousand hippo hunters blew river water from their nostrils. In a voice all the more strange for its calm, the commando leader ordered his men to fetch the unconscious prisoner and throw him into the river. The inert body sank swiftly, as if gripped in an undertow, and the faces slid back under the water.

Afterward, nothing could persuade the commando leader to return to the bush. He accepted a reduction in rank and was transferred to our unit to serve as adjutant officer. His pressure lamp was never extinguished, and he only left the tent to use the latrine.

On the evening of Weatherhead's death, Bongi marched up to the adjutant officer's desk, saluted smartly, and requested a transfer to another tracking team.

'State your reason,' the ex-commando said.

Bongi hesitated. 'Sir, my team leader is a sorcerer. I saw him today reading omens in Weatherhead's blood.'

Another officer might have dressed Bongi down for talking rubbish, but the adjutant leaned forward. 'Tell me what your team leader read in the blood,' he said.

Bongi hesitated. 'Sir, he told me that he saw death pouring out of a river.'

The adjutant officer dismissed Bongi and summoned me from where I stood eavesdropping outside the tent. 'Your flanker says you're a blood reader.' He cut his finger lengthwise with a letter opener, laying open the small bones and joints. Blood streamed from the ruined finger onto the desk. 'Read it, sergeant.'

Fresh blood is a reflective surface, and I didn't care to look too closely into my own destiny. I looked aslant as it seeped into the carbon paper, reading aloud. *'I see you as a small child standing over your mother. There's coffee spilled on the kitchen floor. Her heart has just stopped. Your father pushes you aside, kneels, puts his head on her chest.'*

'No, no!' The adjutant officer slapped his hand in his own blood, breaking the image apart. 'I don't care about that!' He opened a second finger, and I witnessed another image from his life, this time from his adolescence. *'You're in a schoolyard, reaching into the pocket of a younger student. You're taking money from him, I think.'* Distressed, the adjutant officer sliced his ring finger, pad to knuckle. But he'd been brought up against the limitation of my birthgift. Blood yields random images unbound by time, crystalline moments from the bleeder's past or future. The adjutant buried his face in his hands.

'Is this about the prisoner you interrogated?' I asked.

He looked up at me. The damaged fingers had left three stripes on his cheek. 'It's hard to explain what happened that night in the tent. I was pulling the prisoner to his feet when the lamp went out. I felt his breath on my face and he whispered to me, "Tremble before the Weaver of the Universe, Shaper of the World." I heard the river lapping at the bank, the *crick* of frogs. A fly crawled over the fine hairs on my wrist. Only a few moments had passed, yet it seemed unendurable. Was it God there in that tent, filling up the darkness?' The adjutant tried to wipe his face, but this only made matters worse. The naked lamplight shone white on the desk's liquid surface as he passed out, the letter opener slipping from his bloody fingers. All this happened two days earlier, before the Vampire jets descended on the village and consumed it with fire.

* * *

I woke to the *taka taka* of helicopter blades. Foote ignited a flare on the bank and an Alouette flew out from a curtain of mist and touched down. A passenger disembarked, his features lost in the glare of the low sun, and followed the orderly into the major's tent.

Bongi was turning the pages of *Being and Nothingness* in the new light, reminding me of Weatherhead. It was bad luck to read from a dead man's book. Bongi would cop it on this mission, sure as fate. 'You don't even know how to read,' I told him, the cruellest thing I could think to say.

'You don't need to know the words to believe what is inside this book,' he said.

Bongi ate powdered milk from a foil pouch and stared at the pages. In civilian life, he'd prepared meals at the Portuguese Club. Since he couldn't read recipes, he cooked by his nose, sniffing the air to determine how long to hang the guinea fowl, what spices should be folded into the sauce, when the dish was done. As a scout, Bongi tried to hang on to his identity as a cook, beating and marinating the questionable meat Weatherhead brought back from the bush. But his keen sense of smell began to fail once we took up huffing butane, and when he sniffed over the paraffin stove it was to keep mucus from running into the sauce. All his dishes tasted like thrice-heated leftovers, and he began eating dehydrated field rations.

I heard a voice behind me. 'There's someone I want you to meet.' It was Foote. Bongi and I followed him into the tent where the stranger from the helicopter sat on his haunches in the corner, staring at the knotted cords in his hands. He was barefoot, fatigue trousers rolled above his ankles, a rifle with a sniper scope slung across his back. Three pairs of combat boots hung around his neck; a terr trick, changing boots to confuse trackers. The parrot paced the length the tent. '*Poephol*,' it said.

Major Sowers stood before the mirror, watching me in the reflection. 'Morning, young sergeant.' He'd traded his red outfit for tailored and pressed fatigues. His cheeks had a ruddy glow, makeup maybe. 'Meet your new left flanker, Comrade Zorro.'

Bongi moved close enough for me to smell his powdered milk breath. 'This is what comes of your sorcery,' he hissed.

Foote gave Major Sowers a look. 'Haven't you got things to do?' There was something in the way Foote said this – and in the way Sowers complied – that made me realise the orderly outranked the major.

'Yes, of course.' Sowers bustled out of the tent, starched uniform rustling, the parrot squalling obscenities at his heels. I reckoned Foote kept the actor around as a decoy for snipers.

'We captured Zorro not long after he shot your flanker,' Foote said. 'He's come over to our side.' Comrade Zorro continued to stare at his strangler's hands. It wasn't unusual to turn a captured terr, but to have him replace the flanker he shot was a monstrous idea.

'Why him?' I asked, my voice no longer my own.

'You're the bloody psychic. You tell me.' The new sun

shone through the tent flaps. 'Pack your kits, boyos,' Foote said. 'We're off to recruit some hippo hunters.'

We picked up their trail outside the razed village. One of the terrs was a woman, judging from the proximity of the footprints to the urine-spattered sand. Toes and pads, no heels, the imprint of a squatter. The other was a man. They had urinated together, side by side. Intimates. This was the part I liked about tracking, its facticity. Their tracks ran along the Zambezi, never more than a hundred metres from its bank. Foote kneeled beside me, Major Sowers behind, puffing under the weight of the radio, Bongi on my distant right, Comrade Zorro near left, bound by the river. The man's urine was dark. 'Kidney damage,' I said, 'maybe malaria.'

'Or he's taken some beatings,' Foote said. Sowers walked off, sulking because Foote had ordered him to carry the radio. Comrade Zorro came in to study the tracks.

'Is it true that a sorcerer curses your bullets?' I asked him.

'Yes. These bullets kill the spirit as well as the body.' Comrade Zorro grinned at me. 'No worries, I won't spend them on you. I keep them for my enemies.'

An afternoon wind provided no relief from the heat. Hippos came out of the river to graze. They raised their heavy heads to stare at us. We passed a relay radio station. One of the operators raised his FN rifle and playfully sighted on me.

* * *

The two flankers bracketed me, moving away in open terrain, drawing nearer when the thornbush thickened, always maintaining sight-distance. We followed the tracks north and east for two days. The man's prints grew close to the woman's, his outstep deep. 'He's leaning on her,' I said to Foote. 'When are you going to tell me who we're tracking? You need to keep me informed, or I may miss something important.'

Foote studied me. I'd been huffing on the sly. 'We're hunting the God of the Hippo Hunters,' he said finally. 'His celestial highness got caught up in a sweep by one of our commandos a few weeks back. The interrogator got spooked, tossed the lunatic in the river. Next thing, he surfaces on the far bank, doing his act for the terrs.'

'His act?'

'He goes into this sort of trance, says he's God of the Hippo Hunters, Weaver of the Cosmos, and so on. The terrs think he's mad. Nobody believes him except for this one woman, a sniper, who helps him escape.'

'How do you know all this?' I said.

'Comrade Zorro told us at his debriefing. Turns out the woman's his wife.'

We found berries in their stools. The distance between the prints shortened. They were getting weak. The butane wore off and I found myself back in the material reality of my body. I scuffled as I walked, wondering if Comrade Zorro had allowed himself to be captured so that he could use us to help track down his unfaithful wife and her lover.

We bivouacked that night in a village of one-footed women who prepared for us a chop of round beans and mealie meal. Their fields had been mined, but necessity forced the women to harvest their crops, eyeing the ground suspiciously as they hopped about. The children slapped at moths over the cooking fire and licked their palms. Wet, cheesy patches of white surrounded their corneas. 'Bitot's spots', Foote said, 'from eating too much mealie and not a lot else. Optic nerves rotted clear away.' Their eyes could still see, but the images no longer reached their brains. The children swarmed over Foote's lap, and he laughed and passed out tins of bully beef from his rucksack.

I stood first watch, straining to see into the darkness. The thing about soldiering, the part they leave out of the stories, is the stillness, the crawl of it all.

'The harder one looks at a thing, the less he sees of it.' It was Comrade Zorro.

I opened my tin of lighter fluid and inhaled deeply, waiting for the roar in my ears. 'What sort of things?' I must have asked. Often, when I've been huffing, I hear only the words spoken to me, seldom my own.

'Who can say? Shapes. Lights. Movement. Things too quick for the eye. Secret things that don't belong in this world.'

That night I had a butane dream: *I'm kneeling over Weatherhead, trying to tape the plastic wrapper from a cigarette pack over the bullet hole in his chest to keep his breath inside his body. The mist has dissipated and the sun makes a mirror of the blood. When I tell him I'm sorry, he looks up at me and says it doesn't matter.*

There was vomit on the ground in front of the woman's footprints. I rubbed some between my fingers, smelled it. She'd taken a decoction of foxglove and rue to help settle her weak stomach. 'I think she's pregnant,' I said to Foote. Comrade Zorro had abandoned our left flank and was standing over me. He rubbed two bullets together between his thumb and forefingers.

'Congratulations, old sausage!' Foote said to Comrade Zorro. 'You're going to be the proud father of a bouncing baby God.' Comrade Zorro's eyes flashed as he withdrew to take up his flank position.

'Could we break for lunch?' Major Sowers asked. 'This radio's damned heavy.'

'No time,' Foote replied. The sides of the prints were not eroded, fresh. 'We're nearly on them. If we get the God, we got the hippo hunters.'

We followed the spoor south, along a tributary. Ancient, twisted baobabs dotted the floodplain. 'Come see,' Comrade Zorro said. 'This is the mouth of the Unspeakable River. Long ago Arab slavers were drowned here in their own shackles by the hippo hunters. Put your hand in the water. It's colder than the Zambezi.' I refused.

The sun was fierce and by midday Major Sowers was grumbling audibly. The parrot, silent now, rode atop the radio on the actor's back. Foote tried to jolly Sowers out of his mood. 'Think of the story this'll make. Maybe you can play yourself in the movie. The role of a lifetime!' Sowers seemed to brighten. 'Smile for the cameras!' Foote said.

Major Sowers was smiling brilliantly when the sniper shot him. He'd turned to face Foote, so the bullet entered at a right angle, shattering his teeth but otherwise leaving him untouched. Comrade Zorro returned fire and I heard a cry from the tall grass. Bongi swept around and we closed in to find a naked man, his head cradled in a woman's lap. He glared at me from behind a mask of mud. 'Tremble before the Weaver of the Universe,' he said, holding me fast in his pale gaze, 'Shaper of the World, Speaker of All Languages, Teller of All Stories, Origin of All Words, Begetter of All Things!'

Foote held a rag to the prisoner's throat, trying to staunch the wound. The woman used the hem of her T-shirt to wipe his forehead and cheeks, and I leaned forward, hoping to see the hidden face of God. The mud came away to reveal sagging jowls, thin lips and blotchy skin.

'Quick,' Foote said, handing me the sodden bandage. 'Read his blood.'

I kneeled, looking indirectly at the fresh blood. *In it, I see generation on generation of hippo hunters living naked in the weather, surviving by their hands, their lives unchanged since the days of creation when God moulded the first man and woman from the mud of the Unspeakable River. In flood time, women ululate for their drowned children. When the rains end, children play stalking games, exhale and sink to the river bed as they compete to determine who can live longest without air. In drought, the Unspeakable River grows shallow, the women use bark to filter the mud from the drinking water, the hippos move away, and there is starvation. I see hippo hunters standing waist deep in the river, clapping and yelling as they drive a bull hippo onto the bank. Children with war clubs break its front legs, force it to kneel before God as they gut the beast, crawl inside it, and smear their faces and chests with its blood. I see them pour into a village, spurred by God, to drag its inhabitants into the river, embrace them beneath the surface, stroke the heads of the villagers as they breathe the river into their lungs. The river can scarcely support the hippo hunters. There can be no others. I see a brother of the order of Saint Augustine struggling along the banks of the river. His porters have abandoned him. At the end of each day he sleeps with his head on his bible. One night, shadows rise from the river, seize him and pull him roughly down the bank and under the water. They stroke his head as he flails against the muddy bed. The monk wakes face up beneath a forest canopy, half starved, his body ridden with parasites.*

*Feverish, he stands in the presence of a deity more proximate and immediate than the one in his bible. The monk prostrates himself before the God of the Hippo Hunters and asks in a tremulous voice: 'How may I serve you, Lord?'*

I turned away from the darkening ooze. 'He isn't the God of the Hippo Hunters,' I said to Foote. 'He's God's praise poet.'

At sunset, an Alouette brought a camp dentist who repaired Major Sowers's mouth without Novocain, grinding down what was left of the broken teeth and crowning them with grey resin. There was an odour of burning nerves and enamel.

We loaded the praise poet for the God of the Hippo Hunters into the helicopter, his breathing shallow and rasping. Foote prodded him. 'He's no good to us if he isn't their God.' The Alouette rose and banked towards the horizon, bearing the poet away from his Lord.

Foote debriefed Comrade Zorro's wife. She sat against a tree during the interrogation, expressionless, hands and feet bound. Comrade Zorro insisted on being present to ensure his pregnant wife was not beaten. Her name was Comrade Wonder Woman, a sniper in the war of liberation. She was the wife of Comrade Zorro. These three pieces of information were all Foote was able to extract.

That night Bongi stood guard at the edge of camp,

facing the Unspeakable River. Major Sowers wept softly. Foote was on the radio. The snipers spoke quietly. The trick to eavesdropping is to breathe shallowly and stare directly at the source of the words.

'Is the baby keeping well?' The voice was Comrade Zorro's.

Silence.

'Why did you not kill me?' Comrade Zorro asked. 'It was an easier shot.'

'You taught me to shoot officers first.' There was humour in the voice. 'The wind turned my bullet.'

'There are other things that can spoil a shot. The last man I killed, just before I fired, I saw his soul rise from his body. The bullet struck wide of the heart, causing him to die slowly and with much pain.' More silence.

'Is this to be our life's work?' Comrade Wonder Woman asked.

'You would rather sleep with a lunatic?'

'He said he was a voice in the wilderness, making a path for his Lord.'

I listened to Major Sowers weep until Foote told him to shut his gob. Soldiers have no sympathy for the wounded. Bongi called out to the actor from the perimeter. 'You know why the bullet missed?' he asked. 'God is saving you for something else.'

'*Doos*,' the parrot said.

I huffed butane, listened to the nightjars, and imagined

Weatherhead's soul rising above his body just before Comrade Zorro pulled the trigger.

* * *

I woke the next morning surrounded by mist. Comrade Zorro and Comrade Wonder Woman were gone, uniforms and rifle discarded on the bank, their roles as snipers incompatible with the image each saw in the other's eyes. I ejected the sorcerer-cursed bullet from the chamber and pocketed it.

We came to an empty village where we found a cooking fire still burning beneath a vat. The inhabitants had been brewing beer. I switched off the safety on my rifle. There were four houses; roofs newly thatched, fresh daub on the walls, the ground broken and ready to plant. I walked past overturned bowls, the spilled mealie meal covered with ants.

There were muddy footprints coming from the water. The hippo hunters left spoor, therefore they existed, the ontology of man tracking. I examined the scatter of dirt where they had dragged the villagers back into the river. There was something disturbing in the hippo hunters' prints. Many of the warriors were women and children.

'Remarkable,' Foote said, eyes flashing.

A few hours' walk brought us to a vast canopy of misshapen trees. Foote turned to me. 'Wait on that rise with the radio, sergeant. If we don't come out by morning, get on the horn and rain hell down on them.'

Major Sowers flashed Bongi a ravaged smile. 'Is this what God has saved me for?' He adjusted his beret to a cocky angle, picked up his obscene little bird, and followed Foote onto that liminal stage. Bongi lighted a Madison and started after them.

'They're insane,' I told him. The right flanker turned, shrugged, and handed me his cigarette. By the time he disappeared into the riverine canopy, I'd smoked it down to the filter.

I needed to switch off, so I huffed some butane and settled into an uneasy sleep. *In my butane dream, I kneel over Weatherhead's lifeless body, his pooled blood cupped in my hands. This time I look directly into the sanguine mirror and read my own future. Thousands of hippo hunters surge from the coppery water of the Unspeakable River; young men armed only with their hands, women fighters with infants strapped to their backs, children wielding clubs studded with hippo teeth, eyes glittering behind mud masks. Ancestral spirits move alongside the living, imparting fierceness and strength to their descendants. God rises from the current, urging, inciting. I am in the vanguard, His new praise poet, my face contorted with rapture. Words fill my lungs like brown water. 'Tremble before the God of the Unspeakable River!' I shout.*

I sat up heaving with terror, unable to dispel the after-image of my future. The position of the sun was unchanged.

Below, I saw thousands of dark shapes moving beneath the muddy water towards the canopy of twisted trees where my comrades had disappeared. Soon they would come to drag me before a terrible God who would devour my spirit. So it was written in Weatherhead's blood. A faint hope rose as my gaze fell on the radio. Foote had left me with the means to escape this destiny. I raised the relay station and gave the coordinates for the air strike.

The late afternoon sun hung over the floodplain, suspended in the still air. Silver, bat-like shapes appeared on the horizon, a squadron of Vampires with full bomb racks and rocket rails. Painted on the underside of each wing was a green roundel encircling a lion brandishing an ivory tusk. The sun glinted off the aluminium drop tanks as the bombers released their cargo, concussing the earth, forcing the river to flow backward, consuming the forest canopy in a napalm fire. I huffed and waited for the butane roar.

# *The Leopard Gang*

May, 1973

I WAS KISSING MADOTA BEHIND A PILE OF SANDBAGS when the War of Liberation came to the glen, working my hand beneath the blouse of her school uniform, touching the cotton of her brassiere for the first time. The war didn't arrive in jeeps, their fenders, bonnets, and running boards covered with rebels, come to drag us out of our beds and shoot us on the lawn of our home in the harsh light of our own security lamps. That story happens later. War came instead with the growl of a dog, and a cry of pain and fear that made Madota sit up and button her blouse.

I clambered over the sandbags to witness a grim tug-of-war. A guerrilla soldier clung stubbornly to our clothesline pole, his foot trapped in the maw of my father's security dog, a ridgeback. The dog dragged the rebel earthward by degrees. Because the Rhodesian Security Forces tracked the terrs by the figure-of-eight patterns on their soles, the intruder was barefoot, his combat boots strung over his shoulder. The links of the dog's choke collar rattled with each shake of its head as it separated flesh from anklebone. A poet might have seen in the man a sort of backward Christ, his face pressed against the pole, arms wrapped around the crossbar, but there's no poetry in a fifteen-year-old boy determined to lose his virginity, and I saw only an old man screaming.

Behind me, Madota tucked her blouse into her waistband. I'd spent the better part of an hour opening the garment one-handed, my thumb and forefinger working the mother-of-pearl through starched buttonholes as my other hand stroked the pleats of her plaid skirt. In opening her shirt, I had exposed a swell of brown flesh against the bleached whiteness of her secret undergarment. Two silver rings hung from a thin metal chain around her neck. We both understood that a new line had been drawn between us, that the next time I coaxed her to the sandbags, this open blouse would be my entrenched position. My assault on Madota's maidenhead was glacier-like, unrelenting and slow and inevitable. I meant to become a man, there with Madota in the dirt behind the sandbags, before my sixteenth birthday.

'Leave off,' I said, pulling at the choke collar, but the dog refused to release the rebel soldier. My father had bought the ridgeback from a trainer in Umtali, a red-faced Afrikaner who beat his animals with his fists, then turned them loose on a dummy whose head and hands were painted dark. No one felt comfortable petting the nameless dog, and Madota would only come onto our property if I escorted her.

It was the dog that had prevented the Shona driver and his turnboy from delivering the sandbags to our door a week earlier. Instead they stood in the bed of their lorry and tossed sandbags and nervous glances at the ridgeback as it paced the edge of our property line with a show of hackles and teeth and black gums. Afterwards, I wheedled and coaxed Madota behind the bags heaped on the shoulder of the road, and there, for the first time, I buried my face in her neck and worried at her school uniform, a haze of dust floating in the late afternoon sun, her brown fingers against my freckled wrist, caressing, restraining.

'Give it up!' I commanded, but the trainer had never bothered to teach his animals to release the painted dummy, and the ridgeback held fast to the guerrilla's foot. I stepped back and pointed to my feet. 'Sit!' I said, and the dog let go of the terr and obediently sat before me, fixing its flat stare on my throat.

The terr climbed from the pole, his weight on his undamaged foot, and regarded us impassively. In me, he saw a pale *murunge* boy who seduced Shona girls for sport, and in Madota, he saw the sort of girl who made poor choices. The rebel was stooped and white-bearded, like Madota's father when he was alive, and she cast her eyes at the ground as she brushed the dirt from the seat of her skirt.

The Shona are a proper people, as were the ancient sisters who ruled the native girls' school and orphanage that neighboured the trust land, members of the withered and forgotten order of Saint Agnes, from whose care Madota sometimes managed to escape in order to join me behind the sandbags against all rules of accepted behaviour.

The terr turned his back on us and began to hobble towards my house, to wait for the police to take him away to prison, there to await his execution. Madota's hand rested on my sleeve, and in this gesture I felt a silent plea. To give him over to our security forces would be to accept his assessment of us. There had always been an unspoken language of touch between her and me, though in the matter of sexual intercourse I refused to listen.

'No, this way,' I called to his back. I motioned to the tangle of wild vegetation behind our house the way a toddler might wave a loaded pistol, or an informant point to a neighbour with whom he'd just quarrelled, a spurious gesture with no regard for consequences. I would help the terr because I felt sorry for him, tattered and bleeding, old and disoriented, and this was the Christian thing to do. Or because I'd become fed up with oppression, and I loved Madota, and so on, the sort of rot that comes early in the story when everybody's still looking for reasons. I draped the rebel's arm around my neck so that I could take his weight. 'There's a place you can hide,' I said, and with this, I stepped into the story that had carelessly rambled into my yard.

The old terr looked at me suspiciously, almost annoyed that he would now be forced to reappraise me. I held my breath, and Madota squeezed my hand; here was a breach in the solidarity between the white people of our country, the cement that held Rhodesia together, and there followed a break in the story to accommodate the enormity of the moment.

That evening, Madota climbed from the window of the crowded barracks she shared with sixty-four other Shona girls, all wards of the church, and she gapped it from the sisters of Saint Agnes. She slowed to a walk when she reached an ancient mahogany whose roots had thrown up a section of the brick wall surrounding the convent – a place, the story goes, where the nuns in their distant youth had met with their Shona lovers. Madota stepped respectfully over the rubble of gnarled roots and broken masonry. It was a sacred tree.

She skirted a desolate plot of ground that on certain days of the year was anonymously decorated with lilies and orchids from the sisters' hothouse, and sped down the mountainside, her bare feet holding the path in the darkness, silver wedding rings jangling on the chain around her neck, until she reached the garden shed. In this way, bringing only her spare school uniform, a picture Bible, and a leather case containing her toiletries, Madota left the care of the sisters of Saint Agnes and joined the rebellion.

Her first duty was to tend to the guerrilla's foot, washing the punctures and tears and applying ointments and fresh bandages that I pilfered from my father's large stockpile of first aid supplies. The terr called himself Granma, after the yacht that smuggled Castro, Che, and a small cadre of revolutionaries into Cuba. Granma had trained for thirteen weeks on the Caribbean island, most of it in the mountains of the Oriente. He'd returned to Rhodesia with bulging calf muscles, a working knowledge of Soviet-manufactured light weaponry, and a ceramic coffee mug. Granma fell into a dream in which an enormous dog held his foot fast in its muscled jaws, and we left him, motionless and sweating, on the dirt floor of the garden shed, outside the territory the ridgeback had marked with its urine.

I led Madota behind the sandbags and removed her shirt. This had become a struggle between us, and we took no enjoyment in it. I succeeded in unhooking her brassiere before the dawn brought its truce, and we lay frustrated on our sides, not looking into each other's faces, the ground hard against our hips and shoulders.

That weekend, while my father and I shifted the sandbags into our house to shore the walls against gunfire and shrapnel, Madota nested in the old gardener's shed with Granma, clearing a small patch of the weedy tangle that had once been a brilliant garden in the days before my father grew too frightened to hire Shona servants.

Her breathy, unused voice sounded like pan pipes as she sang and planted, sometimes a strange and unknown hymn, for the sisters of Saint Agnes were secret psalmists, but more often a bit of nonsense her father had sung to her in her childhood: *There was once a girl, there was once a girl, there was once a girl, let's go to Zinjanja!* Madota planted matinal and nocturnal flowers, and in the late afternoon hours we witnessed showers of purple morning glories close on the vine while moonflowers spread their white petals beneath the darkening sky, and her song floated on their scent, *Who went to fetch firewood, who went to fetch firewood,* and hundreds of species of butterflies sent representatives to the congress that convened in the constant bloom of her garden, *who went to fetch firewood,* and the wind jostled chimes suspended from threads – shards of dutchware blue from Indonesia, stemless champagne flutes, chipped glass napkin rings, and silver spoons pounded flat, an orchestra that swelled and fell away behind Madota's voice as if her breath animated them, *let's go to Zinjanja!* This was not a rebel hideout she was preparing – this point has been clarified in the retellings – but rather a home for the two of us. She planted mint in paraffin tins and set them on the sill of our only window so the mountain wind would rustle it on its way into the shed, and it would always smell cool and fresh inside, until the hot month of November, when the wind chimes fell quiet and Granma's foot began to go septic.

Granma was nearing sixty, stooped but muscular, and he clung to the old Shona belief that all things were woven together into the fabric of the universe. For this reason he never took more than one cup of instant coffee and chicory, though he clearly enjoyed it over any other beverage. 'If I take too much, someone will have to stoop longer in the sun to pick more beans in exchange for the right to remain on their ancestors' land,' he explained. Granma polished his ceramic drinking cup after his daily coffee, wrapped it in an undershirt, and placed it carefully in his rucksack, out of respect, he told me, for the Cuban who'd been in charge of his weapons training. The revolutionary had been a potter in the days of Batista, and the factory owner would not allow time for the cups to cool before the workers removed them from the kiln. The man's fingertips, Granma told us, were like mushrooms.

Granma nursed his daily coffee and watched his foot grey like aged steak, and Madota planted her garden and fetched water and changed the bandages that wrapped his rancid foot, and my father and I stacked the sandbags against the papered walls of the bungalow until the heather print was completely obscured. My father had shipped the wallpaper, along with my mother, from Scotland twenty years earlier, and the African climate had been cruel to both. We piled the sandbags in rows of twenty, floor to ceiling, each tier staggered for cohesion in case any stray rockets managed to clear the towering mesh fence my father planned to erect around the house.

The sandbags concealed the kitchen window and door, eclipsing all sunlight. A single bulb above the table threw shadows over the sink where I scrubbed our dishes, and we grew used to finding particles of dried food on our china and flatware. There were twelve interior doors in the bungalow, most of the rooms with two and three entrances, giving us the impression of many choices. But the barricade of sandbags afforded only one portal to the outside world, and when our rebel executioners finally came to wake us from our dream of security, they would lead us out of the front door into the white halogen light.

Granma's foot prevented him from leaving the shed, so he sent Madota in his stead to meet with the surviving rebels who had crossed with him into Rhodesia. Granma had designated the ancient mahogany at Saint Agnes's as the rendezvous point in the event the cadre became separated, because the tree was prominent on the mountain's crest, and it was sacred, and for other reasons we would later discover. One of their cadre had been lost during the river crossing, drowned or taken by a crocodile, Granma couldn't say. He had turned to pull his comrade onto the bank, but there was only the black, swirling water of the Zambezi. A mounted patrol of scouts fell upon the exhausted and wet guerrilla band, and many surrendered without a fight. Granma threw down his rifle and hid in a tree while the scouts executed their captives, and yet there was no bitterness in his voice as he reached this place in his story. 'What would you have them do, nephew? Arrest my comrades, feed them, give them dry clothes?' he asked. 'That way we could all fight this war forever, and with clear consciences.'

Madota returned with a stooped man and an emaciated boy, not much older than myself, both weaponless, the only members of the decimated cadre to make the rendezvous. October Twenty-Five had been trained in the Soviet Union and took his name from the date of their Great Revolution. He had worked in the refinery in Umtali until the birth of his twelfth child. The other guerrilla had adopted the name Zhanta, after the legendary Shona warrior of the Rebellion of 1896. Like Granma, the two guerrillas had taken revolutionary names to bolster their morale and, in the advent of capture, to shield their villages and families from reprisals.

Zhanta followed Madota into the shed, his left eye welling, its cornea bleached white. The eye blinked and teared constantly, as if trying to rid itself of the naked pupil that floated on its surface like a bit of blown ash. As a child, he'd been taken away from his village to work in the dip tanks because his parents couldn't afford to pay a tax. '*Mhoro*, comrade,' he said to Granma, looking at me with his leaking eye, and I caught the faint scent of harsh toxins. I imagined that the dead parasites he rinsed from the cattle at the dip tank had become for him a metaphor for the Europeans who infested his homeland.

'*Ahoi*,' Granma replied, then lowered himself onto the dirt floor of the shed, his damaged leg stretched before him. October Twenty-Five squatted silently. Of the thirty-seven members of their cadre who crossed the Zambezi into Rhodesia, only the three remained alive, each uncomfortable with his own survival. No one introduced me, and I stood outside their circle, unsure if I was a comrade or an enemy. Granma spread his outdated survey map over a battered trunk, the only piece of furniture in the shed. When I dragged this trunk from the crawl space in the bungalow to our shed, chips and fragments of glass and delft and porcelain and china glaze and longing and heart's desire had shifted like musical sand in the ullage of its depths.

Madota made her chimes from the detritus she found inside the trunk, a coffin-sized steamer lined with rotted toile depicting Napoleon's Egyptian campaigns. Its contents smelled of Scottish mildew, and spindrift, and stevedore's spilt beer, and untreated crate wood, and alien scents of faraway cargo, the wafture of seas and continents. It had accompanied my mother on her sea journey from Scotland, a hopeless chest filled with the sort of frippery that quickly disintegrates in Africa. Because Granma was the only rebel who had previous experience as a guerrilla soldier, he was our leader, and we circled around the trunk that would become our dining and campaign table, and so convened the first meeting of the Leopard Gang.

* * *

Place, rather than time, is the stitch that weaves African stories together, and when Granma told us he knew where a cache of weapons could be found, it seemed preordained that they'd be buried near the sacred mahogany that towered over Saint Agnes's, on a patch of desolate ground scattered with dead and fresh flowers. The previous owner of the weapons, the story goes, was a cadre of rebels who, in the early days of the war, infiltrated Rhodesia with neither reconnaissance, nor planning, nor any local support from the villagers, whom the police alternately bribed and bullied for information. They suffered three weeks of starvation and exposure before they finally buried their weapons and money and uniforms and made their way south across the Botswanan border. Only one member of the cadre, Granma, would return to Rhodesia to resume the *hondo*.

Granma's foot had prevented him from joining us, so there was a childish excitement among the Leopard Gang when we broke ground beneath the waxing crescent moon, playing pirates after treasure. At times Madota's shoulder touched mine as we put our weight to the spades, and an acute awareness of her flooded me, and I felt myself swell against the fabric of my trousers. Although the beleaguered guerrillas had buried the weapons shallowly in their haste to be rid of them, the dry season had turned the mound of earth into the crown of a great skull, and the romance quickly evaporated as the tips of our shovels scraped against the hardpan.

As we dug, I told October Twenty-Five and Zhanta about the twelve lay Catholics, all young Shona men under the direction of a Swiss Bethlehem priest, who had built the chapel, convent, native school and orphanage during such a dry season. A Mother Superior and twenty-four young novices came with the rains, and the chapel sank and canted beneath their feet. After the Swiss Bethlehem father returned to Umtali, the Shona men erected a temporary barracks at a discreet distance from the convent and, according to the story, continued to serve the sisters, first installing blair toilets and a donkey boiler, then a runoff channel to direct the rainwater down the mountainside. The laymen stayed on after there was nothing left to build, repairing all imperfections, save the breach in the wall forced by the mahogany's roots, which provided secret access to the compound.

There was a mandatory hanging clause in the Law and Order Act for anyone found guilty of terrorist activity. Possession of a firearm constituted such an offence, and in our fatigue it was easy to imagine that the hole we dug was, in a way of speaking, our own grave. October Twenty-

Five shuddered and climbed out of the shallow pit to smoke a cigarette beneath the mahogany, and Zhanta threw a shovelful of dirt at him. 'Why do you stand there breathing through your nose while we work so hard? Granma says, "Where one rests, another works double."'

'Granma's always talking. *Zzzz. zzz. zzz.* Where's he now? Who's working double for him?' October Twenty-Five thought Granma was *vuta*, full of airs. 'He also says he'll take on all the sins of our nation. A big job for an old cripple.' Granma was a sinnerist who believed he could save people from evil by committing their transgressions for them. October Twenty-Five spat into the hole where Zhanta dug.

Zhanta's colourless eye glared. He believed Granma was a holy man. Madota and I continued to dig, uneasy in our growing fear that we would exhume the fine bones of smothered infants. It was widely known that the nuns had buried their unwanted babies here, marking the anniversary of each interment with a spray of hothouse flowers. At a depth of four feet, we uncovered a bed of sticks that the rebels had spread over the weapons. I trained my penlight into the shallow pit while October Twenty-Five inventoried the cache: five Chinese AK automatics, seven grenades, one landmine, several thousand rounds of ammunition, stacks of ZANU pamphlets, straps of South African and Rhodesian money, two TNT demolition slabs, a military radio, a PPSH Russian submachine gun, piles of Mao's *Little Red Book*, and discarded uniforms.

We reburied the pamphlets and books, as well as the radio – the Rhodesian Security Forces occupied so many frequencies that it wasn't safe to use it. Madota and I shook out two sets of camouflage uniforms to take home and wash for ourselves. My fatigue shirt had a bullet hole in the shoulder, and when we returned to the shed Madota sat close and taught me how to sew it shut, looping the needle in small, even stitches, my hands in hers, the cooking fire hot on our faces, the smoky chicory from Granma's coffee in our nostrils.

That same night, a leopard visited Granma in a dream, and she told him we would be invisible at night if we kept off the crest of hills where the stars and moon would silhouette us, and she warned us that we must put aside our selfish interests or fail in our rebellion. The leopard was the spiritual animal of Granma's clan, and she advised and warned him in his dreams.

We called ourselves the Leopard Gang in honour of Granma's dream, and we broke off the front and back sights on our weapons to prove we would kill close in the night, and we called each other 'comrade' and fired our empty rifles point-blank at life-size soldiers cut from butcher paper and taped to the rocks. The night wind made our enemies writhe under our imaginary fusillade. On Granma's strict orders, we aimed dead-centre mass, like they teach in Cuba: 'Humans are too hardheaded, and sometimes the bullet will turn against the skull. Better to hit the belly or chest.

That way, you remove three soldiers from the fight – the soldier you shoot, and the two who carry him away.' The mountain wind swallowed the hollow tick of our dry fire, and our silent target practice went unheard by the sticks of police and soldiers who patrolled the highlands; nor did it reach my father as he paced the bungalow's perimeter with the ridgeback, checking locks, testing mesh window coverings; nor did it penetrate my mother's bedroom, where she kept my father's loaded service revolver within arm's reach at all times. Whether she planned to use this weapon as a last-ditch defence against the terrs who would one night burst into her room, or whether she intended at that final moment to turn it on herself, is beyond my ken.

* * *

In September, when the Leopard Gang was still new, we cleared Granma's maps from the steamer trunk and laid on a feast. Granma peppered rusks of stale bread with cinnamon, and we immersed them in his ceramic mug until they were soft with instant coffee and chicory; October Twenty-Five fried beetles that Zhanta rooted from the bark of dead flame trees that had once grown in the garden; I bought scuds of beer and takeaways of fried meat; and Madota stewed a pot of fresh vegetables that had been delivered to us anonymously. Though the Leopard Gang stayed clear of the tribal trust land, we had awoken that morning to find gem squash, tomatoes, cucumbers, maize, pumpkins, papaya, mangos, and courgettes piled outside the shed door. 'There are brothers and sisters everywhere,' Granma told us.

Madota sang a simple blessing over the food, *Keep us well Father*, the music composed the moment it left her mouth, *Guide us in all we do*, grace notes stretching and bending each syllable. I wondered which 'father' she meant: the Christian God of the Sisters of Saint Agnes, as illustrated in her book of Bible stories; Mhondoro, the great tribal spirit of the Shona people; or the spirit of her own dead father. Granma told me to hang some meat outside the shed, and I reckoned this to be some sort of spiritual offering to facilitate the healing of his foot, which I suppose, in a sense, it was.

'Have more, brother,' Zhanta pressed Granma.

Granma refused. 'If I take too much, someone else goes without.'

October Twenty-Five had no such qualms and accepted another scud of beer, then sang the song of the absent lover for his wife who waited in the trust land for his return. *Faraway mountains hide you from me*, the shed's solitary window above him framed the emptiness of the night sky, *while closer mountains throw their shadows at me*, and here he made a fist, for dramatic tension maybe, or some feeling for his woman that had welled up inside him, *Would that I had my war club*, or perhaps this was how the song was sung, with balled fists, *I would smash the near mountains*, and he brought the fist down on the table softly so that it would not disturb his beer, *Would that I had bird wings*, and he made as if he were going to rise, but instead settled back on his haunches, *I would fly over the far mountains.*

His song conjured a buried memory of my parents singing behind the closed door of my mother's room, their harmonies perfectly blended, proof that this was something they'd done often in the long ago, before my father brought his bride to Africa. It was an ancient air, mournful and Scottish. They never sang again in my hearing, and so I'm unable to weave the lyrics of their song into this narrative, nor provide details from behind that closed door to establish a scene, leaving this memory a digression to be edited out, perhaps, in the next telling.

No one spoke at the close of October Twenty-Five's song, and he laughed at my surprise. 'I know how you like to tell stories, nephew,' he said to me, 'and that you say I joined the revolution to get away from my wife and all those children.' Outside the shed, the flies hummed around the meat I'd hung out for Granma. 'Now I'll tell you the truth. My wife's a small woman. When she birthed our twelfth child, the *nganga* told us she wouldn't live through another; if I went with her again, the result might kill her. I had to go somewhere, so I joined the liberation movement.'

'*Ehe!* Why not use a condom, man?' Zhanta asked.

'A condom can fall off, or sometimes they break holes. No, I'm a patient man. There's no quick end to our revolution, and she hasn't so many childbearing years left.'

It took more than a day for the flyblown meat to cultivate maggots, which Madota applied to Granma's gangrenous wound to eat away the poisoned flesh. While Granma screamed into a knotted rag stuffed into his mouth, Madota and I resumed our struggle, hidden in the pruned thicket that surrounded the shed. I had progressed to the point where Madota was naked to the waist, but despite my coaxing and petting, she refused to yield to me. *Why do we do this?* she asked with her eyes. The contest might have lasted all night had October Twenty-Five not discovered us when he left the shed to relieve himself. 'This sort of thing endangers everyone,' he muttered, returning with a full bladder to watch over Granma.

That morning, Madota burned out the maggots with a glowing stick, and Granma fell into a deep sleep that lasted two days. When he awoke, he refused to take any of the instant coffee we'd made for him, and he gave his ceramic mug to Madota, and he told us his dream. 'In my sleep, the leopard told me our first target. We attack the sisters at Saint Agnes tonight.'

Zhanta's eye stared at Granma, and Madota seemed to sink into herself. I retreated from the circle of rebels. Up to this point, it had all been playing soldiers and talking.

'They're only old women, comrade,' October Twenty-Five said.

'Those old women with their Jesus. He's more dangerous than soldiers.' Granma's foot appeared smaller beneath the bandages. 'A proper saviour would commit our sins for us, so that we might be spared.'

'Is this what we trained and planned for?' Zhanta asked. 'Warriors are supposed to die in combat, but nuns!'

'Just so!' Granma thumped the chest, and its contents shifted musically. 'How many such acts can we stomach? It's time for a new war, one so ugly nobody can face it. The old one's gone on too long.'

'They aren't hurting anybody,' I said. It had been my practice to remain silent at these meetings, and my voice sounded thin and childish in my ears.

Granma settled back on his haunches and stared at me. 'When I was a small boy, a messenger from the Ministry of Lands informed my family that our ancestral homestead had been designated as white and our cattle would be confiscated to make room for their convent and orphanage. No one's blameless, nephew.' And here was the reason his story kept circling round to the ancient mahogany tree.

Zhanta's bleached eye wept in its socket. Shortly after his release from the dip tanks, guerrillas had come to his village and promised his mother they'd send her son to England to study so he could become a leader when majority rule came. They took him across the border into

Zambia, where they gave him a khaki shirt and trousers and a new name and sent him to Algeria for training. Each night, Zhanta pictured the faces of his family and fought to remember the exact position of each house in his village. 'We'll never go home,' he said miserably.

'This is something you've just now realised?' Granma said sharply.

'I didn't join the liberation movement to kill nuns,' October Twenty-Five said.

Granma placed his hand on October Twenty-Five's shoulder. 'No worries, comrade. I'll take their deaths upon myself.' In these last days, the old revolutionary spoke with gravity and portent, as if he were reading scripture.

I collected water in buckets from the bungalow's kitchen and we ritually cleansed ourselves in preparation for the attack, lathering and rinsing our genitals and armpits. No one else stared when Madota joined us, but I couldn't look away from her nakedness, the water that ran down her belly and off the hair between her legs, and I quickly rinsed and covered my hardness. We dressed and drew leopard spots on each other's faces with burnt sticks, and we set off together to Granma's new war, because we were too frightened to face it alone.

* * *

I'd leave off the rest, but a story ossifies over time and there's no changing it. The Leopard Gang moved through the breach in the wall, towards the unlit chapel where the old nuns, it is said, danced slowly in each other's arms, their eyes closed, remembering. Madota and I took our place with the submachine gun behind the rubble of bricks thrown up by the mahogany tree. From here we could watch the road and provide covering fire for our comrades. The convent shone in the moonlight like the walls of heaven in Madota's picture Bible. This story was supposed to be about how I lost my virginity and became a man, but somehow Granma had turned it inside out until it was all about killing nuns, and there was no longer any time for coming-of-age. My blood was up when I raised the submachine gun and trained it between Granma's shoulder blades.

Perhaps Madota read my intent, for she unbuttoned her fatigue shirt and let it fall to the ground. The silver wedding bands that hung from her neck shone against her skin. The larger ring had belonged to her father, who raised her, the smaller ring to the mother who'd died outside her memory. Granma limped into the darkness, and I sighed as I lowered the weapon, and the mountain wind swept away my breath.

Madota raised her arms and I removed her undershirt, humming inside with satisfaction as I kissed her face and neck and breasts and nipples. Madota showed me how to arrange her body beneath me and, after a few misguided thrusts, guided me into her. Below us, an armoured car wound its way up the mountainside followed by a five-tonner filled with soldiers who sat on sandbags to protect their testicles from landmines, their cigarette ends glowing like rats' eyes. I wondered who in the Leopard Gang had betrayed us. I tried to roll over to the submachine gun, but Madota pulled me back to her. I couldn't find my breath, her beauty and the moment stretched out before me. I heard the squeak of axles as the vehicles moved closer, and the rustle of dead petals from the nuns' hothouse flowers beneath us. Perhaps Madota relented not because she loved me, but rather so she could cease to love me, or maybe there, lying on her fatigue shirt beneath the immense moonshadow of the mahogany, she imagined herself in the marriage bed we would never share.

The first report of Granma's rifle came to us from the convent. The nuns, some say, recited in unison as they were exterminated, *The Lord is my shepherd, I shall not want*, and it has been reckoned that the interval between each shot was precisely the amount of time it took Granma to hobble over to the next kneeling sister, *He maketh me to lie down in green pastures*, and with each line another voice fell away, *He leadeth me beside the still waters*, until only one sister was left to deliver the final line of their dwindling psalm, *and I will dwell in the house of the Lord for ever.*

The rattle of the armoured car and the five-tonner continued to grow closer, Granma fired his final shot from inside the convent, my flesh was overwhelmed, and here was the reason I joined the war of liberation, to bring Madota to this moment of selfishness, and I rutted and roared and shut out the rumble and clatter of vehicles and soldiers and gunshots, my eyes closed to her impassive stare so as not to spoil this beautiful moment when I became a man.

Exhausted, I listened to the crack of the soldiers' FN rifles and the deeper pop of the Leopard Gang's Chinese assault rifles as they returned fire. I could barely lift my head to see October Twenty-Five catch it on the lawn of the chapel. A bullet in the chest turned him to face his executioners, a second in the neck, a third in the groin. He must have rejoiced at this last wound, for he was no longer a threat to his own wife, and he lay on his side and bled into the ground, and he sang the song of the absent lover until there was no more breath to carry the words to the nearby trust land where she waited for him. Zhanta's dying silhouette moved between the trees amid the wink of the soldiers' flash suppressors, the restless, bleached eye now sightless, his arms and legs dancing crazily as he fell, only to miraculously rise again in his village where, it was said, he was seen by his mother and her cousin. There was no sign of Granma during this brief skirmish outside the chapel, and the news service would report only two bodies recovered.

I closed my eyes and dreamed of Madota in some future, faraway place where I could never find her. *She cradled an infant in her arms, a girl child that looked like her mother, but with blue eyes and a ginger cast to her hair.* I reached out to touch my lost family, but their skin was as rough as the wool of Madota's fatigue shirt, and my fingers came away sticky with blood in the place where she had lain, but now was gone. If the mahogany had not sunk its roots deep into the earth over the centuries, it would have turned away, having seen enough, as I ran into the darkness of the forest.

* * *

The branches of the sacred tree now support an epilogue to this story – chimes made from broken rifle sights, silver wedding rings, and the shards of a ceramic coffee mug, a sign, perhaps, that Madota refused to drink from Granma's cup. The caretaker of the empty convent bought the chimes, she recalled, at a *musika*, before the police shut down the native market and scattered the vendors, from a woman who carried on her hip a coloured child with ginger hair. I received my call-up notice on the second anniversary of the Leopard Gang's attack on the sisters, and was given two weeks to report for induction into the Rhodesian Security Forces.

My father, worried that the underbrush might provide the terrs with cover, hired a bulldozer to level the ground between the bungalow and the security fence. Some nights,

I crossed the floodlit area between the sandbagged walls of our house and the mesh fence, past the ridgeback that patrolled the broken ground, the stump of its docked tail stiff and unwagging, and through the surrounding tangle of new growth and deadfall to the place where the Leopard Gang had once sat and planned around my mother's hope chest, the shed now dark and the roof collapsed. The crepuscular moonflowers still opened their white petals though, and the wind continued to gather hollow notes from the chimes, and these were reasons enough to draw me there.

The Portuguese had lost Mozambique, and the new government there welcomed the boys of the *hondo* to operate from behind the closed frontier that bordered the eastern highlands of Rhodesia. From their new base camps, the terrs could easily cross the free-fire zone on foot, or come to us in the night, crowded onto the running boards and bonnets of jeeps.

The sound of their engines woke me, and I heard them shoot our security dog, and still I didn't leave my bed. The bungalow's many doors offered only illusory escape routes.

Neither my father nor mother registered any shock at the sight of the hooded rebels who had crowded their dreams since they landed together in Africa. The terrs set fire to the bungalow and we all fell back before its heat. My father would go to his death ahead of us, neither courageous nor cringing, but resigned, as if he hadn't any place in this new world where it was no longer a good thing to be white. My mother followed him passively – perhaps her pistol had clattered to the floor when she reached for it, and they found her scrabbling on her knees in the darkness. Or she had placed the barrel in her mouth but could not make herself pull the trigger. Regardless, the pistol was useful only to ward away night fears, like the ridgeback that lay motionless beside the burning house, its tongue lolling.

They shepherded us away from the house and made us lie down on broken soil where they would bring us to still waters. This was the path of righteousness, and though we lay in the shadow of the glen, I feared no evil, for Granma stood there before us, terrible and deathless, with his walking stick and his Chinese assault rifle, and I took such comfort as I could in his presence.

Granma stood above my father, the barrel of his rifle pointed dead-centre mass, and he retreated a step to avoid the backsplash of gore. My mother took my father's hand and he squeezed back, the only sign of affection between them I would ever witness. At least they would have this, the dying together. My father bounced as the bullets *thupped* into his back, and my mother wailed as she fully realised for the first time since my birth that she was in Africa, a rending ululation that resonated even after Granma took her death upon himself.

I buried my face in my arms as Granma's uneven

footsteps grew closer, and I shuddered at the touch of his rifle against the back of my head. A breath of wind filled the hollows of the glen like pan pipes, and from somewhere within the foliage outside the security fence, Madota's bric-a-brac chimed like bells for a wedding, *There was once a girl*, and I wanted to marry her and hold our daughter in our arms, *There was once a girl*, and my story no longer belonged to me, any more than the ancient sisters of Saint Agnes could lay claim to the tales I'd invented of their Shona lovers and smothered children.

Certainly there followed the staccato of automatic gunfire, but only muted sounds penetrate such moments and register on the memory. The soft tangle of music from Madota's wind chimes, *Let's go to Zinjanja!* The crackle of flames that burned away the covers of the sandbags, melting their contents into walls of opaque glass.

Granma broke training and pushed his rifle against my head, hard enough to make the barrel slide at an oblique angle, and the first bullet turned my skull without penetrating it, as he always warned us might happen if we didn't fire dead-centre mass, and the rest streamed harmlessly into the ground. My shoulder settled against my father's, and my mother's dead fingers touched the wetness of my anointed head as I fell into darkness, and now that the rebels had finally come, we were a family; my father, my mother, and I.

At this point, the Shona water drawers might conclude

their storytelling with 'Day breaks'; or a child with the rote 'The end'; or, in the psalmody of the sisters of Saint Agnes, 'Amen'. But endings sometimes go and come without the story taking notice. Granma's story, I suppose, is still alive with atrocities committed so others will be spared, and Madota's story flows with her breast milk into our daughter, while the story of my father and mother continues along a path this earthbound narrative cannot follow. My own story invariably circles round to the night when Granma spared me to answer my call-up notice and become a soldier on the other side of the same fight, his disciple in the new war, a storybook of fresh offences open before me.

# *The Centre of the World*

December, 1972

For dinner, I warmed an opened tin of meat paste in the convection oven, a massive appliance that in times past accommodated a prison loaf large enough to feed thirty-nine boys. The cooking smells rose with the heat into the rafters of the empty dining facility.

Days come to an abrupt end in the eastern highlands, and by the time I rose from the table the view of the glen had already been replaced by my reflection on the window-panes. I switched off the radio, silencing the Christmas carols and war bulletins. Guerrilla soldiers had fired up a farm in northeastern Rhodesia in these, the closing days of 1972.

As the last and sole ward of the Outreach Mission for Troubled Boys, it fell upon me to put out the lights and lock up. A framed map hung above the exit, paper continents arranged against a sea of blue felt. Africa rode too high on the equator, Rhodesia slightly left of middle, locating the mission at the dead centre of the world. Outside a man was unhitching a dented horse trailer from the Very Reverend's Land Rover. Mrs Tippett stood on the rectory verandah, making certain the man left the blankets and tackle which were not part of the purchase agreement. The Very Reverend had retired for the night. Since the Prisons Department cancelled its contract with the mission, he slept more than he was awake, leaving his wife to supervise the dissolution of his life's work.

'Where are you off to?' she asked me.

I shrugged. The stables no longer needed mucking. Earlier in the week a representative from the Rhodesian Security Forces had collected all the mission horses, excepting the mare that drowned in the river. Mrs Tippett turned back to the rectory wherein her husband slept, the windows shuttered against his failure. 'Go on then,' she muttered.

I watched the man drive away with the battered trailer. Once, when the trailer was filled with horses, a green mamba had crawled inside and was stamped to a pulp. This was how the dents had been made. It was Ibzan who told me this. He used to say I collected stories like other boys collect dead bugs. In my pocket was the notice I'd retrieved from the garbage:

NOTICE OF CREMATION AND DISPOSITION

H. Takafakare Crematory

'Pay your last respects, not your lifetime earnings'

This is to respectfully inform concerned persons that the
burning and disposal of all remains correlative to the
deceased will be conducted by end of removal day.

I started along the dirt track that cut across the empty compound. Each morning women from the trust land raised their yokes and tramped down the mountain path through the mission to fetch water from the place where the river ran deepest. In their stories they referred to the track as Three Man Road. Before their relocation to the trust land, the water drawers had inhabited a village on the river near a sacred kopje where heaven joined with earth. Always they beat the ground with their walking sticks as they followed the track that took them back to the river of their youth. Their descent into the glen took less than an hour; the laden climb back to the trust land consumed the balance of their lives.

As they walked, the women took turns reciting a communal narrative that began in a time when God and animals still spoke to people. On the occasions when I accompanied them, the women spoke English, happy to have an audience. Their stories revolved around place rather than character, and symbolism took precedence over plot. The cadence of their voices rose and fell with the beat of the walking sticks. And when the final words were uttered, '*That is all*,' and the women found themselves stranded in the present day, someone would cry out, '*A story!*' evoking a chorus from the others: *'Bring it!'* and the water drawers would begin again, reaching back into the days of creation.

I followed the track past the darkened dormitory that had once housed the criminal youth of our nation. These days Rhodesia needed her troubled boys for the war, and any interest in their redemption had evaporated. A soft tremor ran through the ground, making the soles of my feet itch. The glen lay on the southernmost boundary of a tectonic plate that stretched the length of Africa. It was a shifting, unsettled place and such quakes were common, though nothing ever came of them. The track crooked around the abandoned chapel, then traced the riverbank half a mile to the foot of a kopje that rose up from the bottom of the glen. Some ancient cataclysm had sheared away the summit, giving it the appearance of a colossal altar. A pillar of smoke spiralled up.

I began my climb, stepping along one of the twin wheel ruts that angled across the steep face. Snow fell as I neared the top, the flakes warm on my cheeks. I brushed at them and my fingers came away grey and greasy.

The ground grew level beneath my feet as I reached the flattened crest. In the darkness I could make out a brick oven that bulged and billowed amid a field of ash. A breeze-block house stood at the oven's mouth, illuminated by its flames. Chimes hung from the eaves, hollow bones that twisted and came together in dull, yet musical, clacks.

The owner of the field was named Mr Takafakare, a failed sweet potato farmer given to great fits of coughing. He stood over a charred husk that had once been the neck and shoulder of the drowned mare. A lorry had been backed up to the oven, a chain saw in its empty bed.

'Come to see the horse-burning,' Mr Takafakare said. I blinked through the pong of charred hair. The cremator gave a short bark of laughter that trailed into a phlegmy burr. 'You almost missed it, young sir.' He produced a perfectly white handkerchief, cleared his throat, and spat. The wind lifted flakes of burned bone and tissue into a swirl of carbon waste that rose and fell on the field.

Mr Takafakare had bought the field to grow sweet potatoes, and later added the kiln as a side business. He came on the idea after listening to an African Service radio broadcast in which an agriculturalist from the Ministry of Lands touted carbon as an excellent source for fertiliser. Mr Takafakare quickly discovered there was no market for sweet potatoes grown in human ash, and the path of his life turned away from farming and towards burning. For twenty years the oven exhaled the marrow of blackened bones into his face, forcing him to retreat each night into his house where he buried his nose and mouth in freshly laundered linen handkerchiefs. Therein he spat and blew the corporeal residue of landless Shona, low-caste Indians, vagrants of mixed race and diseased livestock.

Mr Takafakare broke the mare's cremains in half with

his spade, and they reared up in a flurry of sparks and ash. The oven flared, bathing the scene in white light, and I saw a girl standing atop a ladder against the roof of the house. She held a laundry basket on her hip, the tip of her nose barely visible beyond the line of her cheek. Moses-in-the-boat grew in a window box next to her, pointed tongues of purple and green wagging in the blasted air. The girl's skin and hair were a uniform grey, save for the brown of her forearms which looked as though they had been recently immersed in water. I watched her spread her father's handkerchiefs to wind-dry on the asbestos roof. My face grew hot. I was uncomfortable with strong emotion: an inherited trait.

The cremator followed my gaze to his daughter. He might have told me to go home, but he knew I'd come from the mission and he didn't want any trouble. Ash rose in devils that swirled through the lower rungs as the girl descended the ladder with her empty basket. Mr Takafakare buried his face in his linen handkerchief, blew noisily, then presented her to me.

'This is my child, Madota.' It is a custom to give children names that reflect a family problem at the time of the birth. Mr Takafakare called his daughter *Madota*, which in the Shona language means ashes. She stood before me in the light of the oven, enveloped in silence. 'A demon lives inside her,' Mr Takafakare said. 'She cannot speak.'

I followed Madota into the house. The furnishings were

spare: a cooking pot and three metal bowls; a cardboard box containing groceries for the week; the typewriter and thesaurus which had produced the notice in my pocket; a sprung mattress, dark and shiny in the place where Mr Takafakare lay alone each night in his own sweat; a neatly-made doss where his daughter slept; and four grey volumes, Winston Churchill's *The History of the English-Speaking Peoples*, each with a facsimile signature of the former British prime minister scrawled across its cover in cramped, golden script, the handwriting of a megalomaniac. Their former owner was a teacher at the trust land school who died intestate. Mr Takafakare had taken the books with the corpse as payment for the latter's removal, and now kept the volumes stacked on the floor for use as a stool.

An unframed photograph of Mr Takafakare's dead wife was affixed to the wall, her wedding ring suspended from a tack. Mrs Takafakare's constitution had been defeated by the fine layer of human ash that covered every surface and utensil of that unclean house. It was said she left behind a corpse so diminished that when her husband folded and fed it into his oven the flames only licked at the shroud before subsiding. In desperation, Mr Takafakare doused his wife with petrol, and she went up in a bituminous cloud that filled the sky until a cleansing rain erased it two days later.

Madota wiped the ash from the kitchen table before seating me in front of a large bowl of peanut butter soup.

It tasted faintly of carbon, and I realised she had heated it atop the brick kiln. Her almond eyes followed each spoonful of soup to my mouth. I stared back, suddenly aware that I was eating her dinner.

I poured the unfinished soup into the sink and sat atop *The History of the English-Speaking Peoples.* Madota squatted on her haunches beside me and the earth trembled lightly as we looked out of the window into a galaxy of stars that wavered in the heat of the brick oven. Her fingers were corded with muscle and tendon from a lifetime of wringing handkerchiefs. They squeezed my hand with a silent request. *Talk to me.*

I'd never spoken at length to a girl before and, as the warmth of her hand seeped into mine, I began to recite the stories I'd collected from the water drawers, braiding one into the next. 'This happened in a time,' I began, 'when people still listened to God and animals.'

As I spoke, Mr Takafakare looked up from his mattress, distressed with the way things were turning in these, the last months of his life. I had seen blood mixed with ash and mucus in his handkerchiefs and knew that soon Mr Takafakare would be fed into his own oven.

The night wind rolled off the mountains, carrying away the heat from the oven, and the mare's remains cooled and fell to join the rest of the forgotten animals and ancestors that blanketed the flat summit of the kopje. Outside hyenas, lured by the smell of charred meat, ploughed the field with their noses, breaking bones with their jaws and filling their bellies with ashes.

* * *

Four streams flowed down from the mountains that walled the glen. They came together to form the river, a topographical feature that, coupled with the abundance and variety of fruit trees, convinced the Very Reverend that he'd found the location of Eden. He lobbied the Ministry of Lands and National Resources to bulldoze a Shona village and shift its inhabitants to the trust land on the periphery of the glen, that he might establish the mission upon the geographical origins of his faith.

Mrs Tippett and I ate fried eggs at opposite ends of the dining facility, our flatware unnaturally loud against the dishes. The Very Reverend no longer rose for breakfast. When the mission's funding got the axe, the older boys were offered commuted sentences to join the Rhodesian Security Forces, while the younger ones were sent to industrial schools to serve out the remainder of their time. With only a month left of my sentence, I'd been allowed to stay while Mrs Tippett disposed of the mission's assets.

I could hear the voices of the water drawers outside as they went down to the river with clay urns suspended from their yokes, always following the dirt track across the mission grounds. Half crippled by age, they refused the convenience of the communal tap in the trust land, preferring instead to fetch their water and gossip at the river. The Very Reverend had ordered an end to this trespass, but his servants refused to interfere with the women. I sometimes sat on the chapel steps as they drew water, listening to the words stream from their mouths.

Mrs Tippett surprised me by speaking. 'I need you to help me dress the Very Reverend and bring him out onto the verandah.'

'I've got things to do,' I said, rising to leave.

Mrs Tippett pushed the eggs around on her plate. 'When I was your age,' she said finally, 'I also believed the world revolved around me.'

Outside, two men struggled to push a pump organ through the double doors of the chapel, an uphill battle. The chapel had been built too close to the river and the altar-end was sunk deep into the mud. Red locusts crunched beneath my feet, spilling their eggs into the dirt, a sign, according to the water drawers, that the rains were coming. The women had warned me away from the kopje. They believed cremation was the worst form of desecration; that without the body, the spirits of the burned would become homeless and unpredictable. I arrived to find Mr Takafakare forcing a corpse into a crouching position. The brick kiln was only four feet square.

'Back again, young sir. I'm afraid my daughter must go

into the mountain to collect camphor basil to help with my coughing.' He shook his head regretfully. 'Come back next week.'

Madota's fingers settled lightly on the ball of my shoulder, *Come with me*, so I accompanied Madota down the kopje, her father staring after us. We walked along the river bank, our feet sinking in the black vlei, and I felt as if I were moving in a dream. 'Here's where the mare drowned,' I said. 'The one your father was burning when I first came to your house.' Already it had faded into a brief anecdote to associate with the moment of our meeting.

Three Man Road climbed out of the glen and into the mountains, past the ancient mahogany tree, a convent that housed orphaned Shona girls, the thornbush where my godfather buried my umbilical cord. We passed the foundations of a coriander plantation abandoned by Franciscan monks – Manicaland is littered with the ruins of forgotten missions – and I told Madota how, in olden times, the friars would move naked through the groves at night, fertilising the rows of coriander with their semen. The ground shuddered softly beneath us and we held hands for balance. The track crossed the mountain highway where vendors and market goers choked on the dust and diesel that filled the mouth of the trust land. My calves ached as I struggled to match Madota's pace, her form seeming always to hover ahead and above me, ringed in light, a sign that the air was thinning and my mind was starved of oxygen.

My words became lost in the roar that filled my ears. Three Man Road came to an end in a profane place where God moulded Past, Present, and Future into a single creature that chased itself in circles. All this I had learned from the women as they drew their water from the river. Deadfall blew across the clearing. 'South-blown leaves,' I said, parroting the water drawers, 'rain to follow.'

Madota turned back to me, and her fingers found the base of my skull. *Kiss me.* I leaned towards her face, and her mouth swallowed my words before I could give them voice. Above, the sun moved unnoticed in its sky, the mountain air collected the moisture it had dispensed at dawn, and clouds erased the glen below.

The river, straightened by age, bisected the glen into perfect halves. Each morning I walked its banks to Madota's house, past the place where the drowned mare had lain for two days undiscovered, its stomach bloating with combustible gases that burned so fiercely that they melted the oven bricks. In order to prevent further damage to his livelihood, Mr Takafakare took to crouching by the mouth of the warped oven, gauging the heat by the intensity of the blast that struck him full in the face. He had endured this awful proximity for almost a month before resolving to travel across the mountains to Umtali to purchase a pyrometer.

Mr Takafakare had never left the glen, so he asked me to accompany him. The low clouds hung motionless around us as the lorry struggled up the mountain face. Mr Takafakare stuffed camphor basil into his mouth while he drove, grinding it into a leafy bolus that filled all the gaps in his teeth. I spread a Survey Unit Reserve map across my lap, ready to call out directions once we reached unfamiliar territory. Rhodesia had been featureless before the English-Speaking Peoples came to chart and name it, one of Churchill's 'empty places of the globe'.

'Why do the water drawers think the kopje is sacred?' I asked.

The lorry whirred and juddered up the steep grade. Mr Takafakare chewed on the camphor basil and my question. 'In the beginning of the world,' he said, 'God tore apart the mountains and buried the village in ash. When our ancestors saw that the kopje had been cut in half, they took this as a sign that it was a sacred place.' Three Man Road floated before us on the clouds. 'They began to bury their dead here, in a crouching position, shoulder to shoulder, generations upon generations, until the ground was filled. This is why I was allowed to buy the field. Even the Europeans refuse to live in this place.' He wanted to say more, but he fell into a coughing fit that peppered the windscreen with festive flecks of green and red.

The lorry rolled to a stop when we reached the mountain highway. Mr Takafakare turned in his seat and looked down on the glen. Perhaps he was afraid that if we continued, we would drive off the face of the earth. He remained twisted in his seat, staring back on the road he had taken, the unmuffled engine idling and backfiring. Finally, he executed a three-point turn on the horizon of the world, and we returned without the pyrometer.

That night at the mission, I dreamed Mr Takafakare was pushing me into his oven. I awoke crouching beneath my blanket, flames lapping at the wallpaper. The Very Reverend had splashed diesel fuel over the dormitory floorboards and lighted it. I wrapped myself in my bedclothes and crawled through the smoke towards a gauzy rectangle of starlight framed by flaming curtains. Outside, I threw off the burning blankets and rolled in the dirt, my lungs heaving.

The building was a lost cause by the time I reached the water hose, so I soaked the ground to keep the fire from spreading to the rectory. The Very Reverend quoted scripture as Mrs Tippett led him away, the sparks catching and dying in her hair. 'Take heed to thyself,' he shouted at me, 'that thou offer not thy burned offerings in every place that thou seeist.'

Mr Takafakare was an outcast among the people who engaged his services, so he did not object when I offered to ride with him as he conducted his final removals. On these occasions he recited accounts, punctuated by coughs and throat clearings, of the first ancestors who founded the bulldozed village. Mr Takafakare brought along the power saw when the removal was something large; say a bull that had succumbed to black-leg disease. A dolly was required for medium-size removals such as a fighting dog, its teeth sharpened with metal files, wounds daubed with leopard's bane in a last ditch effort to prevent blood loss and rouse the animal from shock. In the case of something small, say an infant dead of tuberculosis, Mr Takafakare would conduct the removal in a dignified manner with gloved hands.

Once we removed one of the water drawers who had died in the trust land. We took her from a single-room house, its breeze-block walls cracked and seamed from seismical stress. A communal patch of stunted mealie struggled to survive in the granite and rime soil. Madota travelled in the back with the corpse while I rode in the cab next to Mr Takafakare, his head tilted back to keep blood from streaming out of his nose. He down-shifted the lorry as we passed through the mission, slowing almost to a stop. 'Here is the place where the dead woman was born. She was my cousin.' Mr Takafakare chuckled, then fell to coughing. 'Don't look so surprised,' he said. 'It was my village as well.' A thin trickle of blood stretched from his nostril to his lip. He nodded towards his daughter. 'She also knows all the stories of our village, stupid girl.' I looked over my shoulder to the lorry bed where Madota lay across the blanket to keep it from blowing off the corpse. She was mouthing words to the bundle, the stories of a village she never knew. Mr Takafakare stared at his surd daughter in the rearview mirror. 'Small matter, young sir,' he said.

'We have lost our place in the world, and our stories mean nothing now.'

The rains, summoned by the spawning locusts, came to the eastern highlands, filling the glen. The river burst its banks and swollen currents swept away the mission chapel, leaving only naked pillars that canted in the vlei, indistinguishable from the handful of concrete headstones that marked the graves of boys and servants who'd died at the mission since its founding. There was rain enough to overfill the urns, but still the women came down to the river for their water. They shrugged when I told them that Mr Takafakare could recite a story for everything within the horizons of the glen. 'How would you know if he was lying?' one asked.

In the grey days that followed, the field atop the kopje became a lake of char. While Mr Takafakare struggled through the sheeting rain to fire his oven, I remained indoors with Madota, reading to her the stories of the English-Speaking Peoples which Churchill had taken and bound in volumes, his masterwork organised into chapters, books and volumes – divisions, regiments and battalions of words that advanced inexorably until they overwhelmed his audience.

* * *

My court sentence expired amid a series of unsubtle omens. The earth quaked and shook the glass panes from the window over the cot I'd set up in the stables, and I woke beneath a blanket of broken glass. Crows flew in through the empty frame and nested in the rafters, spattering my pillow and bedclothes with their white faeces.

One day, Mrs Tippett put her luggage and husband out on the verandah and locked the rectory. Disnested, the Very Reverend peered out at the compound through the grey lens of rain. His boys, horses and servants had been taken away to fight on different sides of the war, and the mission had the look of a razed military barracks. I held an umbrella over Mrs Tippett's head while she loaded the detritus of her life into the back of the Land Rover. The Very Reverend had located his faith in the centre of a map, but as he looked through the windscreen, he seemed not to know where he was. They drove away, leaving the buildings to collapse on their foundations and the land to become as it was in the beginning: a profane, uncreated place without form and void.

The absence of the Very Reverend and Mrs Tippett left my routine unaltered. I rose from the spattered cot each morning to help Madota pick camphor basil for her dying father and search the ash for hollow ear and finger bones suitable for chimes. At sunset, I lay beside her on the roof with the drying handkerchiefs, making shapes out of the clouds in the red sky, while below us Mr Takafakare fed his oven with scrub mahogany and corpses. The flames continued to burn ungoverned without the pyrometer, and he kept the oven door agape, judging the heat by the force with which it struck his face and blistered his lungs. The sweat evaporated before it left his pores, and his skin became indistinguishable from the oven's brick. I reckoned he would die before the rains came again, leaving all his stories sealed within his voiceless daughter.

'There. A horse,' I said to Madota, pointing at a cloud, but already the wind had pulled the image apart, and it looked as though flames were coming from its back. We descended from the roof with the dark to take our places amid the volumes of *The History of the English-Speaking Peoples.* Madota listened while I spun out a filament of lore to drape across our sliver of world, my words clacking together over our heads like the dull music of her bone-chimes. Whereas Churchill was driven to account for all the English-Speaking Peoples across the globe, I recounted only the lore that fell within my horizon. We differed, he and I, only in the scope of our compulsions.

I talked myself to sleep, my head cradled in Madota's lap, and dreamed of us alone in the valley as it had been in the beginning. *An unbroken canopy of ancient forest flanks a winding river. The granite mountain spills out fire and magma, the ground undulant and volatile beneath our feet. Madota leads me into a grove of young fruit trees, her fingers speaking with subtle pressures against my arm.* I woke to the sound of phlegmy throat-clearing, my hand on Madota's breast, Mr Takafakare standing over us. 'Perhaps you should go now, young sir.'

The sun burned away the mist and sparked against quartz deposits that shot through the jet granite mountain, forcing me to squint out over the glen from where I stood in the splintered threshold of the dining facility. Winds rippled through the orchard, turning each leaf in light and shadow. The previous night someone had prised open the door, ransacked the pantry, and stolen the flatware, dishes, food, tables and chairs, as well as the frame and the blue-felt backing for the Very Reverend's map. The paper continents swirled like leaves at my feet.

The water drawers stumped along the track that ran through the mission compound. They numbered fewer than when I had arrived at the mission a year earlier. As young brides, their husbands had been press-ganged to improve the glen with grass buffers, dip tanks, drain strips, galley dams and a highway to bring the bulldozers that would push over their village. Now the women lived as widows amid breeze-block houses and dusty fields pegged out in grids, and their granddaughters drew water from a tap.

Above, I could see the brightly coloured umbrellas of the vendors who lined the entrance to the trust land. A column of armoured cars raced past them along the mountain highway, reducing its graded surface to scree beneath their solid rubber tyres and plated steel. Once, mid-sermon, the Very Reverend had led his congregation of servants and troubled boys from the chapel to the river. 'Look,' he commanded us. 'Fix this place in your hearts, so you can return in the dark times to come.' The mission boys and servants would return to the glen in the coming years to fight each other in a war of repression and liberation, and the ground tremors would be replaced by a concussion of rockets that would shake the sacred kopje apart, spilling out the crouching bones of the village ancestors.

The mountain shadows had retreated by the time I reached Madota's house, leaving the valley bathed in sunlight. The rains had just ended. Newly-hatched locusts swarmed, devouring the tongues of Moses-in-the-boat that filled the window box. Mr Takafakare stood over a sectioned cow. I went over to help him clean the chainsaw but he waved me away. 'Why do you always come sniffing about with all your talk! Leave us alone, or I will take Madota far away from you.'

I laughed at this. 'You can't even leave the glen.'

Madota's chimes shook, though there was no wind, and I realised the ground was elastic with tremors. Mr Takafakare tried to menace me with the chainsaw but it wouldn't start. He tore through his house in a fit of temper, kicking the cooking pot, overturning the water bucket, upending the cardboard box, strewing groceries. He filled the box with Churchill's volumes and dropped them at my feet. 'Take them and go.' He wanted to say more but a racking cough seized him. He stood before me, waiting for his lungs to quiet, wishing me away. Soon his chest would grow still altogether, as the earth would one day cease to shudder and sound Madota's bone-chimes.

Madota watched me from the threshold of the disordered house as I descended the kopje shouldering the burden of *The History of the English-Speaking Peoples.* There came to me the cracked, halting voices of the water drawers as they returned from the river, laden, and I set down my books and listened to the broken rhythm of their gait, the thud of their walking sticks, the telluric drone of shifting plates of granite. Always, they had bound the glen together with their lore. Without them to remark on the connection, the red locusts would no longer lay the eggs that brought the rains to the mountains, the river would run dry, and the glen would become a furnace where sacred places warped and rifted, the world unmade.

# The Wide Boys

November, 1971

THE OUTREACH MISSION FOR TROUBLED BOYS had been built by prison labour on unsettled ground with predictable results. Doors fell from their hinges. Windows rattled softly in their frames. Jephthah, the ancient houseboy and bell ringer, roamed the compound each dawn with a hammer to pound wayward nails back into rough-hewn fruitwood that was soft with age and scored by beetles. The wood had been harvested from a nearby orchard – plum, cherry, peach, pear and apple trees grown from seeds sewn outside memory.

'Listen, novice! Twenty years ago there was nothing where we now stand.' Ibzan, the cook and assistant sacristan, liked to tell old stories to new arrivals as he guided them through their first day at the mission. 'It took just six days to put all this up,' he'd say with a sweeping hand that encompassed the rectory, dormitory, dining hall, stables, chapel, outbuildings – the eastern horizon of

Rhodesia, 'and everything has been falling to the devil ever since.'

The convicts who built the mission had been brought in chains from the remand prison. For six days they began and ended their workdays in complete darkness. On the final morning, one of the labourers buried his hammer in the guard's skull and the prisoners ran together, down the embankment and into the river, where they perished in its currents. 'God is just,' Ibzan concluded.

The ancient orchard formed a brittle canopy over a kraal where horses snorted and stamped and tossed their heads. A tribe of boys gathered for the Blessing of the Horses at an altar on the rectory lawn. The granite altar had been quarried from the mountain that held the mission in shadow. I'd arrived late the previous night and slept beneath a horse blanket, locked in the tack room, my head on a saddle.

The Outreach Mission for Troubled Boys was a last resort for the wayward white youth of our nation, petty thieves, vandals and bullies, mostly – wide boys who grew up in the reformatories and industrial schools.

Butterflies dotted a bed of liquorice that abutted the rectory. A figure walked towards us across the lawn. The sun was brilliant on his white robe, obliterating all fold and shadow, the garment two dimensional in its radiance. He called out: 'Cook!'

Ibzan stiffened. 'Yes, Adam.'

As sacristan and stableboy, Adam carried the authority of their employer and spiritual director, the Very Reverend, and that of his wife, Mrs Tippett. A crude image of Saint Anthony, struck from pig iron, hung from a chain around his neck. 'Go fetch the other servants,' he commanded.

Ibzan spat when the sacristan turned his back. 'See how he walks, *sha sha sha*, with his holy costume and religious medal. I tell you this: Adam was here when they built this mission. But he did not run into the river with the others. He was a young boy, skinny enough to pull his wrist out of the manacle.' The cook looked at me, as if for the first time. 'You like stories, novice?'

I nodded.

'Good! You will leave here with many stories.' Ibzan left me outside the dormitory. Across the lawn, the Very Reverend, founder and self-ordained minister of the Independent Anglican Church of Manicaland, took his place behind the altar, heels lifted, back ramrod, pompadour constructed of hair and tonic, stretching his frame up as far as it would go.

'Quit goggling and come along,' Mrs Tippett said, pushing past me. She wore a sweater over her sack dress and hugged a clipboard to shield her breasts from my indecent gaze. Apart from a woven bracelet of wind flowers, she was bereft of jewellery. I followed her into the dormitory where I would live out my thirteen-month sentence, a convicted peeper.

* * *

The dormitory smelled of sweat, carbolic oil and dead snake, forcing the woman to breathe shallowly through her mouth while she turned out my rucksack and rummaged through my belongings. Mrs Tippett confiscated my father's field glasses, penknife and military service pin. 'These will be sold to offset the cost of your food and housing,' she said, ignoring my protests.

Outside, the Very Reverend's convocation was underway. 'We are gathered here before God Almighty,' he said, 'to bless these horses in the name of Saint Anthony. Lord, smile upon this fellowship of men and beasts.' He drew back his lips to reveal teeth that were perfectly, astonishingly black. The objects of the blessing circled the kraal. A mare pranced at the head of the herd, her forelegs fully encased in steel from hoof to mid-pastern. She was an ill-proportioned creature, short-necked with outsized hindquarters. A confirmed kicker according to Ibzan. I counted thirty-eight horses in the kraal, not including the mare. One for each boy.

'Take these.' Mrs Tippett piled two thin woollen blankets, a foam rubber pillow, a bible and a paper schedule onto my outstretched arms. 'You'll sleep there.' Mrs Tippett indicated a gap in the line of bunks. A folding cot lay on the floor. 'There's no more proper beds,' she stated without apology. 'The Very Reverend will join you presently.' I stood with the issued items still in my outstretched arms and watched her hurry out of the dormitory.

Through the window I could see each boy leading his mount from the kraal to receive its beatitude. They were a closed-face lot, lean from months in the saddle, freckled and burnt, hair bleached by the sun. One struggled as he came through the kraal gate.

'Hold fast,' the Very Reverend told him. 'Horses want a master.' He squinted up at the animal brought before him. 'We place this beast in Your keeping. Make it a perfect instrument of Your will.'

It took two servants to lead the mare from the kraal for her blessing. A third, Ibzan, enticed the horse forward with bits of liquorice root. They kept their eyes on the ground, taking care that the mare didn't crush their feet with its steel shoes. She balked as she approached the altar, refusing the blessing, head down, weight forward, ready to kick out with her hind legs.

'*Chenjerai!*' Ibzan called out in Shona. *Watch out.* The servants dropped the bridle and backed away.

'Speak English!' Adam said sharply. 'God's language.' He flailed his hands and yelled after the mare, chasing her back into the kraal, the final blessing unbestowed.

The ground shuddered as the boys queued up to receive the Eucharist, and Adam held the paten beneath the Very Reverend's hand in case he should fumble the host.

The slapdash buildings heaved and muttered on their foundations. Behind the kraal gate the mare stood still, ears forward, intent on Adam's every movement.

The Very Reverend stretched out his hand, palm down, and the congregation knelt as one before him. 'May this mission,' he said, 'serve as a beacon on this continent of dark negation. Amen.'

'Amen,' the congregation echoed.

After the blessing, the Very Reverend greeted me from the threshold of the dormitory. 'You're the peeper,' he said. He held a chafing dish of liquorice root. 'Don't hang your head. No temptation takes us but what's common to man. The wife settle you in?'

'She stole from my kit.'

'You'll be giving your everlasting soul to God,' he said. 'Don't begrudge Him the rest.' His attention shifted to the dish of liquorice. 'It's from the rectory garden. There's nothing that won't grow here.'

'When do I learn to ride?' I asked.

His small fingers grasped a piece of liquorice. 'After your baptism.'

'I'm already baptised.'

'Not by me.' The Very Reverend placed the root on his tongue and sank inward, his lips and lids closing out the world. 'Liquorice has been with us since King Solomon's day,' he said finally. A black tongue ran across his purple lips. 'The pharaohs were buried with it. Liquorice sustained Napoleon on the battlefield. It promotes industry, provides spiritual balance, diminishes the libido, alleviates constipation. Have some.'

The liquorice was electric on my tongue, and my mouth became a fount of hot saliva. I could feel twin black worms of drool wriggle out from the corners of my lips and dangle from my chin. In desperation, I swallowed a bit and my throat and sinuses burned with it.

The Very Reverend regarded me for a moment. 'How do you hope to profit from your time with us?' he asked.

'I want to find God,' I said brightly, thinking this was what he wanted to hear.

He sprang forward and pinned me against the wall, his forearm across my throat. 'Now listen, you jumped-up little pervert. Don't think you can play me for a fool.'

I nodded, unable to speak.

He released me and turned towards the door. 'You'll do fine here, novice. Just keep your head in the scriptures and out of the windows. The other boys will come round to introduce themselves.'

I unfolded the cot and stretched out. Before long, a flood of boys pushed into the dormitory. They wore belts, bracelets, and bolo ties made from snake hide. A rotten smell emanated from these poorly cured accessories. The boys formed a line before my cot, youngest to oldest. Each struck me five times as they sang a queer little song, the first blow falling with thumb knuckle foremost, *Tom Thumper*, the next blow with the index knuckle extended, *Ben Bumper*, then the middle knuckle, *Long Larum*, the ring knuckle, *Billy Barum*, and a sideways blow from the pinky knuckle, *and Little Oker Bell!*

Mrs Tippet's paper schedule shaped my days: rise before dawn; muck the stables by lamplight; a boiled egg for breakfast; clear debris from the mission grounds; weed and water the Very Reverend's liquorice bed; another egg at lunch; two hours of bible study followed by an hour of forced prayer led by Adam; and in bed before curfew, an orange sliver of sun framed in the dormitory window as it disappeared behind the mountain.

By the time I finished mucking, the other boys had already saddled their mounts and ridden out from the mission, whooping like American cowboys as they beat the bush for snakes. I would not see them again until they returned for my nightly beating. They refused to speak to me, yet there was no rancour or unnecessary force behind the blows. I learned the best way to take them, curled up in a ball, my pillow wrapped round my face. Afterwards I lay motionless in my bed while the other boys rubbed carbolic oil into their saddle-sore thighs, whispered among themselves, became drunk with wine fermented with snake meat, and fell asleep in twos and threes.

* * *

The rains moved into the glen, obscuring holes and roots and stones, a time for horses to step carefully. I watched the mare paw the ground with her massive shoes, roll in the mud, buck and fling her heels in a capriole. No one passed through the kraal gate unless Adam was there to pacify the creature. Foundations sank into the ground. Fruitwood doors swelled in their jambs and had to be shouldered open. When the ground was too wet for riding, the boys sulked about the stables and flung manure at one another.

Things went missing: the Sanctus bell, a letter opener, the chafing dish that held the Very Reverend's liquorice root. On the occasion of these thefts, Adam would turn us out in the middle of the night and select one boy at random to be lashed with a leather belt. The number of strokes varied according to the Very Reverend's humour, as well as the offender's hair colour and handedness. Ginger-headed, left-handed boys such as me were considered resistant to discipline and in need of enhanced correction. 'Father,' the Very Reverend would say, raising the belt above his head, 'teach this young man to profit from the suffering

You've put in his path!' The Independent Anglican church of Manicaland was not in communion with the See of Canterbury, and the Very Reverend answered only to God and the Prisons Department.

The rains moved off the mountain and the water vanished into the earth. *Horse weather*, Adam called it, a time when the herd capered and rutted, sure now of their footing. Each Sabbath, the Very Reverend would press me to submit to his baptism. If I gave up my mulish behavior and became a blood-bought Christian, I could learn to ride. The Very Reverend promised to grant me authority to walk on serpents and overcome all the power of the enemy, and I would take my place among the mob of boys that swarmed over high ground and low bush, ridding the glen of snakes.

Like all the servants, Adam was forbidden to ride for fear he would steal one of the mission horses and gallop north across the Zambezi to join the guerrilla soldiers. I sometimes paused in my work and watched through the stable window as the sacristan stared across the pasture, past the chapel, to the river. The mare stood in the kraal, ears forward, immobilised in perfect concentration, her gaze fixed on the same point on the bank.

In accordance with the Very Reverend's remedial diet for troubled boys, no supper was served; a full stomach encourages dreams. When I was too hungry to sleep, I broke curfew to creep between the rows of cots and footlockers and boys – their faces guiltless in sleep – and I would steal over to the dining facility window to listen to the servants deal cards and gossip across the kitchen table. Izban, the cook and assistant sacristan, recited stories, while Elon, the kitchen- and altarboy, speculated aloud on the cards his opponents held against their chests. Jephthah, the aged houseboy and bell ringer, sat silently across from them, accepting the hand he was dealt. They were all former inmates of the remand prison, paroled, hired, and baptised on the same day. As a condition of their employment the Very Reverend had re-christened them with Old Testament names and required them to take up positions in his ministry. Once, as I looked through the sacristy window, I saw the naming bible, opened midway through *The Book of Judges.* Whenever a servant ran away, his name was struck from the page.

When the Judges of Israel retired for the night, I roamed the mission compound, peeping in darkened windows, rummaging through the outbuildings where the tractor, tackle and tools were kept. Although the rains had long departed, the flat, eaveless roofs still sagged beneath stagnant water that swarmed with mosquitoes. At this hour, mounted scouts from the Rhodesian Security Forces could be seen charging up and down the mountain steppes, a drove of centaurs in silhouette.

Winter came upon the mission, and the ground dried and shrank back like the skin on a mummy's face. During the outdoor services I sat on the lawn next to Mrs Tippett, our hands joined in prayer. She dressed simply in a grey wool suit and her flower bracelet, the only jewellery the Very Reverend permitted. Her palm emanated heat and discomfort as we listened to rambling sermons in which eggs figured prominently. Following the service, Ibzan baked us a prison loaf.

Eleven months of my sentence passed in this way. There's a restless comfort in isolation and routine. The mind, disengaged from the world, comes unsprung.

* * *

It was still night when the mare staved in the kraal gate and ran amok in the rectory grounds. I stood with Mrs Tippett in the false dawn and watched the spectacle. The mare's teeth glistened in the waning moonlight as she walked backward, pulling the Judges of Israel by the lead. The Very Reverend was away at the remand prison, witnessing for the Almighty. The Judges struggled to keep clear as the mare reared and pawed the air. Jephthah lost his footing, and the others dropped the lead and scattered, freeing the mare to let fly her heels.

The other horses stamped the earth, restless at the mare's antics. It was the third time in as many days that the mare had gone round the twist, always a welcome break in the monotony of court-imposed religious instruction. One of the mare's shoes caught Jephthah under the chin, splitting his jaw lengthwise.

'Please God,' Mrs Tippett prayed. 'Grant me strength to cope with murderous horses, Africans, and wide boys.' She looked pointedly at me.

Mrs Tippett watched tight-lipped as the mare began to roll and root in the liquorice bed. Horses and liquorice were the Very Reverend's only luxuries, and he was said to love them above all else in this world and the next. 'Go fetch Adam,' Mrs Tippett said – turning her back on me, the wild horse, the ruined liquorice bed, the defeated servants, all of it – and she retired to the rectory and put out the verandah light.

The chapel had been built on pillars near the river for convenient baptising. Each year the pillars sank several inches into the vlei until the entire structure canted sadly. Bits of wood were wedged beneath the castors of the pump organ to keep it from rolling into the altar.

I found Adam on the steps rubbing lemon and salt into the silver plate. A butterfly lighted on the polish rag and the sacristan looked at me, delighted. 'They taste with their feet,' he said. His cassock was riddled with tiny holes, the result of too many bleachings.

'The mare's got her head up again,' I told him.

Adam looked up from the butterfly.

'Kicked Jephthah in the face,' I said. 'She's in the liquorice now.'

Adam lifted the skirt of his cassock as he raced through the mud towards the rectory. I ran after him, past the unmucked stables, the darkened dormitory where the wide boys slept in dreamless exhaustion. We arrived back at the rectory to find horse and servants in a wary truce. The mare stood motionless amid the up-ended liquorice, ears back. Jephthah lay face down in the mud, the other Judges crouched near the open kitchen door, ready to bolt inside if the mare charged.

Adam draped his cassock over the gate and looked off into the mountains, rubbing grass between his palms to make a soft, swishing sound. Ignored, the mare came over to investigate the noise, bumping him gently and touching her nose to his face. If butterflies taste with their feet, who can say through which medium Adam and the mare communicated?

'Mwari!' Izban exclaimed in wonder as he opened the kraal gate for Adam and the mare.

Adam struck the cook open-handed across the face. 'Mwari is the god of beasts.'

The mare stole Adam's reach-me-down cassock from the gate and galloped into the kraal, waving the garment from her mouth like a carnival flag, head up, tail curled in high spirits.

Ibzan rubbed his cheek as he watched Adam chase after

the mare. 'Adam opens his mouth and the Very Reverend's words come out.' The cook gave me a sideways look. 'Do you know it was Adam who killed the prison guard all those years ago? He still speaks of it in his sleep. But he was clever enough not to run. Of course, the Very Reverend refuses to believe that such a sweet-faced boy could do such a thing.'

I went back to the stables to finish the mucking, show over. Manure stuck to the straw inside the stalls and I shovelled it without enthusiasm. I'd grown sluggish and cross from the Very Reverend's prescribed diet. I leaned on the handle and looked up at the mountain. A thin trail of smoke rose from the clearing where the scouts were laagered.

The rains were coming again, a time to fallow the pastures and sow pigeon grass. After I finished my mucking, I watched Adam as he tried to start the tractor without success. From the kraal, the mare also watched him, stamping to get his attention. The steel shoes sent sparks off the rocks.

'Cook says you killed a prison guard,' I said through the window.

Adam stiffened. 'Ibzan is foolish.' He stepped down from the tractor and stared out to where the mare stood, one ear pointing forward, towards the river and the mountains beyond, one ear back towards the mission. 'A horse can look two ways at once. When her ears go in different directions, so go her eyes.' Adam turned to me. 'Why do you resist baptism? Do you enjoy your beatings?'

I had no answer to this.

Adam opened the tractor bonnet and leaned over. He stared at the empty bracket beside the tractor engine, wiped his hands on his trousers, then looked at me. 'Somebody has stolen the battery.'

*Free time is the enemy of troubled minds*, a sentiment Mrs Tippett had posted on a sign above the dormitory exit. After mucking the stalls, I reported to the dining hall to set places for the other boys.

I paused at the window to look in on the servants. A pot of water and eggs roiled over a lighted stove. Ibzan was carving swine into chops for the Very Reverend. We were not allowed to eat meat as flesh was considered too stimulating for troubled boys. Jephthah sat at the kitchen table holding his ruined jaw with both hands. Elon sharpened a knife on a whetstone. He spat in the direction of the kraal. 'When Baba Zai comes back he will break that horse or shoot it, please God.' I'd discovered that the servants called their employer *Baba Zai* when they thought no one was listening. Father Egg. The insult was doubled in that it was delivered in the Shona language.

Ibzan covered the chops with a sheet of newspaper to keep the flies away. 'He will never shoot that creature. Come peel these carrots.' These were for me. The Very

Reverend prescribed a corrective diet for each of us according to our flaws. As a peeper, my lunch consisted of steamed carrots for healthier vision and a boiled egg. Everyone got the egg.

Elon pared the carrots while Ibzan wrapped a rag, chin to crown, around Jephthah's ruined face. The split jaw was already turning purple where the shoe had made contact.

Ibzan spoke soothingly to the old houseboy. 'It's all right now, Jephthah.' Then to Elon, 'We need the Very Reverend's hair tonic.'

Elon nodded. 'Why does Baba Zai put such shoes on that horse?'

Ibzan knotted the rag beneath Jephthah's chin. 'To hide its toes.'

'You mean hooves,' I said through the window. 'A horse has hooves.'

The cook squinted out at me. 'I know what I say. That horse is unnatural. This is why the Very Reverend covers its feet with steel shoes.'

'Pay him no nevermind.' Elon beckoned to me with his knife. 'Come inside.'

I remained at the window. The slats had been left unplastered and stripes of morning sun fell across the west wall. Generations of servants had sanded and polished the concrete floor to a marble smoothness.

'Before that horse was properly birthed, her mother

was killed by a leopard,' Ibzan said. 'The mare spilled out from the torn womb, unfinished. God is just.' The cook studied me for a moment. 'You want a cuppa?' He removed the eggs from the pot and poured the boiling water over some instant coffee. 'How much sugar can a boy like you take?'

Jephthah moaned piteously. I shrugged. At fifteen, other people's troubles were nothing to me. I watched the cook spoon sugar into my cup until the coffee was thick with it.

The Very Reverend returned with the rising moon and commanded Adam to turn us out of our beds to stand before the granite altar in our underpants. The stolen tractor battery lay in the mud. The Very Reverend's hair was wild, the coil of his pompadour hung over one eye.

A murmur rose from the formation of boys.

'Put your tongues back in your heads!' Adam barked.

On the verandah, Mrs Tippett embroidered a frontal for the altar. The Judges of Israel emptied the dormitory, bringing everything out onto the lawn, upending mattresses and rummaging through footlockers. The wind sailed one of the blankets across the lawn and Adam brought it back to Ibzan.

'*Mazviita*,' the cook said, thanking him.

'English!' Adam hissed.

The Very Reverend stood before the altar, watching the

judges complete the search. He grubbed in his pocket for his comb but came up empty. Ibzan dumped out the contents of the last footlocker and looked up at his employer, shaking his head.

The Very Reverend spat in his hands and smoothed back his hair before addressing us. 'I found this battery in the kraal. An interesting thing. Someone had smeared liquorice root on the terminals. When the mare licked the battery, she received a nasty shock. Anyone want to take credit for this clever piece of work?'

No one stepped forward.

He strode over to where I stood and put his face inches from mine, sniffing my breath for his missing hair tonic. 'You're smart enough, I'll grant it,' he said, 'in small, beastly ways.' He whirled and stormed to the verandah and led Mrs Tippett back by the arm. 'I've given you boys the opportunity to confess and atone,' he yelled out to us, 'but you have spurned it. So now this innocent and good woman will suffer for your trespass. Tonight, while you sleep, Mrs Tippett will work to restore my liquorice bed. She will resume this labour each dawn until the responsible party comes forward to take her place. Think on that as you lie in bed, in sin and guilt.'

After the mission returned to sleep, I left the dormitory. In the sidereal light, I could see scars in the lawn from where the mare had battled the Judges of Israel. A shadow moved sluggishly against the rectory: Mrs Tippett, squatting in the liquorice bed, trowelling mud over the exposed roots. I listened to the leopards and hyenas and scouts as they hunted the animals that went down to the river to drink under the cover of darkness. The scouts had come to the granite uplands a year earlier to beat the bush for a cadre of guerrilla soldiers. They had found them, killing most and chasing the survivors across the border into Botswana. The scouts had returned to the glen, their role in this story not yet ended. It was after midnight when the Very Reverend finally allowed his wife to brush the dirt from her arms and feet and re-enter the rectory.

But he did not follow her back inside. Unseen, I shadowed him across the mission grounds and took my place beneath the stable window. The mare stood inside, ears back, tied to a post. Adam was there too.

'She's a hot-blooded horse, a good keeper,' the Very Reverend was saying. 'See that kink?' The mare's tail flashed in an S. 'We'll take that out of her.'

Adam stared at the ground. 'You said it would be a sin to break her.'

'She's almost nine years old. I swear on my faith I won't let her go to her maker an unblessed barn rat. The Very Reverend approached the mare with some sugar cubes in his outstretched hand, let the horse smell them, take them. The mare nickered softly while he stroked its rump, back, and muzzle. Without warning, the Very Reverend drew back his fist and punched the horse behind the ear. The mare's forelegs folded. She fought to keep from rolling onto her side, then struggled back to her feet. 'See that? Most horses would've gone down.'

Adam looked away and swore softly in Shona.

'Speak English,' the Very Reverend said. 'The Devil'd have us speak in a mob of tongues, give him his way.' He worked a thick cotton rope between the mare's back legs, then encircled it around the horse's ankle and passed the loose end through the neck piece. 'Take hold,' the Very Reverend told Adam, and together they pulled smartly on the rope, bringing the hind foot forward until the mare stood on three feet, unable to straighten the bound knee. They released the hobbled horse into the kraal and she hopped away, fighting furiously against the rope. At last fatigue set in and the mare began to shake and whinny. The Very Reverend offered her a sugar cube and spoke gently, clucking, whistling, caressing her neck as Adam fetched the hose and watered the dirt at the horse's feet. When the earth was saturated, the Very Reverend threw the mare to the ground to roll helpless in the mud. He leaped on the underbelly of the toppled horse and began to sack her out, slapping her on the neck, forelegs, and withers with a burlap bag, working around to the belly and genitals until she was desperate to breathe. Horses are thin skinned, reacting to the slightest touch, and the mare laid her ears flat against her skull, mane standing on end like the hackles of a dog. She curled her upper lip, baring her teeth at the Very Reverend. For two hours this continued until the mare remained perfectly still in the mud. 'That's enough for today,' the Very Reverend said, rising. 'She's halfway gentled.' He walked towards the rectory, leaving Adam to rub butter into the mare's rope burns.

The scouts continued to squat on the mountain, racing their horses through the trust land, overturning cooking fires, trampling mealie patches, exacting hut taxes, market taxes, dog taxes, beating young Shona men caught outside after dark. Their lieutenant ruled the glen like a warlord.

Each night we listened to the mare's piteous cries as the Very Reverend sacked her out. Some oaths are harder to break than to keep, and though the Very Reverend might unwish his vow, he could not now leave the horse unbroken.

I continued to haunt the kitchen after curfew, drawn by the lighted window. Flies and funk floated above a pile of snake skins heaped beneath the sill, forcing me to breathe through my shirtsleeve as I looked in the window.

Ibzan sat with Elon at the table, smoking a hand-rolled cigarette. 'Is he drunk yet?'

Elon was using a serrated knife to scrape away bits of flesh that clung to a hide. The snake's eyes still glittered fiercely. He looked beneath the table. 'No.'

'You need to go ahead anyway. There's no more hair tonic. It's time, Jephthah.' I heard a muffled assent from beneath the table, and I stood on the pile of snake skins to see better.

Ibzan looked up. 'Oho. The skulking boy.' He handed the cigarette to Elon and rose from the table.

I lost my footing and fell face down, the skins smooth and dry against my cheeks. A thumb and forefinger closed around my wrist and pulled me to my feet. 'Still awake, hey? Come inside,' Ibzan said. 'I'll give you something to make you sleep.'

Inside, Elon regarded me through the smoke and the network of red veins that covered his eyes. 'Why you always lurk at our window?' He offered me the cigarette. 'Take some.' His hand was slick with snake flesh. The lit end glowed weakly and the tip was wet with spittle.

'I don't want any,' I said.

Elon leaned forward and gripped my arm. 'You won't nick on us now?' He looked at me hard. 'When Baba Zai returns, maybe we tell him we caught you looking at his wife through a window, eh?'

Ibzan's face broke into a broad smile and Elon released my arm. 'It's only a little dagga,' the cook said. 'Come smoke with us. We're all wide boys here.' Outside, the hyenas called out to one another. Ibzan smiled at me. 'Even Baba Zai was a wide boy once. He was a jockey before he promoted himself to Very Reverend status. Jephthah saw him race at Borrowdale Park. Hey, Jephthah?'

Jephthah nodded blearily. Two empty bottles of hair tonic and an open tackle box filled with handtools lay beside him.

'Riding horses was the Reverend's birthgift,' Ibzan continued. He took the cigarette from Elon, drew on it, then handed it to me. 'When the Very Reverend grew too old to ride, he became a bookmaker, well known in all the knocking shops. We all have two lives. Hold the smoke in your chest.' I filled my lungs and held my breath. 'Yes, just so. Now tell me – isn't this better than boiled eggs?'

The dagga tasted like foetid mud. I leaned back in my chair, muzzy-headed. Elon stuffed a cotton wash-cloth in Jephthah's mouth to absorb the blood and screams while Ibzan pushed an awl through the houseboy's cheeks and tried to stitch the broken jaw together with the picture wire.

* * *

Each morning we rose to find the mare prancing in the kraal, the other horses turning on her every move, the kink still in her tail. On our way to the dining facility, we averted our eyes as we passed Mrs Tippett stooped on her knees in the raw light, tending to her husband's liquorice until the sun bleached the sky.

More things had gone missing in the night. A tin of meat paste. A bag of salt. Adam and Ibzan conducted daily inventories of the pantry. Jephthah's jaw continued to worsen until he could no longer speak, eat solid food, or hammer wayward nails, and clapboards began to fall from the buildings like dead leaves. At eighteen months, Jephthah had been in service the longest, not counting Adam who'd been there in the beginning, and so the Very Reverend decided to make him a Companion of Saint Anthony before sending him away to die in the trust land.

There was a brief investiture ceremony. Adam, who'd received the medal three years earlier for painting the stables, served as Jephthah's sponsor. The Very Reverend draped a black cloak around Jephthah's shoulders. 'For your many months of service to this mission, you are now a Companion of Saint Anthony, the highest honour the Independent Anglican Church of Manicaland can bestow upon a layman. May your example inspire the boys.' Adam helped him to his feet and the Very Reverend draped the medal around the drunken houseboy's neck. Jephthah, Companion of Saint Anthony, would be escorted to the trust land the following day.

A dry harmattan blew over the mountains during the

night, and my mouth was sticky when I rose and went to petition the Very Reverend.

Apart from the verandah, the rectory was devoid of architectural detail. The Very Reverend had ordered the ceilings built low to save on construction materials and winter-heating oil, and to give himself the illusion of height. I studied a reproduction of a gothic painting through the parlour window: Saint Anthony of Abbot, gilt halo, black cape fastened around his shoulders. He stood on a pedestal, melancholic before farm beasts, the poor and the afflicted. The painting leaned against the parlour wall where it had hung before the wire was stolen.

The Very Reverend stepped out of the rectory, surprised by my presence. Below us, Mrs Tippett turned the soil in the liquorice bed, folding in the morning's coffee grounds. I swallowed. 'Permission to speak, Your Reverence.'

He looked out over the kraal at the horses bathed in the new light. 'Speak, novice.'

'Please, sir. Bring out a doctor to look at Jephthah. Let him stay.' Mrs Tippett looked up from the liquorice. Despite her efforts, the leaves had shrivelled and were turning to mush.

The Very Reverend embraced me. 'I've prayed for this. I'll hold Jephthah's job for him while he recovers. Mrs Tippett will call for a doctor as soon as she's through here. I imagine you'll want to be baptised in the morning.'

That night, after curfew, I lay on a pile of horse blankets and listened to the wind whistle through the beetle holes bored in the soft fruitwood, the only source of ventilation. On the Very Reverend's orders, I was kept locked in the tack room to keep me from running out on my baptism. I tried to read scripture by torchlight, but my spirit and the batteries were weak.

Before dawn, I heard the bolt slide. Ibzan pushed his head through the tack room door and looked down on me. 'I saw the light, novice, and decided to look in on you. I am going to join the war of liberation. Take care of old Jephthah. I have given you all my stories. Remember them.'

There was no breakfast that morning. In the camp above the mission, we could hear the rattle of equipment as the scouts mounted up to give chase to Ibzan. I was double-minded about his departure; in the uproar that followed, my baptism was postponed.

Mrs Tippett's brother, an undersecretary in the Prisons Department, came out to the mission, and I watched through the rectory window as he dressed down the Very Reverend. 'This really gives me the hump, Russell,' the brother-in-law said. 'We're not running a halfway house for terrorists. You lose any more of my boys, I'm going to have to cut you off.'

I stayed too long at the rectory window and was forced to work through lunch to finish the mucking. Adam brought an opened tin of meat paste to the stable and we squatted over it, sticking our fingers in and licking them. 'I hear you will be baptised,' he said.

'Yet again,' I said sourly.

'Sometimes it does not take the first time.'

Our conversation was disrupted as the scouts rode through the mission compound in formation. It was the first time I'd seen them up close. Apart from the white officer, they were an integrated lot: Shona, Ndebele, Rhodies, Boers, Indians and a few of mixed race. The uniforms were as irregular as the soldiers – slouch hats, berets, bush caps, wool caps, camouflaged T-shirts, field jackets, shirtless, most in shorts, combat boots, ankle-high hikers, even a pair of black canvas gym shoes, rifles of all description slung, holstered, or carried in hand, their jacket webbing festooned with cartridge and grenade pouches, canteens, knives.

Adam watched them through slit eyes. 'They will hunt the cook and drag his body through the mission as an example for everyone.' He buried the empty tin in the horse manure and wiped his knife on his trousers.

'Cook says the mare has toes,' I said, changing the subject.

Adam stood up to leave. 'It's good Ibzan left before he

filled your head completely with foolishness.' From the kraal, the mare followed the stableboy's every movement with her eyes.

'She hardly looks like a proper horse,' I said, remarking on her odd proportions.

'This is the way horses are supposed to look. She is an African horse. In bible times, King Solomon used to send his agents across the Zambezi to purchase our warhorses. Don't shake your head at me. The Sun Warriors of Great Zimbabwe rode into battle.' Adam and the mare fixed their gaze at the same place on the riverbank that bordered the mission. 'I'll tell you her secret name,' Adam said, nodding towards the mare. 'She is Nigeste Negest, named after the Queen of Kings, empress of the Solomonic Dynasty. Do not repeat it to anyone.'

Each dawn Mrs Tippett tended the liquorice. At high noon, she would lay down her trowel, straighten painfully, and retire to the rectory. Once, when she had quit for the day, I went over to inspect the bed. The water had already dried on the leaves, leaving a white film. I picked one and touched it to my tongue. It was salty. Mrs Tippett was poisoning her husband's liquorice.

I was woken roughly and taken from the dormitory. The starlight still illuminated the hollow fruit trees that had long ceased to blossom or bear fruit. Their branches were bare, save for some empty beehives and a smattering of leaves that grew in tufts, like hair from an old man's ears. A horse neighed and snorted in the kraal and I knew it was the mare.

Wide boys and Judges lined the banks, stamping their feet and yelling as the Very Reverend and I went down into the river. I struggled to stand against the rushing current that threatened to sweep me away, my toes curling against the muddy bed.

'On this day, you leave the egg and are born into the spirit,' the Very Reverend said, and he thrust my head underwater. I struggled and emptied my lungs of air, but still the Very Reverend pushed down on the back of my head, holding me under to make sure the baptism took this time. The rushing current muted the sound of the yelling boys as I choked on water that tasted of fertiliser and insecticide, and again I was baptised, a twice-bought Christian.

They left me heaving on the bank, the wind drying my face and clothes, and I fell asleep.

* * *

The cook once told me that there's always more than one ending to every story.

The earth shook me awake and I found myself alone by the river. It was not the unsettled ground that caused this disturbance. Four hooves struck against the hardpan almost as one, *crump*, then again as the horse and rider launched themselves into the air, *crump*, and louder, *crump*, the hoof beats reverberating through the riverbank.

It was Adam, riding to the river with the equipoise of a Spanish Don, posting forward, his weight over the mare's withers, never mind that he'd never been astride a horse. The mare's steel-encased hooves forced her to high-step as she galloped. No rider had ever mounted the mare, nor would any do so again. They raced headlong down the bank and splashed into the water, their bodies stretching and reaching forward, each urging the other on. Perhaps this was what Adam and the mare had been imagining as they stared together at the river. When the horse reached its depth and the current began to carry her downstream, she struck out for the far bank, her wake an arrow pointing to dry ground.

Her forelegs encased in heavy steel, Adam's weight on her back, submersed to her ears, the mare was forced to follow her head. To drown her, a rider would need only to pull hard on the reins, to the right or left, forcing the mare to swim in circles until she tired. Adam pulled to the left.

Despite the nightly sackings, the mare was unnaturally strong and Adam's forearms swelled as he struggled to keep her from reaching the banks. Among humans, the horse had allowed itself to trust only Adam. Only at the end, when her heart gave out from the strain of this final baptism, the mare's eyes dilated and rolled in fear, and her lips shrank from the bit.

The death cry of a drowning horse is both terrifying and heartrending, and it came as a relief when the river filled the mare's lungs and she sank beneath her rider.

Adam rose on the far bank and began walking towards the mountains with his saddlebag filled with stolen silver.

Again we were roughly woken and ordered from the dormitory to stand in our shadows beneath the stars, this time by the lieutenant who commanded the mounted patrol of scouts. From beyond the woodline I heard snorting and whickering and the shaking of bridles. The lieutenant dropped his hand to his side, and his scouts thundered from the trees with a show of rifles and pounding hooves.

Something trailed from behind one of the horses, a heavy carpet dragging from a rope. When the rider crossed before the assemblage of boys, I saw the carpet was in fact a man being pulled by his ankles face down across the lawn. The body rose and fell fluidly as it passed over stone and root.

'Adam!' the Very Reverend called as he ran out of the rectory and knelt beside the figure. But when he turned the body over to administer the final rites, he drew back.

It was Ibzan who looked up at him. The cook still clung to life, struggling to speak.

I stepped forward to listen, but Ibzan's voice did not carry. The Very Reverend placed his ear over the cook's mouth. Perhaps Ibzan had been saving the breath inside his dying body in order to deliver these final words unto his spiritual director and employer. The blood drained from the Very Reverend's face when he heard them, and he took a very long time to rise from his knees.

There was no blessing that year on the feast day of Saint Anthony, patron of horses and breeders. Rather, Elon and I waded into the current until the water reached our chests. I dived beneath the surface and swam to the dark silhouette that stood mid-river. The steel shoes kept the mare mired in the riverbed, and the current streamed through her mane, as if she was running against the wind. Her eyes gazed up to where the sun played on the water's surface. I braced my feet on the river bottom and tried to pull one of the hooves from its shoe. I wanted to see if the mare had toes as Ibzan had claimed, but the foot had swollen in the river and I could not get it off.

Elon and I paddled against the river's current, taking turns underwater with the hacksaw, our eyes closed to the roil of silt and blood, until we had sawed through all four of the mare's legs, allowing her to float to the surface. The corpse got away from us in the current, and it would be two weeks before she was found downriver in the rushes.

There were no more assemblies on the rectory lawn, and the granite altar disappeared in the tall grass. The Very Reverend diminished with each day until he became fully contained in his small frame. His black teeth faded to grey, and his unpomaded hair floated like a halo about his head.

Elon ran away, and his name was struck from the bible. The wide boys continued to rise at daybreak to ride across the glen, poking their long, hooked sticks into the tall grass, rodent burrows and trash heaps. They slept in the stables with their mounts. From the dormitory window, I watched them return from the hunt, shirtless, their faces painted with blood, saddles heaped with gleaming skins, the snake eyes still fierce in their gaunt, diamond skulls.

Without the rigours of Mrs Tippett's schedule to keep my mind occupied, I found myself standing outside her bedroom window at night, watching as she opened the top drawer of her dresser. She removed its contents, each item wrapped in an undergarment, and arranged her trove on the vanity table. The Very Reverend's pocket comb. The pewter chafing dish that had held her husband's liquorice. The Sanctus bell. Adam's Companion of Saint Anthony medal. My father's military service pin. The socket wrench used to remove the battery from the tractor. Mrs Tippett caressed each item, traced its contours with her fingers.

She pushed the service pin through her earlobe, stared at herself in the mirror. In the flame of her conversion, Mrs Tippett had given everything to the Very Reverend, but now the fire had gone out and she wanted it all back. I moved closer to the window to watch her rat her shabby treasures back into the drawer, her face blurred, the glass opaque with my breath.

# *The Story-Ghost*

June, 1971

My father and I travelled in our customary silence, listening to the pistons' rapid fire, the *dik dik dik* of bugs hitting the windscreen, the rush of wind. The heat fell away with the horizon, and I breathed shallowly as the British Ford climbed the mountain highway into the starless sky. After a year in the lowlands, I could no longer fill my lungs.

My father pushed the car to desperate speeds, drawn home by some unseen force. We overtook a lorry filled with soldiers, the lighted ends of their cigarettes floating in the darkness like rats' eyes. I stared out the window as we drove past the trust land crossroads, the river of my baptism, the thorn tree where my umbilical cord was buried, my reflection superimposed on the landmarks of my childhood. The granite mountain that overlooked the glen seemed diminished, sunken into the earth. A powder snow fell against the windscreen, unheard of in the eastern highlands. Even the seasons had changed in the year since I ran away from home to become a man.

My father narrowly avoided a blind pedestrian who tapped his way along the highway with the tip of a closed umbrella. No one else was afoot.

Phantom shapes galloped alongside the car just beyond the treeline, flashing between the acacia and scrub mahogany, matching our pace.

The sensation of motion did not cease when my father turned into our drive and switched off the motor. We remained in the car and listened to the ticking of the cooling engine block. Through some trick of shadow and perspective, the bungalow appeared warped and swollen, the clapboards bowed outwards with old secrets. A familiar tightness spread across my chest, and I nearly took my father's hand. Wordlessly, he roused himself from the driver's seat.

Inside, the story-ghost waited for us, a seething, roseate mist that smelled of pipe tobacco. It had grown in my absence, bloated and ubiquitous.

I went to the bedroom where my mother sat in her Queen Anne chair in the light of an Italianate lamp, its spelter cracked during the voyage from Scotland. The painted bulb reflected iridescently in her eyes. I wondered if my year-long absence even registered with her, if time passed at all in that dark room. The woman refused to see what she could not understand, and so she was blind to the story-ghost that pinioned her to that chair.

The house had deteriorated while I'd been away: floorboards were sprung, crown moulding separated at the joints, clocks frozen, corners draped in dustwebs, the stove pilot light extinguished. I stood at the kitchen window. A chill mist shrouded the overgrown garden, muting the roller's song, dimming the moonlight.

A voice called out from the wilderness: 'Divinations! Prophecies!' It was the blind man my father had almost run down on the highway, tapping his way towards me with the tip of his umbrella. 'Pasts uncovered. Secrets unveiled. One dollar.' He wore a wool coat and sunglasses, his head shaved like a holy man's. 'The future is here, your true nature waiting to be revealed.'

I opened the door, and he paused in its threshold, rattling a box with his free hand. 'This house is out of balance,' he declared. 'Perhaps one of your ancestors is aggrieved. For a dollar I can put it right.'

I led him into the kitchen, and the blind man placed the box on the table and shrugged off his coat. There were words scrawled on the box in a large, uncertain hand: *Omen reading. One dollar – One Hour. No refunds after five minutes.* The doorstep diviner scratched his bottom and settled into a chair. 'Let's kick on, then,' he said. I watched him open the box, gather the bones into his hands, and cast them into the lid. He fingered the ossicles, rolling his eyes behind the dark lenses, making a show of it. 'Bring me a dollar and I'll tell you what the bones say.'

He grasped at the dollar I held above his head, forgetting he was supposed to be blind. I stepped back, laughing. 'I thought you couldn't see.'

He looked sullenly at me from behind the dark lenses, returned the bones to the box, and closed the lid.

'My great-grandmother was a diviner,' I said. My father kept an ancient photo hidden in his study between the pages of *Readings for the Railway.* It was taken in Cape Town: a Xhosa woman, ritually scarred, smoking a pipe at a bar table where she read futures. 'Go on,' I said, pointing to the bones. 'Give them a throw.'

The doorstep diviner looked down at the bones and shook his head. 'We don't need to pretend. Just give me the dollar.' He shifted in his chair, reaching deep into the back of his trousers to scratch vigorously. 'Tapeworms,' he apologised.

I waved the dollar in the air, watching his eyes follow it.

'Maybe I can help you after all,' he said. 'I know what you want to know. All boys ask me this question: "What sort of man will I become?"'

'I'm already a man,' I said.

The diviner stopped scratching his anus. 'Oho! A man. I should have seen it straight away. A boy's soul is a shifting, inconstant thing. In men, it becomes fixed. Have you had time to learn what sort of man you are?' He snatched the dollar out of my hand. 'There's a way to find out.'

My mouth became dry. Outside, there was a distant yowling.

He picked up his box and stood. 'Time for me to leave. I want to be home before the half-beasts begin their prowl.' It was a story the trust land Shona told their children: each midnight, lisping half-beasts roamed the glen, resuming their quest-without-end to become wholly human.

The doorstep diviner held the umbrella before him, blind again. 'I sleep in the sacred mahogany tree that grows next to the convent near the trust land. Come visit me there, young friend. Bring a dollar and I'll tell you where you can go to see into your soul.' He tapped his way along the animal track that vanished into the overgrown garden.

* * *

The sun rose on the first day of my return, a white dawn, shimmering and relentless. I went out on the verandah which overlooked the glen.

Nothing remained of my childhood. Loggers from the Forestry Commission had clear-cut the mountain, leaving it naked and shrunken, the trees sold to a nearby sawmill which produced industrial-grade lumber for pallets and coffins. A rough path had been forced through the bush, as if by a herd of animals. I followed it in.

Dead snakes were strewn by the pathside, their carcasses flayed. A wake of whiteback vultures fought over the pallid remains.

There was a disturbance in the earth. The grass rippled and whispered, a mystery on this windless day, and an uneasiness settled over me as the whitebacks rose clumsily into the air, abandoning their carrion. Then came the snakes; pythons, spitting cobras, shield noses, puff adders, gaboons, mambas surging from the tall grass in a panic. They swarmed around my ankles, their skin dry and glistening, then vanished into the tall grass as quickly as they appeared. I put my ear to the ground. There was a faint rumbling, a swelling percussion of hooves, and I dropped flat in the tall grass.

A mob of boys on horseback thundered past, yowling like wild beasts. Each carried a pole with a thin metal hook which they used to scour the bush, overturning rocks, poking into burrows, whipping at the grass. Strings of snake skins hung from their saddles. These were the galloping shadows I had seen from the car window the previous night, the animal cries that had frightened the doorstep diviner. The dense bush swallowed the riders, their mounts, and the thunder of hooves, leaving me to wonder if I'd seen anything at all.

I was still in my pyjamas when Mrs Tippett arrived with a tray that held a frilly bible, a dish of ash, and a plate of scrambled eggs gone cold. My father had been forced to ask her to care for my mother while he fetched me back home. She was pallid almost to the point of albinism, translucent skin over a network of fine veins. It was my heritage, I suppose, this longing for achromatic women. Apart from a woven bracelet of wind flowers, she wore no jewellery.

'You've come back, then,' she said, her voice atonal, disapproving. I wondered if this was because I'd left home, or because I lacked the strength of character to stay away. 'If I'd known you'd be here, I'd have made more eggs,' she said. 'We're all of us eggs. In the spiritual sense, that is.' The unmusical voice trailed away. 'What the Very Reverend says, at any rate.'

Mrs Tippett paused at the threshold as she came up against the story-ghost of my great-grandmother. She crossed herself and quoted Job: *As the cloud is consumed and vanisheth away: so he that goeth to his grave shall come up no more.* Having thus reassured herself of its non-existence, she pushed through the apparition.

I followed her into the room where my mother sat in the dark. Mrs Tippett switched on the lamp, set the tray in the invalid's lap, and opened the bible. The words of Christ were printed in red letters to set them off. She'd sewn a purfled cover for the book, quilted batting to soften the Word. The cover also served as a pin-cushion for her sewing needles.

I moved closer, the length of one of her pale, hairless arms. The air conditioner blew full on her as she read, freezing her breath and hardening her nipples against her cotton blouse. She gripped the quilted bible, her eyes locked on mine, quoting from memory now: *But if thine eye be evil, thy whole body shall be full of darkness.* The story-ghost drew nearer. A backward needle stuck deep into the pad of Mrs Tippett's index finger, and she dropped the bible onto her lap. 'Oh, life,' she said.

I stared at the droplets that punctuated the red text, my own blood rushing. Mrs Tippett looked up from her bible, stared at my crotch, and turned away.

'God forgive you,' she said.

I spun around to face the wall, waiting for my erection to subside.

Mrs Tippett spat in the dish of ash, mixed in the saliva with her finger, and painted a cross on my mother's forehead. 'I'll pray for you,' she told me as she retreated from the room, her obligation discharged. I listened to her quick steps against the floorboards, dishes rattling on the tray, the bang of the screen door. My mother, unsaved, wiped the ash from her forehead with the back of her hand.

The study was the heart of the bungalow. In Cape Town, in the days of my great-grandmother, it had been a place where bargirls lounged on stools, or moved against one another on a small patch of dance floor as they waited to be chosen by any of the silent, drinking men who would take them through one of the house's many doors. It was the room where my great-grandmother once smoked her pipe and divined the blighted futures of those who entered that place. Often after hearing a bit of his unhappy destiny, a man would spill more money on the table and insist my great-grandmother tell him more, and she would read on until daybreak, exhausting his future and wallet. My father had had the house disassembled and moved away from the sea, overland to the eastern highlands of Rhodesia, leaving behind a brick foundation, a pile of sprung mattresses, and his African ancestry. The floorboards still smelled faintly of lavender. Peeling paper revealed glimpses of flesh-coloured wall. The study was a favourite place of the story-ghost.

My father lay on the iron bed, the story-ghost settled on his chest. I stood in the doorway and watched him sink deeper into the mattress as the story-ghost forced him to heave and struggle for each breath. I kicked the iron bed. 'Go sleep somewhere else!'

The story-ghost released him. Iron legs scarred the painted floorboards as my father dragged his bed into one of the empty rooms of the bungalow, thus abandoning the study, its books, and all authority over me.

Vast shelves lined the walls, floor-to-ceiling, the topmost accessible only by stepladders that rolled along a track the length of each aisle. My father's carpenter had underestimated the weight of Western knowledge, and the low-grade African mahogany bowed and creaked plaintively each time a book was removed or replaced.

I browsed the shelves of my study, taking down books at random: *Wealth of Nations, The Lost Horizon, Modern English Usage, A Subaltern's War, Technics and Civilization, Great Expectations.* Stories to instruct and stories to pass time. Stories for staying awake and stories for falling asleep. Stories for holding, for turning in one's hands. Stories of lands and peoples, facts and myths, human and inhuman truths. Stories like picture windows. Stories to trouble the mind.

For three days I read, letting the words wash over me. I fell asleep mid-sentence, picked up the narrative thread upon waking, chain-reading one volume after the next. Each book was a story-ghost – bound, covered, and shelved – and they each demanded an audience.

Time thickened. Lifetimes passed before me. New words crowded out the old ones from my childhood. I tracked the days by the morning song of the rollers, the sound of the British Ford coughing to life as my father began his commute to Umtali, the midday stifle, the night screams of the swifts. I left the study only to use the toilet and to drink water from the kitchen tap.

Immersed in the books, I hardly noticed the presence of the story-ghost. The air smelled of sea salt and kelp.

I heard the flutter of canaries' wings. Parrots cursing in tongues. A Victrola played from somewhere in the room, *Dusk and the shadows falling.* I listened as my great-grandmother's pipe-worn voice rasped along. *O'er land and sea.* I knew the words before they were sung. A heaviness stole over me, as if I were lying beneath a stack of woollen blankets. I let the book fall to my lap. *Somewhere a voice is calling, calling for me.* It was the story-ghost that had sent my father to fetch me back to this room. I exhaled pipe smoke.

Perhaps I would still be lost in that room, the world a better place for it, had the lights not gone out. I went onto the verandah to investigate. There were whispers and stifled giggles in the darkness. Small faces peered from the tall grass – trust land children, scaring themselves with their proximity to the story-ghost. I chased them as far as the highway, where I found a python hanging, blackened and eyeless, coiled around a blown-out power terminal where it had sought safety. In the distance I heard galloping hooves and boys hollering as they drove the snakes before them. The moon had begun its descent, time for the half-beasts to rouse themselves. Unable to continue my reading, I allowed my feet to take me where they would.

In story there is direction behind even the most aimless wandering. My thoughts turned to Mrs Tippett, her pallid flesh, and my feet turned towards the Outreach Mission for Troubled Boys. A light went on as I passed the rectory. I found myself hiding in a stand of fever trees.

And so I was there when she came to the window to stare out into the dark sky, her lips parted, heavy-eyed, hair alive with the static electricity that filled the cool air. She cupped her pale breasts in her hands, giving them youth and lift, and for a moment she appeared a girl no older than me. Her hand dropped to her belly, then below, out of view. She moved away from the window, and I abandoned the cover of the fever trees and stood among the climbing onions that grew beneath the sill, watching as Mrs Tippett drew the nightdress over her head and kneeled on the mattress, naked save for the bracelet of wild flowers. I lowered my gaze to her shallow navel, the wispy pubic hair. My breath crystallised in the chill mountain air.

All my life, danger would come upon me while I was looking hard in another direction. There was movement on the edge of my vision. A rustle and sigh of leaves. Shapes moving low and swift. Night adders writhed at my feet and the climbing onion came alive. Too late I heard the stampede of hooves, the whooping boys. I was still standing outside the bedroom window when they burst from the fever trees and lay into me with their long, snake-catching sticks. One knocked me down. Another held my neck against the ground with its curved metal end. More sticks beat and jabbed at me while I writhed on the hook.

* * *

My father was of a generation that judged one another by their school colours, the shine of their shoes, the condition of their heels. He stood behind me on the morning I was to be brought before the magistrate, threading his school tie through my collar. A week had passed since my capture and disgrace. My father looked over my shoulder and into the mirror. 'You've grown in the year you were away,' he said.

I felt suddenly small. 'Not so much,' I said.

My father guided my hands as together we tied a double Windsor, passing one end of the tie under the other, round and over, above and through. In the mirror I saw him open and close his mouth, as if he were about to speak but thought better of it. He'd been unable to look at me when the police brought me home. We shaped the knot, working it tighter around my throat. 'There,' he said, satisfied.

My father took me out onto the verandah and showed me how to polish my ox-blood wingtips for the magistrate, melting the paste wax over a can of Sterno, dipping a chamois into the liquid and rubbing it onto the toe, into the crevice where the upper was stitched to the sole, working the wax in ever-smaller spirals until the shoes shone like satin. He had taught me to read. Spit like an African. Keep secrets.

I set down the shoes, and together we stared out at the dew glinting in the new sun. My father startled me by speaking without necessity: 'There is sweet music here that softer falls than petals from blown roses on the grass.' The words stuck in my mind coming from someone so unpoetical. Stories told in retrospect invite future memories, and time jumps the track. Long after his death, I would read these lines again in a volume of Victorian poetry. My father was only parroting Tennyson, but at that moment, on the verandah awaiting my trial, the words were his own.

Neither I nor my father spoke at the trial. The court had been established in a furnace room behind the headquarters of the district police. The electricity went out briefly: more snakes in the power terminals I imagined. There was a delay as a road flare was ignited. The usher bade us all rise and I waited for an imposing magistrate in a powder wig and black robe to make an entrance. Instead, a slight figure dressed in khakis stamped into the room without acknowledging anyone. Sweat ringed her collar and armpits. She paid no attention to my tie and shoes.

I did not hear the magistrate's words as they were delivered in the flickering light of the road flare. Rather, her assessment registered in my memory to be played back on future nights as I lay awake in my bed. The magistrate told the court that I was a wide boy, spiritually flawed, a neurotic little thug who deserved a sound birching if it were left up to her. Rhodesia would stand or fall on the strength of its young men, and God help us all if my sort was indicative of the entire generation. But fortune smiles on the wicked, second chances and all that. The Very Reverend had considered my circumstances. Absent father, afflicted mother, et cetera. No way to raise a white child. Monday next week I would report to The Outreach Mission for Troubled Boys for a period of no less than thirteen months. Next case.

The magistrate's words kept me from sleeping that night. I quit the house and took the path to where the doorstep diviner lay in his sacred mahogany tree, his spine curved into the bough, legs elevated against the massive trunk. The tree was riddled with beetles and seemed in danger of collapsing beneath its occupant. The diviner shimmied his bottom against its bark, seeking relief from the tapeworms.

I cleared my throat. 'You told me there's a place I can go to look into my soul.'

His foot slipped against the trunk and he nearly fell from the tree. 'Maybe that's not such a good idea, now I think on it.' He looked down on me for a moment. 'God keeps us from such knowledge for a reason.'

I held up a dollar. The diviner wrestled a moment with

the temptation, then shook his head. 'Better to find out at the end of your life what sort of man you are. It makes no matter then.'

I climbed onto a massive root, reached up, and brushed his hand with the bill.

He snatched and pocketed it in one motion. 'Oh, oh, oh. Are you certain you want to do this?'

The mouth of the trust land is lined with vendors' stalls and the graves of children killed by lorry drivers. Morning traffic flows away from such poor places and, unable to hitch a ride, it took me an hour to make it to the market on foot. Street sellers squatted before legless tables, over kerosene stoves and cooking pots, beneath umbrellas, atop slabs of granite, in derelict cars forever parked amid the expanse of transistor radios, paper sacks of fried takeaway, plastic sunglasses, soapstone animal carvings, spools of ringspun yarn, gallon tins of Frytoll, woven placemats, rolls of baler twine. Two soldiers played cards atop the turret of an armoured car, the barrel of its cannon pointed into the crowd of market goers.

Long ago, the story begins, a little boy came here to beg. But trust land Shona give nothing away, so he began to sketch the souls of passersby on bits of refuse paper. Thus captured, he bartered the souls back to their owners in exchange for food. The boy grew fat on his earnings. This is what the doorstep diviner had told me for a dollar.

A haze of gnats and dust hung over the market. I bought a beer from a vendor and took my place in the long queue of Shona waiting to discover their true nature. As I waited, I ate the purge nut the diviner had given me the night before. 'It will help rid you of evil,' he explained, 'so that your soul will perhaps appear less dark.'

The Illustrator of Souls perched on a small hump of earth where the trust land road meets the highway. Though competition was fierce for these choice spots, the boy had held this place uncontested for as long as anyone could remember. His child-belly rested on his knees, a stack of flattened paper sacks beside him. Toothless, he chewed on a piece of biltong with gums as hard as bone. When my turn came, I placed the beer before him.

'Draw my soul,' I said. The purge nut had left a bitter taste.

The boy picked up a piece of charcoal and, without looking at me, scribbled furiously on a paper sack. He tossed the drawing at my feet.

I stared at the image. It was nothing more than a series of tiny, jagged lines that blurred into a black smudge. The drawing stirred my guts, and I vomited black bile that smelled of burned milk and mildew and carbon and vegetable rot. Even the gnats would not light on it.

I kicked the bottle over, spilling beer on the boy's feet, and I ground his charcoal beneath my heel, leaving a smudge on the road identical to the drawing on the paper sack. The Illustrator of Souls shrugged, his drawing validated.

An overland truck sped past on the highway, narrowly missing several children who shrieked with laughter as they ran out from between the stalls. The vendors looked up, relieved that more valuable space would not have to be given over to graves for children killed in traffic.

Another sleepless night brooding in the study, books scattered at my feet, as I waited to be sent to the Outreach Mission for Troubled Boys. My father brought me a tray of biscuits and quickly retreated. I could no longer remember why I had run away from this place. I sat in the study and listened to the footfalls of barefoot bargirls. Outside, I heard the screech of seagulls. The crashing of waves. My great-grandmother's voice: *A story, let it come.* The words came from my own mouth.

I was roused by a rapping on the window, the doorstep diviner wanting to find out what I'd learned from the Illustrator of Souls. He peered into the thick miasma of story-ghost that filled the study.

'God blind me!' He angled for a better look. 'How can you people live under a roof with this thing?' He scrambled in through the window. 'Look how it pushes out the walls so.' He passed his hand through the story-ghost.

'It's the spirit of my great-grandmother.'

The diviner studied the apparition intently. 'It's no such

a thing, my friend. Your great-grandmother's long dead, her spirit gone some other place altogether. It's her story that throws this house off-balance. You say your great-grandmother was a diviner?'

I nodded.

'Ehe! It's a terrible thing when a diviner gets separated from her own story. You listen to this story-ghost?'

'Yes.'

'Now there's real trouble. This evil thing is eating your past. It won't be satisfied until it has swallowed you completely.'

Outside, a muster of penguins brayed in the surf. He was right. I was living in my great-grandmother's story. 'You're a diviner. Can't you chase it away?'

'Now you're talking nonsense! If I had powers, would I suffer from tapeworms?' He paced the study, bones rattling in the box. 'My mother used to drive such things away.' He stopped still, staring down at the box as if he'd never seen it before. 'We should consult these.'

'I thought you couldn't read them.'

'Truthfully, I never tried.' The diviner removed the lid from the box. 'These are just old pork bones I boiled. I sold the ones my mother left me. Even so, I cannot leave a friend to be eaten by a story-ghost. Come bring me a dollar. Let's rattle the bones to get the story-ghost's attention.' He produced some pepper-bark, a box of matches, and an ox-tail whisk. 'Everything, it's all right now.

Goodbye, my friend.' He pocketed the dollar and pushed me out into the hallway.

Wisps of smoke came from under the study door as the diviner burned the pepper-bark. I heard the boiled pork bones roll in the box lid. There was hand-clapping, the swishing of the ox-tail whisk, the diviner working hard to give me my dollar's worth. Later there were voices, too low for me to hear. It sounded as if they were conducting secret negotiations. I fell asleep in the hallway, my ear to the door.

The study was empty when I entered the following morning, story-ghost and diviner both gone. I searched the house, but it too was bare, its life force departed.

Days passed, sluggish and blurry, while I waited for my sentence to commence. I took to carrying the dark smear of my soul folded inside my breast pocket as I tramped through the untended garden. Some mornings, I found fawn tufts of fur impaled on pointed branches, and I wondered if they had come from the half-beasts, the unformed creatures that existed in the margins between the material and spirit worlds. The fur smelled of musk and carrion and mist.

I pestered neighbours' servants, market vendors, tavern owners, asking after the doorstep diviner, but no one remembered him, his existence erased. Who can say why he offered himself up to the story-ghost? Perhaps he wanted a new past, even if it belonged to someone else. Or he was tired of sleeping in a tree with only his tapeworms for company. Or he did it for the dollar.

Some exorcisms are more successful than others. My father took up pipe smoking on the verandah, and when he thought no one was near, he whistled a popular tune from another time. And for as long as it stood, the bungalow would continue to shift and creak on its foundation, as old houses will, the wind whispering through its loosened window frames.

# *The Raw Man*

Ulwaluko Ixesha (Initiation Time), 1971

WHENEVER A STORM BLEW INLAND, THE run-off from the kopjes turned the road into a sump. I'd slogged the muddy path for two days before I learned its name – Imfene Road – from a Xhosa cyclist who regarded me as a dog, no offence intended. He was a young man, perhaps one year beyond his initiation. 'This isn't a good road for children,' he told me, glancing at the falling sun. 'Especially at night.' He raced away, the rear wheel splattering his backside with mud.

I followed Imfene Road past flowering mimosa trees, through low bush and tall grass, vast fields of wild pineapple, clusters of abandoned huts with collapsed roofs. It wasn't a proper road, but rather a ghost track etched by prehistoric animals, beaten into hardpan beneath the hooves of cattle, then graded by order of the South African Roads Board.

A lorry sped by, its driver ignoring my efforts to wave

it down. I'd covered eight hundred miles on the tramp, fifteen longitudinal degrees on the globe in my father's study, always moving south and east, towards the edge of the continent. I was invisible in my filth and rags, my emaciated body moving without volition, carrying me into the heart of the Ciskei, birthplace of my great-grandmother.

I met a woman who balanced an enormous bundle of kindling on her head as she walked. She offered me a tomato, but my stomach rejected the fruit in a liquid rush.

A battered estate car announced itself on the horizon with backfires and dust, slowing as it passed. It made a wide turn in the field, jouncing back onto the road beside me. The driver leaned across the seat to open the passenger door, breaking wind with the effort. The handle came off, and he swore in Xhosa. Hollow palatal clicks gave rhythm to the oaths. He motioned for me to open it from the outside.

The engine threatened to stall, and still I hung back. 'Get in, nephew, get in!' the driver called. The words came out thick, as if his tongue were too large for his mouth. He fiddled with the knobs on the silent radio, his eyes wandering in their sockets. I saw perhaps a dozen severed baboon arms piled in the backseat, their stumps black with flies. One stretched a hand towards me, its withy thumb and forefinger pointing like a pistol.

Another backfire from the engine and I leaped away, throwing myself into the brush and scrambling beneath the branches on all fours. I lay prone in the shadows while the driver bungled through the thicket in pursuit. The air was hot and wet, and he stopped to mop his forehead with a khaki shirtsleeve, crying out to the dusk: 'Nephew! Nephew!'

The driver abandoned his search with the sunset, and I watched from behind a screen of foliage as the car bounced away in the direction from which it had come. I remained hidden long after the vehicle disappeared over the horizon, listening to the wind in the leaves.

I resumed my trek, walking until my cracked feet could no longer feel the road and I veered off into the bush. When I fell back against the earth, my legs continued to crawl in the air, unable to cease their walking. The bible in my father's study had it wrong; it's not the flesh that's weak. I quit my stubborn, dying body and rose high into the air where bats swooped and screeched around me.

* * *

Day broke and I looked down on a vast tract of pineapple that stretched into the distance. A flock of rock-pigeons flew against the morning sun, shadows fluttering over the road, and I wanted to join them, ready to begin my eternity. Instead, my body stood and stretched and resumed its walking, and my spirit followed, a hovering figment tethered by some unseen thread.

My body travelled along the road, beyond the golden fields, past the fighting ground where men pummelled one another with sticks while their sweethearts looked on, to a village of round houses with thatched roofs and narrow doors that faced away from the distant Indian Ocean and its monsoons. Old men wore red blankets and smoked from long-stemmed pipes. Unmarried girls, naked to the waist, crushed maize to meal. They looked away from my body where it walked along the road in its makeshift turban and filthy rags, its skin grey with dirt. On the outskirts of the village, my body came to a shebeen of daub and wattle, its asbestos roof strung with Christmas lights. Shadows pooled beneath the battered estate car that had stopped for me the previous day. Raucous voices and tinny radio music emanated from the open front door.

My body crossed the threshold and collapsed within, releasing its hold on my spirit. The clientele stood over the discarded corpse and spoke all at once. I was curious to see what would happen to my remains, but my spirit floated up through the ceiling. The shebeen shrank beneath me, hills falling away, the horizon curving as the earth spun below, and my gaze followed Imfene Road east until it became a track canopied with flat-crowned trees that dead-ended against a beach of thrusting rocks, raw-sugar sand, and pounding ocean. Still rising, I looked down on the ocean in wonder until it disappeared beneath clouds of startling whiteness.

* * *

A foul liquid ran down my throat, and I woke, choking, back inside my body. A grum, red-eyed woman sat beside my doss with a bowl and spoon. Music and conversation floated under the door. I looked about the room: folded clothes on a shelf, a curtained sleeping closet, an enormous cooking pot over a dung fire.

'Ho! He's awake.' The driver of the estate car appeared over the woman's shoulder. I struggled weakly against the blanket that pinned my arms to my side. 'How does the day find you?' His intestines thundered and a pong filled the room. 'I apologise.' He chewed absently on a necklace made of roots doubled around his throat. 'I was born with healthy digestion. God doesn't make sick people.' He thumped his ribcage and belched. 'I'm your Uncle Yizo.' I shut my eyes to the possibility that this madman was a blood relation, and darkness overtook me.

For a week, the woman poured spoonfuls of her filthy brew into my mouth, jarring me, sputtering, back to consciousness. 'Maybe he won't die,' she said to Yizo each time I opened my eyes. Sometimes there were others in the room, old people. The woman knew the lineage of everyone in the village, all the way back to God. She recited their bloodlines for tobacco money, and the oldsters nodded as she spoke the familiar names.

My shrunken stomach expanded and the woman forced more of the broth down my throat. 'You're even fairer than I imagined,' she said, regarding me with her crimson eyes.

'Who are you?' My voice was raspy from disuse.

'She's nobody,' Yizo said from behind the curtain. 'Call out "Woman" if you need her.'

The cooking pot began to bubble over, and acrid smoke drifted into the woman's eyes as she stirred. 'Sleep now,' she said, and I drifted back into unconsciousness.

I woke late one evening and watched through slit eyes as the woman smoked her pipe at the window, framed by the stars. There was a ginger cast to her hair, faint freckles beneath her dark complexion. A baboon perched on the sill, chattering softly into her ear. I heard snoring through the curtain of the sleeping closet.

'My name is Zenu,' she said, turning to me. A flayed baboon arm bobbed on the roiling surface of the cooking pot, its grey meat falling off the bone. Zenu saw me shudder. 'It's medicine.' She puffed rapidly on her pipe to keep it lit. 'To help you recover your strength.'

When I next woke, the sun was streaming through the window. Zenu stood over her husband with a knife. Yizo shifted in his chair to examine me. 'Brilliant, nephew. You're still alive.' His stomach gurgled against his belt. 'They said you would come.'

'Keep still,' Zenu ordered, cutting away her husband's hair.

'Who said?' I asked.

'The night voices,' Yizo answered. 'They speak to me in my dreams.' Zenu pinched bits of his hair and cut them away with her knife. 'People think I'm simple,' he went on, 'but my brain works – only a bit slower, more careful. The voices spoke to me again last night.' He swallowed and belched. Zenu lathered his scalp and began shaving the remaining stubble with a razor. 'Ai!' he cried out. Blood seeped through the white of the shaving cream over his forehead. 'Cut me again, you red-eyed witch, I'll knock the magic out of you!' He stood and mopped the cream from his gleaming skull. While Zenu finished sweeping up his hair, Yizo took the dustpan outside. He paused at the door to make sure his wife was not following.

I no longer fought against the medicine, and when I was strong enough to stand, Zenu dumped the remnants and filled the enormous pot with curry and vegetables. The dung fire billowed smoke, blackening the walls and reddening her eyes. I'd grown so accustomed to the shebeen that I no longer heard its nightly racket. Zenu removed the bedpan from my doss. 'You're strong enough to use the privy.' She tossed me a pair of Uncle Yizo's khaki trousers. I winced at the urine stains on the crotch.

My skin glowed beneath the Christmas lights as I stepped out into the night. There was no electricity in the privy and the walls had been painted black to drive flies up the air vents where they were trapped by screens. The wind was still as I emerged, yet there was a rustling in the undergrowth beyond the car park. A naked figure stepped out from the bush, translucent in the moonlight, genitals hanging slack and low with age. The apparition leaned into a phantom wind, its wispy hair rippling against its skull, though it was dead calm where I stood frozen in its gaze. A wind devil rose up at the spectre's feet, circling its ankles in deasil spirals.

I ran wild-eyed into the shebeen but no one took notice. The cacophony of clinking bottles, raised voices, blaring radio and laughter failed to escape through the asbestos roof, and the noise fell back in a heap upon the men, burying all thoughts of their kraals and families. They sat in klatches, drinking from the same scud of sorghum beer, each taking draughts by order of his initiation year, calling out for more beer and bunny chow, sopping up the curried vegetables with bits of their bread bowls. Shards of mirrored glass had been set into the concrete walls, creating the impression of another fragmented world that abutted ours. The air was heated from the press of bodies and the brick oven filled with baking bread. Zenu and a young girl tended bar.

'Ghost!' I shouted, pointing to the car park.

Zenu looked up sharply from behind the bar, and Uncle Yizo fell silent in the middle of a story. 'You've seen him, then?' Uncle Yizo pushed me into a chair. 'Let's drink, nephew!' The beer smelled like a kraal, but I downed it, trying not to make a face. 'Brilliant!' he exclaimed. 'If you're strong enough to drink this piss, you're ready to learn how to fight with sticks!'

Zenu cleared a place amid the empties and a new scud appeared without comment. Two raw men gravitated to the fresh bottle. It had been twenty-one years since Uncle Yizo's initiation. As the senior man at the bar, he drank first, and after the bottle made its rounds, drained the dregs. He spat and smoked by turns, and his cigarettes were still burning when he threw them on the saliva-soaked floor where the young men retrieved them.

Uncle Yizo lifted a hip and broke wind. 'Bloody grasshoppers. I've got to be going.' He finished the last swallow but made no move to rise from the chair.

Zenu laughed from behind the bar. 'You're always *going*. You're *going* to paint a sign to put over the door. You're *going* to raise the prices on the chalkboard.'

'And when are you *going* to give me a child?' he yelled back.

'Who was the ghost, Zenu?' I asked.

'Don't speak her name in my presence, nephew! May God never curse you with a barren woman,' and he swore that he'd been cheated on his wife's bride price and would never be able to pay it all. His eyes followed Zenu as she quit the shebeen. Uncle Yizo gave the young men more beer to hold their attention while he resumed his tale, and

I followed Zenu into the backroom where she stood over the cooking fire, stirring the curried vegetables.

'Zenu?'

'Yes, child.'

'Who is the ghost outside?'

Zenu lit her pipe and took a long draw. 'Once there was a woman who left this village to live among the Europeans. She stayed with them for so long that her child was born white. Another child came, a daughter, but she was not so white, and so she was given to the boy to serve and watch over him.' Zenu's voice took on the incantatory quality she used to recite bloodlines. 'The firstborn son grew up to marry a fair woman who gave birth to a fair boy. But his second child, a daughter, was dark.' Zenu picked up the blanket from my doss and wadded it into a tight ball. 'He smothered this one,' she clenched the blanket, 'and buried her body in the garden. A year passed, maybe more, and his mind slipped. He began to wander through all the rooms of his house, into the garden where he had buried his daughter, out into the road, each day further and further from his family and the house that looked out over that grave. One day he kept walking, his head cocked to one side, as if there were voices in the blood that roared in his ears, and he did not stop until his body brought him to a road that led him to this village, the place of his mother's birth.'

'The ghost I saw.'

'Just so.' The pipe smoke curled around her nose and into her eyes. 'In this village he met a woman who was also simple, and they had a child, Zenu, which means Scotland.'

'He's your father,' I said.

She nodded. 'Your paternal grandfather.'

* * *

The next morning Zenu woke me early. 'Yizo is waiting for you in the shebeen. Be careful with the sticks,' she warned. 'That's how your uncle lost his wits.'

Outside, Yizo handed me two fighting sticks – one with a wicked looking knob at the end. I examined the red-stained wood and reckoned that this was the stick that had crippled the man's intellect. I sliced it through the air, whooping, and Yizo delivered a stinging blow to my knuckles. 'Mind your fingers!'

For the first few mornings we fought in slow motion, Yizo showing me how to swing and parry, but soon we were fighting in earnest, our left hands wrapped in cloth to spare our knuckles, refusing to cry out as we administered and received welts and cuts and bruises. Yizo was surprisingly fast, deflecting most of my strikes.

Afternoons, we ran. At first I limped as the gravel bit into my heels. 'No, no! You run like a honey badger.' Yizo sprang out into the road. 'You must leap from the ground before your foot even falls.' He bounded lightly across the road. 'Like an eland.'

I ran beside Yizo until my lungs were blown and I asked to rest. He stared at me incredulously, then glanced back over the expanse of winding road. 'But we're still in sight of the village.'

I stopped breathing on the second day, but my feet took no notice as they fell in time with Yizo's. We slowed briefly to watch baboons forage in a pineapple field. One stood off from the rest of the troop, watching us. Yizo shuddered. 'That one is a sorcerer's familiar. Probably a man once. You can lose your spirit on this road after dark.'

On the third day of running, my heart stopped beating, and Yizo and I were elands racing against the setting sun to reach the village.

Each night I returned with swollen knuckles and calloused feet, sometimes a closed eye or a lip split to the gums. Zenu whistled when I entered the shebeen. 'Yizo was always a madman with the sticks.'

One evening, when the music from the shebeen was especially loud and my injuries kept me from sleep, I went to sit on the verandah. I saw Zenu leave the bar with a bread bowl filled with bunny chow, the baboon walking in her steps. The ocean wind had risen, and I reckoned there would be a frost. I shivered as something white moved through the underbrush. The ghost of my father's father emerged to accept the offering. She tried to touch its colourless skin, but the naked apparition faded back into the bush.

After a month of stick fighting, hard lumps of muscle grew around the tops of my shoulders, cords stood out from my forearms, and scar tissue hardened the line of my brow. Yizo beamed. 'I was cursed with a barren wife, but God corrects all imbalances in good time. Now I have a son.'

One day I told Yizo I wanted to go to the fighting ground and challenge the larger boys.

'Ho! They'd break open your skull like a pineapple,' he told me. 'You can't even beat a man with grasshoppers in his stomach.' He held the sticks out before him. 'Let's begin.'

My temper had returned with my strength, and I walked into the whirlwind of Yizo's sticks without parrying, answering his blows with my club stick, beating him about the ears. He fell back on his rump at my onslaught, his legs stretched in the air, and I saw an opportunity to end the fight and earn the right to join the larger boys. I swung the club-stick between Yizo's legs, full force, bang in the groin. On the verandah, Aunt Zenu shook her head.

Yizo leaped easily to his feet. 'Brilliant, nephew!' He laughed at my astonishment. 'Why are you staring? I'm a man!' Zenu turned and went back inside. 'I tell you, nephew,' he continued, 'there's much worse pain, and it hurts the same whether you lie on the ground or stand on your feet.' I pretended not to notice that he'd wet his trousers.

Yizo's digestion grew worse. One evening I saw my aunt place her lips to her husband's distended belly and make a seal against the flesh. She took a deep, sucking breath, pulling his skin upward until it stretched taut. Her cheeks began to vibrate and hum. Zenu put her hand to her mouth, and a grasshopper crawled out onto her palm.

* * *

They brought me to a man so old even Zenu couldn't remember his name. The villagers simply called him M'dala, which meant 'old man'. M'dala gave my aunt a sour look and told her to wait outside by the kraal, but she followed him into his house anyway.

Yizo spoke softly, as if in the presence of an ancestor. 'I heard you will be conducting an initiation. I hoped you might take my nephew.'

The old man examined me and frowned. 'Don't try to think so hard with that rattled brain of yours. I'll go to prison if I initiate a white boy. Go away.'

Zenu spoke up. 'The boy is Xhosa. Only his skin is white. His great-grandmother by blood was Ukusaba, daughter of Ngamathamb.'

It had been over one hundred years since Ukusaba had

left the Ciskei, but M'dala's eyes widened when he heard her name. 'His skin is even whiter than his grandfather's.'

'You knew my grandfather?' I asked.

'Be quiet!' Yizo said. 'People are talking.'

A stooped man came to the door, and M'dala led him out into the kraal. I watched the visitor choose a young cow and lead it away. 'Mark that,' Yizo told me. 'That man's wife died in childbirth and he has no money to buy milk for the baby. M'dala is lending his cow.'

M'dala returned, pleased with himself. 'How can I enjoy a happy life when a child's stomach is filled with water?' Zenu muttered at this, but M'dala ignored her and turned his attention back on me. 'He's young, you know, but perhaps an exception can be made.'

Yizo beamed as we walked home. 'This is a great gift! Not one of your white ancestors knows the day he became a man!'

On the night before M'dala came for me, my body refused to sleep. I was still awake when Zenu entered the room, her hands covered with dirt. 'How many boys will be going with you?' she asked.

'Two,' I said.

Zenu sighed and lit her pipe. 'In better times, dozens of boys would be initiated, and there would be dancing contests between raw men from every village along the road. Now our men wander away to work in the mines or on the docks. Those who remain spend all their time and money at Yizo's shebeen. And still he begrudges my bride-price.'

'How much was it?'

'Little enough. Yizo agreed to provide food for my father and me. We were starving. No one offered to lend *us* a milking cow.' Zenu's pipe glowed in the darkness. 'Yizo thought my father would die soon after the marriage. Instead, your grandfather grew plump on my husband's food, lying day and night on the doss on which you now sleep. Finally, Yizo chased him out of the house.' She knocked the dottle from her pipe into the cooking fire. 'So now he lives in the bush, hiding his skin beneath a layer of ash.' Zenu removed a bundled scarf from between her breasts, placed it on the shelf, and went into the shebeen to dismiss the bargirl and turn the last of the patrons out into the night.

I listened awhile to Yizo's snoring, then climbed up on a chair and retrieved the bundle. I untied the scarf and stared at its contents: a ball of Yizo's hair, matted with dirt.

* * *

We went down to the river. M'dala instructed each of us to construct a beehive hut out of sticks covered with empty cement bags, because there wasn't enough foliage to thatch it in the old way, and he ordered us to shave one another's heads. With each command, I felt as though generations of initiates moved within me, their shorn hair commingling with mine on the muddy bank. 'Mind you bury your hair where no sorcerer will find it,' M'dala warned.

Yizo and some of the old men from the village came out to perform rituals that once had some meaning, but were now lost in tradition. Each boy was given a knobkerrie carved from mimosa wood, a braided bull's tail to wrap around his head, and an undyed cotton blanket – 'White, for purity and holiness,' M'dala explained. We immersed ourselves in the river, and the current purled in my ears with the same incantatory tone that Zenu used to recite the bloodlines of the village. We smeared butter over our bodies, rubbed antheap on our faces and chests to harden ourselves, and M'dala declared us initiates.

Yizo brought a white goat, which was slaughtered and charred over a fire of green palmwood until bitter with carbon. The initiates ate from the sinewy forelegs while the men dined on the tender flanks, and in the distance we heard the women wail for their lost children.

On the last night of my childhood, I slept in my beehive hut and dreamed that the baboon came to me and whispered with my Aunt's voice: *This is why your body brought you here.*

The surgeon arrived as the sun rose over the river. He was as old as M'dala, and there would be no one to take his place when he died. He entered my hut, waving an assegai. 'Rise up on this day of your manhood!' he cried. 'Where is the dog, this thing I have come to make into a man?' He brandished the assegai at me, showing no surprise at my pale skin. 'Leave this dog, Evil and Badness!' These were the old words, the few he still remembered. The rest were lost. He chased me outside where I stood shoulder to shoulder with the others, our eyes forward, jaws and fists set against the coming pain.

M'dala and the other old men surrounded us in case we tried to run away. Without warning, the surgeon pulled on my foreskin to stretch it away from my penis, and he worked the assegai in a circle, pulling at the prepuce as he sliced. Pain shot up to my chest, numbing my fingers and toes. It seized all my muscles, even stopping my heart, and my lungs became rigid and airless. Still the surgeon cut at me, and still my body refused to flinch or cry out.

Each pain has its own scent, and this one smelled of fresh leaves and iron shavings. As the blood of my boyhood pooled at my feet, I stared down at my distorted image. Behind me, I saw the reflections of countless generations of Xhosa boys, now old men or ancestors, at this defining moment of their manhood, and still my body didn't flinch, even as the surgeon threw the ring of my foreskin to the ground.

'You're a man!'

I retrieved the gobbet of flesh and replied as M'dala had instructed: 'I'm a man!'

The surgeon moved down the line, circumcising the other boys, and we set out in separate directions with our severed foreskins clenched in our fists.

I cast the remnant of my childhood onto an anthill, and the ants crawled over it and pulled it inside their mound, leaving me with only a singing pain in the wound where it had been.

For the first week I lay alone with my misery in the darkness of my beehive hut, where I sweated and bled into the straw. M'dala brought mealies and water mixed with antheap to sustain me in my recovery, and he covered the wound with leaves from a sneezewood tree bound with pulped rushes.

On the eighth day, the men came out to inspect me. They stepped back when M'dala removed my poultice, and Yizo looked as grey as the flesh around my groin.

'The ants must not have eaten all of the foreskin,' M'dala said. 'If a sorcerer found it, the cut will never heal.'

The wound filled with pus, and the smell of my pain grew rancid. A single, high-pitched note filled my ears, and as I lay still on my back, bathed in fever, I realised the keening was coming from the vocal cords of my body as it voiced its suffering across the initiation camp, past the river to where the women of the village held vigil for their sons and nephews and grandchildren. The women joined their ululations to mine, sharing my agony, and as a new wave of pain shook me, all the birds in the trees shot up as one into the sky, their beating wings concussing the night as they lent their screeching to the cacophony that stretched to the horizons.

I floated away with the pain and fever, leaving my singing body below, my spirit running light as an eland across a vast panorama of continents and seas.

When I woke back in my body, the baboon was framed in the doorway. I shook my head, and when my vision cleared, the figure watching over me was my aunt. Zenu gathered me into her arms and carried me out into the sun.

Custom forbade all contact between initiates and females, and Yizo waved her away. 'Leave off, woman! M'dala will take care of him.'

Her eyes flashed. 'Like he took care of you?' Yizo gave her a pleading look and glanced at me, but she went into the beehive hut, swept out the blood-encrusted straw, and rubbed cow dung into the dirt floor until it looked like polished stone. She brought me back inside and removed M'dala's poultice. My genitals looked as though they'd been sculpted from the foetid mud that lined the banks of the river.

That night Zenu lifted and cradled me. I struggled weakly against her embrace. 'Put me down, woman. I'm a man.'

'Is it?' Zenu said. She carried me to the river and we

watched, hidden in the rushes, as Yizo bathed beneath the moon. My uncle turned towards the bank where we crouched, and I shrank back from the image. Yizo had no scrotum or penis, only a dark patch of pubic hair.

Back in the beehive hut, Zenu examined the dead flesh between my legs. 'Yes, you have a man's body now.' She made a new poultice for my genitals from the fat and crushed bones of a river snake and covered this with mud.

'Does anyone else know about Uncle Yizo?' I asked.

My aunt nodded. 'The entire village. M'dala inspected his wounds.'

'Then why does he pretend you're barren?'

Her pipe had gone out and it hung loosely between her cracked lips. 'Men are always pretending in front of one another.'

The following morning, Zenu stretched me across the backseat of the estate car and Yizo drove us to the sea, as the voices that spoke to him in his dreams had instructed. The upholstery smelled of baboon fur and dried blood. The car kept to the winding road, its wheels following the ruts, until the track ran up against the ocean. Zenu and Yizo carried me into the surf, immersing my mutilated genitals in the salt water until I passed out.

That night I woke to the sound of a struck match. I crawled to the opening of my hut to watch as Zenu set fire to the ball of Uncle Yizo's unearthed hair. She added dried husks of grasshoppers to the fine ashes, grinding the mixture with a wooden spoon until it became a coarse powder. The embers glowed in her pipe, illuminating her bloodshot eyes as she uttered her wirra. She ladled curried vegetables into a bread bowl, stirred in the hexed powder, and carried it across the camp to where Yizo sat at the fire, waiting for his dinner.

I healed, and the time arrived for my coming out. M'dala showed me how to wrap my doek around my head in the manner of an unmarried man. I was given a new blanket, the red wool of my people, and the knobkerrie that my uncle had carved and blackened with smoke. The old men chased me to the river. '*Hamba hamba!* Go like a small, lowly man should go. Look not to the past, it is burning behind you!'

I heard the crackle of flames as they fired my beehive hut. I washed in the river and covered my shorn skull with animal fat, slapping it roughly on the top of my head, my face and chest, down each leg. Then I rubbed clay into my glistening skin until I shone like a ghost.

'Now you must lead a good life, with no more nonsense,' M'dala announced.

The villagers smeared white clay on their faces and held a beer-drink on the fighting ground. I danced with ankle rattles made from cocoons collected from the branches of mimosa trees, and the old men told me I was a man, no longer a dog, a thing.

Yizo wasn't drinking. 'Too many grasshoppers,' he told me, and he went home early to receive instruction from the voices that came to him in his dreams.

The other raw men stood before their sweethearts who inspected their fresh scars and led them into the tall grass. Aunt Zenu seated herself beside me in the gathering darkness. 'Look around you,' she said. 'The land is exhausted. Our herds have thinned. The wars are over. Our men are lost. Circumcision only determines the order in which they drink.'

The stars pulsed in the sky, while the men drank and danced listlessly.

'Did you ever meet my father?' I asked.

'Once. His body brought him to this place.' Zenu tamped a wad of tobacco into the bowl of her pipe. 'But he ran away before the surgeon arrived.' She laughed at my astonishment. 'There are no coincidences here.'

She rose and walked to the edge of the fighting ground where her father stood naked and covered with ash, leaning against the wind, waiting for his supper.

The sun rose over the beer drinkers, and the villagers turned their white faces to where I sat in my man's body. Heat shimmered over the road, and my eyes dried in their sockets as I stared out over the village.

# A is for Ancestors

## The Rains, 1969

R *is for Rain.* In *Fructman's Illustrated Dictionary for Little People*, a duck holds an umbrella against the slashing rain drops.

The rats came with the rains. Nights, we heard them skitter inside the walls and beneath the floorboards of the bungalow, the scrabble of their tiny claws following us into our dreams. Mornings, sawdust fell through cracks in the beadboard ceiling and into our oatmeal as they gnawed at the beams, wearing down their long teeth. Afternoons, they slept in the stifle beneath the corrugated iron roof, and the house fell silent.

There was a burr in Mr Gordon's 'R's, an affectation acquired during his year in Scotland, where he met Mrs Gordon. Perhaps he travelled to that country because he'd heard the women are so very fair. 'Rrats,' he'd say, looking down on the spoor that peppered the kitchen counters. He dredged it up from the back of his throat. 'Bloody rrats.'

In this, my twelfth rain season, the days played out by degrees, like the attic air that chilled with the advance of the mountain's shadow. The season brought two types of rainfall to the glen: a deluge of heavy drops that beat on my head until it throbbed, and a soft mizzle that crawled under our collars and between the seams, weaving dampness into the fabric of our clothes. At dusk, when the vermin began to stir from their dreamless sleep, Mr Gordon would rise from his supper of bubble and squeak without excusing himself and climb the ladder to the crawl space with a plate of tinned meat to bait the spring traps. He also took a beer to drink as he stooped under the iron roof, breathing in the day's accumulated heat, and one of his ponderous ledger books – the coup de grâce, I supposed, for any rat that might survive the snap of his traps. Perhaps he cherished this time away from me and Mrs Gordon, because he remained there, reading aloud from the massive ledger by torchlight, until the air grew cold beneath the moon. His muffled, disembodied words drifted down on us with the sawdust; a litany of receipts and expenditures, his *Book of Numbers.*

On average, Mr Gordon filled one ledger book every three weeks in his careful hand, pencilling all the transactions of his life into its ruled margins. Each ice cream he bought for me on haircut day became an *Accounts Receivable*, and each time I completed a household chore he noted a reduction against my debt. Every tank of petrol was an *Asset* to be amortised over the mountain roads he drove each day to and from his furniture store in Umtali. The brightly coloured scarves he bought for Mrs Gordon were entered as *Goodwill.*

Years ago, Mr Gordon had ordered his carpenter, Sundayboy Moses, to construct a monolithic file cabinet in the office above the furniture store to house the ledgers – a wall of great drawers, floor to ceiling, each as large as a steamer trunk. The joints in the cabinet were seamlessly bevelled, and the drawers glided on runners lined with stainless steel ball bearings taken from the wheels of derelict tractors that littered the trust land. It was the last piece of furniture Sundayboy produced – his masterpiece before he limped away northwest towards the Unspeakable River where God resides.

Sundayboy's departure left Mr Gordon's store with four employees: Mr Tabori, a sales associate who'd fled to Rhodesia after the fall of fascist Italy; two stockboys, Now Now and Pamwe, who worked for daily wages unloading and uncrating furniture in the mornings and running deliveries in the late afternoon; and the cleaning lady, Mrs Moses, who scrubbed Mr Gordon's toilets, emptied his waste bins, boiled and bleached his shirts and underpants, and rubbed paste wax into the heavy wooden file drawers her husband had made.

Mr Gordon would no longer abide Africans in his house,

so I became his servant. I fetched him his beer and jigger of scotch when he returned from the furniture store each night, massaged his knobby feet, polished his ox-blood shoes, and lived as a squatter on his property.

The bungalow existed in a remote glen in the eastern highlands of Rhodesia, outside of time and the world. My calendar was based on the growth of my hair. Two crew cuts marked the passage of a month, twenty-four a year. On the first and third Wednesdays of each month I joined Mr Gordon on his commute to Umtali. He inspected my head before we set out, his fingers rooting through my bristles. 'You have your mother's hair,' he'd say, satisfied.

I had to take his word for this. Mrs Gordon kept her hair pinned tightly beneath a scarf, protection against the air conditioning unit that blew full force, even during the raw nights that sometimes accompanied the rains. Scottish forebears hung on her walls, fixed and deathless in their sepia worlds – five grown sons standing around a seated patriarch, a small boy in pigtails and a kilt, a Royal Flying Corps pilot. They stared down on me with lithic eyes, folded hands, tight mouths. I only entered her room when she summoned me with a bicycle horn. She remained silent when I entered, my arms covered with gooseflesh, to place a tray of cold food over her knees and retreat with a sloshing bedpan.

Mr Gordon and I never spoke of passing. The matter

of our ancestry was an understanding between father and son, something to keep from my mother. Our secret filled all the rooms of our house up to the corners and crevices, leaving hardly enough room for the rats.

We began our commute before the sun cleared the mountain and filtered through the rain clouds into the bungalow, though never into my mother's room which faced west, its heavy curtains drawn. Mr Gordon hunched over the steering wheel as he piloted his British Ford along the mountain highway, scanning the ridges for guerrilla soldiers who sometimes infiltrated the eastern highlands to rev up an isolated farmhouse or waylay a motorist. The windscreen blurred and cleared with every pass of the wipers, offering us intermittent glimpses into a landscape of ambush.

Fear and logistics kept casual motorists at home. Petrol and automobile parts had run short, and older cars were abandoned on the road's shoulder where they had broken down. At times it seemed that Mr Gordon and I were the sole inhabitants of all creation as we sped along an endless stretch of rain-enveloped highway that wound through an empty and silent universe.

Once we rounded a blind curve to find a felled tree blocking our way. The car slewed on the wet pavement while Mr Gordon fought the skid, the massive ledger flew forward into the dash, and we came to a stop amid the branches and leaves. A dozen wild-eyed and unshaven

Shona with glistening machetes emerged from the shadows to slit our scrag where we sat, hooked in our safety harnesses. Mr Gordon held the ledger before him like a shield.

But lightning had killed the tree, and the mountain winds had blown it over; these men were part of a road crew come to clear away the debris. We watched them work, lean muscles showing through ragged yellow coveralls that left shoulders, knees, ankles, sometimes even genitals exposed to the guti weather. They sang a crazy song, *wari wari wari*, while they stripped the branches from the tree and hoisted the sheared trunk off the road, down into the ravine. Then they trotted off in unison, still chanting the same two syllables in a sort of nonsensical invocation to their god Mwari, the rainmaker. Their voices rose and fell with the wind, *wari wari wari*, as they vanished into the mist that gathered between storms, blanched silhouettes that rose and fell in loping strides.

It was late morning before we arrived at the Shona barbers – Mr Gordon didn't fancy paying a pricey stylist for a crew cut, nor did he like the idea of a European inspecting our hair too closely. The barbers saw our white skin and seated us immediately in adjacent chairs. I pretended to read *The Umtali Post*, turning the pages at the same moment as Mr Gordon. While the barbers ran clippers over our skulls, Mr Gordon handed his newspaper to me and pointed to the lead story. There was a picture of an overturned motorcar on a mountain road. Bullet holes riddled the door panel. I gazed at it, picturing myself inside.

'What's it say?' he asked, pointing to the article. 'I forgot my glasses.'

The clippers buzzed in my ears.

'Well then, go on.' I shifted in my chair.

'Dammit boy, read it!' At this outburst, both of the Shona barbers ceased their clipping, unsure if they should continue.

I stared dumbly at the newspaper.

Mr Gordon knitted his brows. He pointed to the headline. 'Read this then.'

I shrugged.

'Bloody hell,' he whispered, all harshness gone from his voice. 'You don't know how.'

I was illiterate at twelve, a testament to Mr Gordon's commitment to secrecy. Six years earlier, he had taken me to a military boarding school for boys outside Salisbury, but we left abruptly after meeting with the headmaster. On our way home, Mr Gordon pulled over and shut off the engine. He stared through the windscreen, his hands gripping the wheel, fighting the direction his life had taken. An admissions application lay between us on the seat, along with a crumpled release form which, if signed by a parent, would allow the admissions board to conduct a background investigation into our family. A formality, but the very idea frightened him out of his senses, and I'd been allowed to stay at home with no more talk of school.

We sat in our barber chairs in silence for several moments. 'Of course you can't,' he said softly. The Shona barbers resumed their clipping, and bits of hair fell about my neck. With a flourish that seemed almost choreographed, the barbers spun our chairs to face the mirrors and together Mr Gordon and I absently nodded our approval.

'Come on, then,' he said. I followed him as he pushed his way roughly through the queue of Shona men waiting for a free chair. Outside a hard rain pounded our shorn heads, and the dank crept under our clothes and into our skin.

We drove to a bookstore where I waited with the car, watching a team of policemen stop dark-skinned shoppers to inspect their radios, parcels, and purses for shop bombs. A young Shona woman was made to untuck her blouse and turn out the hem of her skirt. There were flashes of lightning followed closely by thunder, clearing the street of potential detainees. The police retreated beneath a newsstand. Fat drops beat like *bira* drums against the roof of the British Ford, made in Rhodesia before the parts embargo. Wind swirled ancestral spirits through the anti-draught window, and the thunder became the stamp of many feet in unison. I was asleep when my father emerged from the bookstore with a copy of *Fructman's Illustrated Dictionary for Little People.*

The book's spine was black with gold pinstripes, reminding me of a suit Mr Gordon had bought but no longer wore, not since the day when an identically attired, especially dark man knocked on the door of our house. It had been years since Mr Gordon invited anyone, servants or visitors, onto his property. The man stood on our doorstep as a witness for one of the religious sects that had sprung up across Rhodesia in those troubled times. It had made a great impression on me, my father and his African doppelganger staring at one another from opposite sides of the barred window that looked out on the verandah, each wearing the other's suit. It must have affected my father also, this mirror into a world that ran up against ours, because he withdrew to his study and left the evangelist standing on our doorstep.

Wednesday was early closing day in Umtali, a relief for both of us, and Mr Gordon was not obliged to linger at the tuckshop where he would read the notices posted on the board over the cash register or inspect the polish on his shoes or crack his lumpy knuckles while he waited for me to guttle my ice cream. We drove home in our habitual silence, the slap of the windscreen wipers, the radio murmuring at sub-audible volume, traffic lights reflecting on the wet pavement that sucked at the tyres.

'From now on you're coming into the store with me,' he said, finally, 'and learn to read like any other white man.' The windscreen blurred and cleared with each pass of the wipers, and thus ended my aimless and unsupervised days at home.

* * *

*S is for store.* In *Fructman's* a jolly aproned man stands before a grocery with empty windows.

The furniture store was located in the shopping district on palm-lined Main Street where Africans waited to make their purchases until after all the Europeans were served. Mr Gordon hated that economic necessity forced him to deal with Africans at all, and he vented his frustration on the shoeblacks who tried to set up on the pavement outside his shop. He kicked at their boxes, spilling rags and tins of polish, before calling the police to move them along.

On the first day of my instruction, Mr Gordon seated me at the unused half of a partners' desk built by Sundayboy Moses. As with the great file cabinet, each piece of the desk fitted snugly into the whole without glue or nails. Sundayboy had helped build Mr Gordon's store and, in its early days, produced much of its inventory. This must have been a birthgift, because furniture making was unknown among the people of the Unspeakable River. They made only what they could carry in their carved boats: knives, clubs, children.

I began my struggle with *Fructman's Illustrated Dictionary for Little People.* The collection of ciphers that corresponded to the picture of a ship started with the same letter as the picture of a bumble bee. 'Ship,' I said aloud, pretending to read. I'd studied the book for an hour and had still not cracked the code.

'It's "Boat".' Mr Gordon reached across the desk, stabbed the letter *B* with his index finger, and said, 'Ba! Ba!' He exhibited the same impatience with his stockboys – particularly Now Now, who responded to all requests for work with 'Yes Baas, I will do it now now.' Among the Shona 'now' might mean two hours or two days. 'Now now' simply meant sooner than now. It was a source of constant irritation to Mr Gordon that he had no means to express urgency to his employees.

My assault on *Fructman's* was interrupted when Now Now arrived late to the store. One of the crowded lorries that brought workers in from the trust land had broken down. Now Now pulled at his grey beard as he stood before his employer. Mr Gordon put on his fatherly face. 'I can't let you stroll in here at all hours, Now Now. My furniture won't unload itself.'

'Yes, big problem.'

'You want to see me run out of business?'

'No, never, baas.'

'Laziness and lack of discipline, that's what.' The Shona stockboy was a decade his senior, but Mr Gordon spoke to him as he would a child.

'Yes, baas, very bad.'

'I'm going to have to cut your pay.'

'Of course, baas.'

'Now shift that lot into the showroom.'

'Yes, now now, baas.' Now Now slumped against the wall as his employer stormed away. He didn't blame Mr Gordon for his troubles. 'It is my ancestors making mischief again,' he said, and Pamwe nodded sympathetically. 'They do not stay well because I cannot afford to bring them meat and beer. The bakkie breaks down, my pay is cut, more bad luck.'

Mr Gordon had packed sandwiches for our lunch. 'Here's some meat for your ancestors' shrine,' I offered, lifting the cold pork from between the slices of bread.

'No, no, little baas. No shrine, no statues,' he said, accepting the gift. 'I am no bleeding Pygmy or Portuguese Catholic. Ancestors nevermind where they get their meat and beer. Anyplace is fine. Go well, little baas, I got to work now.' He settled against the wall, staring at the greasy treasure in his hands. I doubted the offering would make it home to his ancestors.

I ate the bread and returned to the partners' desk to stare at my book until the large block letters blurred on the page. I looked through the window at Mrs Moses's little house, and then studied the top of Mr Gordon's head as he hunkered over his ledgers. His hair kinked noticeably during the rainy season, despite his monthly chemical processes, and he'd taken to shaving a thin, pink parting along the left side of his skull to maintain the fiction that he was a white man.

When our backsides ached from too much sitting, I would follow him out to the loading dock to watch him spit onto the gravel below. My father spat beautifully, another betrayal of his African heritage. He collected the saliva at the back of his throat, not ostentatiously like the red-faced Rhodies who farmed the eastern highlands. Instead he shaped it into an oyster with his tongue and sent it flying through the O of his lips in a graceful arc from mouth to target. He could imprison an ant inside a globule of spit at five paces, an accomplishment of the first order in my eyes. He also whistled perfectly, the dying art of his generation, warbling strange and wondrous tunes that ignored conventional harmonics and stirred something deep inside me.

He was always losing things – his penknife, a tie pin, a fountain pen – and I often found him turning out his pockets or looking beneath the desk on his hands and knees. Each afternoon Mrs Moses would poke her head into the office, her eyes searching Mr Gordon's face, and I wondered if I were interrupting some duty she normally performed in my absence. Before withdrawing, she shot me a cross look that should have explained everything.

* * *

*C is for Church.* A family of little people hold hands at the entrance beneath the steeple. The illustrator for *Fructman's* chose to leave them faceless.

Sundayboy acquired his Christian name because he took odd jobs from neighbouring merchants on the Sabbath, when the furniture store was closed. Perhaps Mrs Moses, returning from her church services, still looked for her husband when she turned the corner into her yard: bent over a cupboard or a chest of drawers, the shavings curling up from the plane in his hand.

Mr Gordon's office window overlooked Mrs Moses's house – a one-room affair constructed of raw pine unmarred by nails, each board joined tongue and groove. Rainwater ran off the asphalt roof onto the unpaved drive where Mr Gordon parked his car.

The Brothers of St Augustine's bestowed Sundayboy's surname because he came to the lonely monastery from the river, floating silent and bleeding in a shallow dugout, his wife guiding him in the current. Though Sundayboy had built the house himself, he never lived within its walls. Unable to sleep inside, without stars, he carried a blanket into the yard and lay down amid the lumber and sawhorses.

For Sundayboy, the shish of tyres on wet asphalt became the rush of a strong current, the soft rain on his face was mist from the river, the diesel rumble of a lorry the roar of a hippo. During thunderstorms he climbed the roof of the house and stretched his hands skyward. It was Now Now who told me how he'd seen Sundayboy stand there with his arms lifted to God, while lightning cast his shadow across the yard below. Now Now witnessed this spectacle from the loading dock, where he was spending the night because Mr Gordon had docked his wages, and the middle-aged stockboy lacked the fare to return to his wife and children in the trust land.

Sundayboy refused to bring a child into this land so far away from the Unspeakable River and the Begetter of All Things. He continued to lie apart from his wife – he in the yard, she in the house – until the cloudless evening when Mrs Moses went out to where her husband slept, hiked up her nightgown, and lowered herself upon him, thus conceiving a child beneath the stars before Sundayboy was properly awake. This too, Now Now had seen from the loading dock, as Mr Gordon seldom sent him home with a full day's wages.

When Mrs Moses's son, Ephat, contracted the mumps, I was sent to sleep beside him in his sickbed. In the garden that flanked the sole entrance to the house, Mrs Moses grew thrift, stonecrop, cast iron, barberry – a stunted, spiky show that grasped and irritated the ankles of visitors who strayed from the one true concrete path that led to her door. The interior of the house was a reliquary of plaster saints and twisted crosses fashioned from bits of frond, collected over half a lifetime of Palm Sundays and nailed to the walls. The house smelled of ammonia and wood-oil soap and discontent.

That night Ephat lay sweating and motionless beside me, bathed in the streetlight that shone through the sole window, his testicles swollen double. At midnight, when he'd kicked away the bedclothes, his mother silently appeared. I watched Mrs Moses as she ran a cool washrag over his feverish body and sang a sort of medicine song, a yodelling chant whose meaning she'd probably forgotten. Her face was hexangular, lean and coffin-shaped in the streetlight from without.

Mrs Moses noticed my open eyes and tried a smile. 'Better to catch this now before you become a man, you want children. You bring this disease home to your brothers and sisters, eh?' She was unaware I was an only child. Mr Gordon never spoke of himself or his family.

'I haven't got any,' I told her.

Mrs Moses digested this bit of information. 'I don't want to be pushing, but is your mother a sickly woman? A woman with only one child is almost sterile. Perhaps she could rub the oil from tsin beans between her legs for fertility.'

Women from the Unspeakable River coveted children

above all else to replace the ones lost to disease, malnutrition, drowning, lightning, and fierce hippos. Mrs Moses leaned over me to kiss Ephat goodnight, and though he was my age, she sang to him as if he were an infant, *Sleep my little one, the night is wind and rain, drops fall in our meal, and the river floods its banks again.* Inside her shirt, hanging on her neck from a chain, I saw a garnet cufflink Mr Gordon had been searching for in his office.

Mr Gordon was the sort of employer who invited theft. Beaded lamps, bookends, throw pillows disappeared from the showroom, fountain pens and notepads from the office. Rather than lose face, he fiddled the books to account for the shrinkage. I also stole from him – a shaving brush, his service pin, liver pills, nail clippers, oddly intimate items.

Mrs Moses looked down on me where I lay beside her son, perhaps considering whether she should also kiss me goodnight. Instead she patted my cheek with a hand that smelled of oil soap and cooking fat, the same tacky composite that covered the surfaces of her house.

Outside, rotting lumber creaked and shifted against the house, untouched since the day Sundayboy stripped down to the dazzling underpants that his wife boiled in bleach and shambled away on his crooked leg, north towards the river of his ancestors, leaving her nearly sterile with only one child. He abandoned his carpenter's tools with his family; the bevel saws and adzes and hand drills buried beneath the muddy gravel Mr Gordon had poured so he could park his car and the delivery lorry within the security fence surrounding Mrs Moses's yard. There was a sign attached to the fence, *Basopa lo Inja*, but the dog had gone with his master and there was nothing left to beware of in that yard. The house seemed to hold its breath, waiting for Sundayboy to return.

That first night I had an incurable case of hiccoughs. Ephat, sweating next to me, said it was a sign of my ancestors calling.

* * *

*L is for Light.* A naked bulb surrounded by a brilliant wash of yellow. This page of *Fructman's* is slightly warm to the touch.

How many people can remember clearly the moment they first began to read? I stared at the illustration of the boat in my *Fructman's.* There was a picture of a sparrow on the opposite page. A wave of understanding flooded my brain.

'Bird,' I said proudly.

'Yes, that's it,' Mr Gordon exclaimed. 'Well done!' He clapped me on the shoulder, and anyone could see my father was proud of me. I took that moment and stored it away deep in my heart. This, then, was the first in a string of words I would read during my lifetime. End on end, they would stretch around the world many times.

Elated, my father decided to take me to the tuckshop for an ice cream. I believe he would have bought this and not even written it into his ledger as an account receivable, had our trip not been cut short. When we stepped outside the store my father froze, his mouth working silently. I followed his gaze to where a shoeshine box lay unattended on the pavement. He found his voice:

'*Bomb*!'

My father hustled me back into the store and we scrambled through the narrow aisles of the showroom towards the back service door, bracing ourselves for the storm of fire and window glass. A customer swore as he stumbled over an accent table, knocking a ceramic vase to the floor. Mr Tabori shouldered me out of his path and I tore my trouser pocket on a drawer handle. A grandfather clock began chiming the hour. Out on the loading dock, Now Now, Pamwe and a delivery driver joined our stampede as we raced down the alley several blocks before anyone thought to call the bomb squad. A false alarm, as it turned out – only an empty polish tin and some rags, the shoeblacks' revenge on Mr Gordon.

When Ephat recovered from the mumps, Mr Gordon took me to the outskirts of Umtali to a clapboard doctor's office. Though his African patients crowded the waiting room and overflowed into the car park, Dr N'gono saw me immediately. Mr Gordon chose him for the same reasons he chose our barbers. The doctor felt my neck and scrotum for signs of swelling and sighed. 'Bad luck you didn't catch this now.' He shone a light into my ear. 'Your father had a bad case, just after you were born. Nearly took him.' As I dressed, I wondered if my father would have risked more offspring if he hadn't caught the mumps in his maturity and left his wife nearly sterile.

I rejoined Mr Gordon on his daily commute along the shadowy mountain roads, returning each night to the bungalow to sleep beneath the rats, and though I continued to see Ephat every day after my reading sessions, he never invited me into the little house again. 'It's the ancestors,' he explained. 'They don't stay well here.' Mrs Moses refused to speak of her hippo hunting forebears, much less provide them with offerings, and so Ephat knew of them only through dimly remembered stories his father had told. They took their name from the river from which they drank, a distal tributary that fed the Zambezi. Because it was forbidden for Sundayboy to give voice to this secret place where God resided, Ephat's ancestors remained nameless.

Outside, neither of us knew how to conduct ourselves in the presence of another child. We climbed the stacks of lumber in silence, staring into the grey sky, or squatted in the yard to recover the ruined tools that had resurfaced with the rains. Our play took shape when Ephat suggested we become hippo hunters, and we fashioned thin spears from sharpened dowels, wading through the deepest puddles in the yard to stalk sawhorse hippos. But these unsatisfactory weapons bounced and shattered against our targets, and we broke tradition and made slingshots from tree branches. I scavenged surgical rubber from the first aid kit Mr Gordon kept in the boot of his car and we experimented with bits of gravel, marbles and hard candy as projectiles. Ephat discovered an ideal size and shape and balance in the tractor wheel ball bearings he extracted from the runners of the heavy wooden file cabinets. We held these perfect missiles between our thumbs and forefingers as we drew back the surgical rubber and released them with enough force to topple a sawhorse.

One day, when my father went down to the sales floor to help Mr Tabori with the late afternoon rush of customers, I saw Ephat enter my father's office with some meat in his hands. I followed, curious, but found no one inside. I dropped to my knees and looked beneath the partners' desk, rose and went to the window and looked out into the yard below, but there was no sign of Ephat. It was as if he'd passed through a portal into the spirit world.

Outside on the loading dock, Now Now unwrapped his lunch, expecting to find a sandwich made from the shank of a goat. The animal had wandered in front of a lorry that was taking him home to the trust land, and the shank was Now Now's share for helping to load its carcass into the bed. He shook his head when he found only two grease-soaked slices of bread inside the butcher paper. 'I swear on my beard, I'm going to beat my wife for this,' he said. He stuffed one of the slices into his mouth and addressed me while he chewed. 'I tell you, young baas, don't come home too late at night if you like meat for lunch.'

I soon mastered *Fructman's*, and this time my father brought me with him into the bookstore and helped me choose: *Curious George*, *The Velveteen Rabbit*, *Goodnight Moon*. Each morning, after the opening rush, it became my father's habit to leave the furniture store in the care of Mr Tabori. We sat at the same side of the partners' desk, his hand on one side of the book, mine on the other, while I read stories to him, shaping my mouth around the sound of each letter until a word emerged. It was tortuously slow going, and my father would provide me with the difficult words only after I'd stared at them for some time. We sat that way, me struggling, my father by turns encouraging and chastising, until midmorning when we took our coffee out onto the loading dock. I held my mug like my father, close to my nose, not using the handle, letting the warmth soak through the ceramic into my fingers, drawing the steam into my damp lungs. As we drank, we watched Mrs Moses work her stunted garden beds. She showed no sign of the chill and wet as she dug and pulled at the ground.

Now Now said that river people are naturally cold and watery, because of the mist. He said that one wet night when he had no money for the lorry to take him back to the trust land, he knocked on Mrs Moses's door, but she didn't answer. 'That's the way of it always,' he said to me smiling. 'When you grow up, you'll weep.'

After lunch, my father would spread before me a daily balance sheet and an income statement identical to his own. Each time he paid an invoice, he subtracted the amount from the asset side of his balance sheet and added it to the expenses in his income statement. Then he handed me the bill to enter into the duplicate set of books I maintained as part of my education in mathematics and finance. Occasionally my father looked across the desk at me as I worked the ledger before me, his own image in miniature. With both of us keeping books, the great cabinet filled at double its previous rate. Each time my father opened a drawer, the wood screeched and groaned from want of the ball bearings Ephat and I had pilfered for our slingshots, and he would rub his forehead and sniff at the faint smell of meat.

At home on Sunday, I read Beatrix Potter to Mrs Gordon, raising my voice above the roar of the air conditioner: *Once upon a time there was a woodmouse, and her name was Mrs Tittlemouse.* Mrs Gordon leaned forward in her Queen Anne chair and listened. *She lived in a bank under a hedge.* In the attic above, Mr Gordon stomped about, setting his traps, and sawdust floated down on us from the ceiling where the rats had gnawed on the beams. *Such a funny house!*

* * *

*H is for history.* On this page, the illustrator of *Fructman's* outdid himself.

The people of the Unspeakable River lived in the weather with nothing to separate them from the wind and sky and killing lightning and storms and floods that the Begetter of All Things fashioned for his children. When Mrs Moses brought her wounded husband to the priory, she must have wondered at the roof and walls that kept the monks apart from God. Perhaps she thought of all the children she could raise to live if she had such a place for herself. Maybe it was she who persuaded the brothers to teach Sundayboy the secret of their wood building when he recovered from his wounds.

Ephat, convinced that his neglected ancestors had visited the mumps on him, moved out of his mother's house and began to sleep in the yard. I was released from my reading to join him there during the late afternoon. The rain fell over us in the yard where Ephat now lived, and stories Sundayboy told long ago resurfaced in his memory like the rusting tools that rose up from the mud. He told me how the hippo hunters immersed themselves in the torrent of the Unspeakable River at the height of the rains, armed only with their fists and voices, to drive a bull hippo roaring and bellowing into the bush. There they forced it to kneel in the presence of a God the tormented beast could neither see nor understand. While the women fell to the ground and wailed for their lost children, the men likewise prostrated themselves before the deity, panting and bloody, beseeching Him to quiet the rains and return the turgid river to its peaceful level. As His shadow of light fell over the hunters and the captive hippo, they became lost in the rapture.

Once, while the men beat the water to raise one of the creatures, a bull rose before Sundayboy. He wrapped his arms around the hippo's head, each hand gripping an ear while great, blunt teeth tore at him.

Mrs Moses poled the dugout containing her husband's mutilated body from the headwaters of the Unspeakable River and down the Zambezi until she came to St Augustine's. There the brothers managed to save Sundayboy's leg and reproductive organs, preserving Mrs Moses's hope that she might still have children.

Ephat also talked about setting out north in search of his father who lived with God beside the remote, unutterable river, but I think he was afraid of what he'd find.

One afternoon my father sent me from the office and I went to the loading dock. Now Now and Pamwe had settled into a sofa they'd unloaded. I caught the end of their conversation:

'Not that I blame him, brother,' Now Now said. 'I'd fancy a go at her myself.' Pamwe nodded his assent and glanced up at my father's office.

'Heyya, what you listening for?' Now Now had noticed me.

'What's a *go*?' I asked him. Pamwe snorted.

'You nevermind, young baas,' Now Now said. He rose from the sofa and called to Pamwe, 'Come shift this inside before the rain comes.' And then to me, 'Go find Ephat and play somewhere else.' To Pamwe again, 'Here, brother, take a side,' and they carried the sofa through the swinging doors and into the showroom.

I called for Ephat at the door of the little house but there was no answer. In Mr Gordon's office above the store, I could hear Mrs Moses, her voice caught between laughter and wailing. I wondered what a *go* with Mrs Moses entailed, and I shimmied up the beam that supported the roof tresses, crawled over the loading dock, and looked in through the office window.

It was a curious thing to see Mrs Moses naked below the waist in my father's lap. I froze, but though Mr Gordon trained his glassy stare in my direction he saw nothing. His fingers grasped at the brown flesh of her thighs as if he would have it for himself, and Mrs Moses wrapped her arms and legs around his waist, pulling him deeper within.

My father's vision focused as he climaxed, and his roar caught in his throat as he met my eyes on the other side of the window. He pushed Mrs Moses from his lap, gathered his clothes, and went into the toilet without looking at the window, leaving this incident to be added to the growing list of things of which we would never speak.

Mrs Moses sat on the chair whereon she had straddled my father moments earlier, rubbing tsin bean oil between her legs. She clamped them together, twice crossed at the knees and ankles to retain my father's arid semen, and remained in this position, her head bowed as if in prayer, for some minutes before she dressed and left the office.

I can't say why I continued to look into that empty room, other than a queer feeling that this scene had not yet ended. The wind blew in from the mountains, driving a thunderstorm over the city. The bottom drawer of the file cabinet glided open by itself, and Ephat climbed out. This was where he'd disappeared the day he'd stolen the goat meat from Now Now's lunch. Ephat made offerings to his progenitors from inside the empty drawer of the monolithic cabinet, surrounded on all sides by his father's craft. We stared at each other, and the window glass reflected the storm clouds that moved across the sky behind me, superimposing them on Ephat's face. His eyes smouldered with hatred for me, who bore witness to his humiliation.

* * *

*A is for Ancestors.* Tear this page from your *Fructman's Illustrated Dictionary for Little People* and burn it.

The next morning Ephat left home to join one of the repair crews that filled potholes and kept the roads clear of scree and deadfall. He slept that evening in the weather on the gravel bank of a highway that wound through the mountains like a river.

As I waited in the office for my father to close the store, I looked down on Mrs Moses where she stood in the doorway of her childless house. The yard had begun to flood, and she watched her husband's abandoned tools rise from the mud and sink again beneath the promised land where Mrs Moses had brought her family to prosper and multiply.

It was the last time Mr Gordon ever brought me to the furniture store. He'd found me a place in The Streams of Living Water House of Prayer and Boys' School in Umtali. The headmaster, a charismatic who called himself Brother Paul, was the very same African who had stood on our verandah in my father's suit, and the masters were all Ndebele from the south: muscular, fierce-eyed men. But they conducted no background enquiries into our family and, as with our barbers and our doctor, Mr Gordon found them less threatening than Europeans. Most of the students were Shona, except for me and three sons of a retired, alcoholic British soldier and his Indian maid. The brothers of The Streams of Living Water administered beatings when we spoke Shona words, or when I wrote with my left hand, or moved my mouth as I read the scriptures silently, or scotched my sums, or pulled my hands away during group prayers, or remained unmoved when the brothers spoke in tongues. I welcomed the beatings that accompanied my immersion into the Streams of Living Water. Someone had to punish me for my secret ancestry.

With my enrolment, haircut day shifted to the Sabbath. Mr Gordon rose before daybreak from the narrow iron bed in his study to cook our porridge. He banged the spoon around the saucepan to send the rats scuttling into the walls before we sat down to eat.

The rains lingered in the highlands, and dark clouds shrouded the mountains, revealing only a few metres of road before us and swallowing it up again in the rearview mirror. Sometimes we heard the faint *wari wari wari* of a road crew singing, but though I strained to make out the grey silhouettes through cloud and rain, I never saw Ephat again.

My father and I had no conversation to distract us from the radio on the way to and from Umtali, instead we listened to news reports of increased rebel activity and motorists waylaid on lonely stretches of highway. We came to anticipate the attack so keenly that when the shot finally came, it brought on the satisfaction that accompanies an expectation fulfilled. It wasn't a bullet, but rather a perfectly smooth stainless steel ball bearing that punched a hole clean through the windscreen, struck my breastbone, and fell to the floormat where it rolled at my feet.

I doubled over, my breath knocked out, head below the dash near the radio. The broadcaster spoke confidentially into my ear as he read the standard procedure for motorists who find themselves under terrorist attack: lie down on the seat or, if a barricade has made it impossible to continue or the vehicle is disabled, move away from the car, find cover, and wait for one of the regular army patrols. I rubbed the spot over my heart where the ball bearing had struck.

My father and I said so little to each other over the course of our lives it seemed natural that we would not speak now. He settled back in his seat, whistling one of his odd tunes, as if there were no point in searching for an attack now that it had already come. We drove on towards our house, wipers slapping, ball bearing rolling on the floorboard, the radio murmuring as if it were in the presence of the dead. By the time my father turned into our drive and switched off the engine, the entire incident had never happened.

* * *

*! is for the unspeakable.* There is no illustration for this on the final page of *Fructman's*, only that single, cryptic mark.

The comical bark of the bicycle horn summoned me to where Mrs Gordon sat in the boneless slump of an invalid. Her chair was turned to the air conditioner that roared full into her face, a windstorm from the Scottish highlands that dried her eyes and rippled the scarf against her skull, the heather and green tartan of her clan flapping over her atrophied legs. It was Sunday, and I could feel more than hear my father's heavy footsteps above as he baited his traps. He never brought the corpses of the killed rats down into the house. At times a faint, sweetly sickening smell slipped through the cracks in the beadboard with the sawdust.

I lifted Mrs Gordon's hand from the armrest to massage it – poor circulation had turned her nails blue – and while I rubbed her fingertips, her knuckles, her palm, I recited a poem I'd read that day, *Alas! Alas! For Miss Mackay*, working juniper oil into the cracked skin, *her forks and knives have run away*, and my mother squeezed my hand back. I dabbed at the milky substance that formed at the corners of her mouth and in the collops beneath her chin, *and when the cups and spoons are going,* and her features softened almost into a smile, *she's sure there is no way of knowing.* Perhaps it was this intimacy, or maybe I could no longer hold our secret any longer, and it spilled out of my mouth before I knew I'd spoken: 'Father and I are coloured.'

Mrs Gordon's hands moved faster than my eyes could follow. The blows stung both sides of my head at once, the first and only time she ever struck me, and by the time I realised she had boxed my ears, my mother had already swept me up and squeezed me against her. I remained dumb in the arms of this carline ghost come suddenly to life. She would have felt the tight curls when she stroked the base of my father's neck in the early days of their courtship, the smell of his chemical process in her nostrils. She'd been our accomplice all along.

'Don't talk rubbish,' she said softly into my ringing ears. The scent of juniper filled my nose almost to my eyes as my mother stroked my face.

That night I had a dream:

*An old African woman in beadwork and an elaborately piled turban stands at the foot of my bed smoking a long-stemmed pipe. She beckons. I follow her up the ladder to the attic crawl space, where hands reach out from the darkness to grasp at my hair and touch my skin. They press against me until I no longer know where they begin and I end, and we become seamless, like Sundayboy's furniture, pieced together with a bond stronger than nails and glue. I smell meat and beer on their breath as they whisper their silent hunger in my ears.*

I rose from this dream and climbed up into the attic. The smell nearly knocked me back down the ladder. My father had left a torch at the edge of the trapdoor, and I switched it on and shone it about the crawl space – a set of vinyl luggage, a streaked mirror, my mother's abandoned hope chest. There were no traps. The torch beam played on the plate of meat my father had brought up earlier and left on a wooden chair, now crawling with rats. Of course it was his offerings, not the rain, that drew the vermin to our bungalow in such great numbers.

The attic smelled of spilled beer, wet fur and the residue of spoiled meat. A ledger book was propped open against the chair back so our ancestors could see the worth of the furniture store to date. The rats shrieked at the torchlight and sank their red teeth into one another in fright and confusion. I stared at this squirming, makeshift altar, my father's secret devotion to his ancestors now manifest. My legs fell out from under me, and I felt myself kneeling and bellowing, like a hippo bullied before the God of the Unspeakable River. Rain fell on the roof in strange rhythms, and the wind sounded beneath the eaves of corrugated iron in notes identical to those my father whistled beneath his breath.

# *The Bones, the Flight, the Destitute Wandering, the Secret Well Kept*

The Harvest, 1856

BE QUIET! PUT MY MEAT AND BEER ON THE CHAIR. A story, how does it go? This happened in the time of *Nongquase*, our national suicide. Smoke from the burning fields swallowed the sun, and corpses of slaughtered cattle littered the savannah. This is not a tragedy. Understand that. Tragedies concern those who suffer for passion only. The Xhosa people sacrificed their herds and crops in order to receive glory, riches, immortality – even old women would regain the freshness of their youth, so spake our prophets.

One of these holy prophets, your ancestor, called himself Ngamathamb, not his real name, but rather our word for 'bones', which is all that now remains of him. He'd made his second wife large with child, and she walked thus – *chug-chug-chug* – hands cupped under her belly, and she sang to her unborn daughter: *The sun sets, the sky darkens, hunger tomorrow.*

'Slaughter and burn all you own!' Ngamathamb

commanded us. Upon this sacrifice the sun would turn in its tracks and set in the east, abundant crops would spring from the ground, vast herds of cattle would thunder from the sea beneath the sacred shadow of Cove Rock, and our warriors would rise up and cut the British to pieces.

So we braced ourselves and went into our herds and fields clasping hope in the right hand and fear in the left, and the oxen bellowed and fell, one beside the other unto the horizon, and we torched the fields and grain stores, and so on, until we looked about and saw nothing under the sky remained for us to ravage. This sad event occurred in 1856, in accordance with the British calendar – after the *Nongquase*, we no longer measured our time in seasons.

Each time Ngamathamb attempted to burn his own crops, the wind blew a storm in from the sea to quench the fire. He went into the kraal to slaughter his cattle, but when he made a small cut in the hide of the first bull, the creature remained quiet, a sign that the ancestors rejected his sacrifice, an embarrassment. Ngamathamb led a new animal to the place of sacrifice and stabbed it, *jah!* but this bull also refused to give voice to its suffering, and so on, *jah! jah! jah!* until he'd left none untried. Then he ran amok with the cows, this one, then the next and again! The animals sank silently to their knees beneath the force of those blows. Finally even the goats were brought forward, and the prophet slipped in the blood as he moved among them, stabbing, but the beasts stubbornly held their row. *Ow*, such luck! Bulls, cows, goats, crops all – the ancestors refused every offering. Ngamathamb tore his crops from the ground and chased the bloodied, hushed cattle from his kraal.

Night fell, and Ngamathamb retreated inside his house and lay down on his doss to wait for the burden of sleep. He would never again open his mouth, neither to eat nor drink nor prophesy. When the sun failed to set in the east as foretold, the women keened, *yuyuyuyuyuyu!* and our warriors sat down on the blackened ground to die. So this begins, like all stories, with an ending.

Time passed. Ngamathamb's first wife lay lifeless at his right side. At his left, also dead, reposed his second wife, her hands clenching me. I was unbreathing, yet still clinging to her milk-skin with my legs, my lips at her dry nipple, our blood motionless. This is the way Ngamathamb's third wife found us when she returned from burying her own father and mother. I tell you all this so you'll know how it was with me. *Yu! Yu! O!* How can a child ever have enough once it's nursed from a lifeless breast?

Now I should tell you that my father's third and youngest wife, the silent one, was skittish and afraid of hands. Ngamathamb had paid a bride price of only seven cows and twenty goats, and because such bargains can nettle the buyer, he often reminded her of how cheaply she came to him. He forbade his young wife to speak his name, or even use words containing any of the syllables which composed it, until such time as she would bear him children. When her conversation dried up, he beat her for sulking.

This woman carefully tied a leather thong around our ankles (Never touch those who've gone on!) and she pulled her husband and two sister-wives into the bush where vultures would gather and leave portions for the maggots, as it was in olden times before we learned to bury our dead. She left me for last, since I was only an infant, and a girl-child at that. But God, composer of the universe, sometimes recalls the dead to life, as a poet might conjure an ancient word whose meaning no one remembers. Before God restored me to the living, he whispered my secret name into my ear, which I withhold from you. If you need something to pass on to your descendants, refer to me as Ukusaba, which means 'the flight'. As my father's third wife carried me into the bush, the leather thong about my ankle, I opened my eyes and stared at her.

My father's third wife burned his house to the ground. You already know that no animals remained for her to offer up to her husband, for whom so much had already been sacrificed. *Ow!* but it agitates spirits when they feel neglected. In death as in life, Ngamathamb wouldn't stay well, and he would continue to bring his third wife hard luck all her days.

This is what one woman did. My father's third wife wrapped me to her belly in a woollen blanket and set out on foot. Let's call her Kubhaca, which means 'destitute wandering'. She sang as she walked: *God is angry, our ancestors gone, their dust scattered, their souls left to wander in the bush.* In this fashion, we left behind that familiar country where the bones of Ngamathamb swelled in the sun, ribs opening skyward to gather in the boundless abundance that he had prophesied. We walked past ridges turned white with the skeletons of Xhosa people who lay dead in rows, like cut wheat. We travelled in sunlight and slept near the road to avoid the wild animals and half-beasts that inhabited the darkness of the bush.

There's more story to tell. Let's be off.

Kubhaca was sixteen when she walked out of the famine into Cape Town, where she became a bargirl in a house on Anne Street, not far from the docks, an ill-suiting occupation for one so frightened of hands. European men visited the house – stevedores, soldiers and sailors.

This house overlooked the sea, and on rare windless days the air would smell of lavender, which grew about the house in sandy beds, and of birds, a hot, mouldy, popcorn scent that squatted over us like a broody hen. All those birds! Garish parrots hung from the verandah in cages and rained curses in all languages down on the jackass penguins that brayed at them from the beach. *Hijos de putas!* the parrots cried out in shrill voices. *Scheisskopfes!* Tame canaries would light on my fingers during the languid afternoons as I watched the bargirls marcel one another's hair. I searched out their nesting places beneath the eaves and cupped my hands around the warmth of their chicks while the mothers screeched at me: *wheat! wheat! wheat!* Lickerish pelicans circled above the house, searching in vain for something to scavenge. So it was.

There was a singing machine in that house. I spent all my free hours listening to the beautiful voice that rose up from it, and I made my notes tremble as we sang together.

A pause in the story to enjoy these careless days of my youth.

There were twelve doors inside the house on Anne Street, and during the course of each night the bargirls would pass through all of them. The pink paint covering the interior walls had faded to the colour of European flesh. We hung lavender upside down on the walls to dry, and sprinkled lavender oil over the cotton sheets as an aphrodisiac and to kill bedbugs. The scent clung to our hair and clothes, separating us from our people who could not abide the odour. When she was no longer fit for any other work at that place, Kubhaca became a scrubber, an anile drab for men to step over while she slopped the floors on her knees, and she rejoiced as the filthy lavender water soaked her dugs because she was free of all those hands.

The story keeps coming. Stop fitching and listen!

It so happens that forgotten and hungry ancestral spirits often go to sea, travelling the world end to end, congregating in port towns. In my fifteenth year on Anne Street, one crawled into my body and tried to speak with my breath. But I resisted and this particular spirit became so angry it turned my lungs to blood. I fell into coughing fits until the bed flooded as I slept, even up to my eyes, and I was drowned and dead in my own blood, commanded to the spirit world for a second time. Never ask me about this place; to hear me describe it would be to listen to the sound of your own death.

Kubhaca brought my body to a European sorcerer who sewed it back onto my immortal spirit. Just so! The stitch marks begin here, at my neck, down between my breasts, longwise, to my navel, an unnatural and barbaric procedure.

Consider. If you're ever lucky enough to return from the dead a second time, never come away with empty hands. I myself brought back a magic that allows one to contest age. Years would fall over me in tens and twenties without marking my appearance, save for these worn-down teeth.

Nothing looked the same when I returned to the house on Anne Street. Blood had filled the whites of my eyes from all that coughing and left a stain that even a storm of tears would fail to cleanse, so what was the point of crying over it? The world had turned red for me, even down to the sanguine canary that flew onto my shoulder to welcome me back.

Here is something! Do you have enough skin for it?

Long ago, when people first came into the world, they could read all manner of things in blood. But they grew squeamish at the sight and had no stomach for the unpleasant things they found there. Certainly, most people lost this skill.

Behold, a Xhosa boy who used his knife to take the life of a bargirl! This took place inside the house on Anne Street after the visitors had left and the bargirls were rubbing lavender oil into each other's backs to help with the aching. Now this boy had once been this bargirl's sweetheart, and for some days now he'd sat on the stony beach among the jackass penguins and brayed up at the house he was forbidden to enter, *aawwwn! aawwwn! aawwwn! awwwn!* Perhaps he spilled more of her blood with his knife than one might expect.

Just then, as I stood over this murdered girl, I saw images, like those projected in a cinema, moving before me in the blood that flowed from her wounds. Later I would come to understand that God had chosen me to bring a forgotten skill back into the world. The bargirl's life purled before me on the floor, and in its depths I read the belly-hunger that drew the murdered woman to the house on Anne Street. I gazed through her dead eyes at the disappointed lover who stood panting and bloody over her body, and I understood why she didn't raise her arms to defend herself against his knife. Relief came with the police who carried the body away and covered these painful images with sawdust. A murdered bargirl was small beer to them.

The other bargirls began to cut their fingers to show me their blood, tortured images that spilled out onto the kitchen table. I learned to throw my voice, first speaking my part, then the part of the ancestors who clouded the bargirls' essence, conversing with them like friends over a cooking fire. I tell you this only to be completely truthful, but that doesn't mean I cheated anybody. This only helped them to believe what I saw in their blood.

Kubhaca's spirit left her when I began prophesying in blood, as she'd already eaten a bellyful of destiny. Shortly before her spirit departed, she told me she ought to have left me in the bush all those years ago to wait with my father for the hyenas. I continued to see her body as it scrubbed at the stains that multiply in such houses, and so she passed from my life, though not my sight.

The bargirls brought meat and beer so their ancestors would stay well in the next world, and in turn these spirits spoke through me: *Nisha! you must leave this house*, or *You disgrace us, Nandi*, or *Zi Zi! How can you be a wife to every man?* The things the ancestors said were hard to hear. Still the girls returned with their blood and their two shillings, plus pence for my tobacco. They placed the money on the table rather than risk touching my hand. I made cuts in my skin with a razor, like this, *tsee tsee,* in swirls beneath my breasts and around my belly, and I rubbed pipe oil into the wounds to bring up the welts, and I was beautiful and frightsome, and I grew plump on the beer and meat of other people's ancestors, and the years flocked over me without leaving a shadow.

Sometimes, for sport, a soldier or a sailor would ask me to prophesy for him, and I'd open a hole at his neck and look into the stain that spread across his white collar and bespoke his destiny: *You will die in battle, but in another place, across the sea*, or, *You will leave this house with a disease and therefore can never return to your wife and children.* When these men left the house there was a hollow sound beneath their laughter, *oh, oh, oh!*

The following event happened on St Valentine's Day when it's said that birds choose their own mates. There was a certain Englishman, the first-born son of a family that owned diamond mines, and his belly dragged on the ground with the wealth of our people. I won't bother to name this fellow, as such things hold little power over Europeans. The moment the Englishman walked into the house on Anne Street and asked me to look at his blood, didn't all the canaries fly away, not to return until the following morning?

Well. My eyes grew wide as I opened a small hole in his neck, surprised that the blood foretold not only his future but mine as well. The stars don't move across the sky just any old way, and even mosquitoes follow a prescribed path through the night. I would bear this stranger two children, though I was already half a hundred years old, so spake his blood. You wonder how I could enter into concubinage with such a one? I've seen canaries caught and eaten by baboon spiders.

'What troubles you?' I asked this fellow, an unnecessary question because the ancestors already know our problems. The Englishman looked down at his bloody shirt, too frightened to speak. He rose and quit the house, leaving the money on the table before me.

This is how I stole the Englishman's whiteness. I'll instruct you in the telling, as it's important to relate this part of the story just so, in case someone might want to repeat the procedure. First, I collected some dirt from under the Englishman's feet and put it in a tin, along with fat from a puff adder and ashes from the burned feathers of a blackbird. Next, I mixed them together with a stick, spinning it between my palms as I called out, '*Englishman! Englishman! Englishman!*' When you reach this part of the story, as you summon my lover, all you need do is rub your flattened palms together – just so! – and your listeners will imagine the mixing stick and the tin and its contents. And so I sat and spun all day over this philtre until he arrived, at length, with the darkness. I led the Englishman through one of the twelve doors to conceive the first of my two children, and he grasped at me and shouted out meaningless sounds because he did not know my name, and he snorted and lowed like a bull whose hide has been pierced in preparation for his sacrifice. By and by, he arose, unbalanced, from where we'd lain together, and he wambled away without direction.

At this point in the story, lie back and hold your legs in the air, ankles crossed, thiswise, to show how I trapped his whiteness inside me.

Following his bewitchment, the Englishman fetched me to live with him in a house so large that clouds formed in its attic. Though it was his birthplace, the Englishman had never seen all its rooms. God's blood! that house contained many choice things, but the most wondrous was a magical box that made toast from bread. Of course, you want to interrupt and tell me about electricity, but you won't convince me that something as marvellous as toast doesn't require at least a little sorcery.

The child grew within me and it kicked and struggled whenever its father spoke. The Englishman was very talkish, and I listened to his words in silence so as not to break his lecture as we lay naked on the floor, eating toast amid ledgers of profits, losses and abuses. He copied these sums from his business books onto charts that covered the walls of the office where we slept together, never mind that this house contained numberless bedrooms. He kept his forehead high as he spoke to those who served him – thus! – like a king, but lacking greatness of spirit. Every waking moment he read and computed, his entire mind devoted to the solution of how he and his family might increase their wealth. The only time his attention wavered from this purpose was when he looked on my body, for which he had a quenchless appetite, or when he heard a sudden, unexpected noise – *bow!* – from a dropped cooking pot, or a bird flying into one of the highest windows of that great house. At this, he would shrink into himself, thinking the Africans had finally come to take away all that made him what he was.

Here's a secret we can share. Unborn babies inhabit the borderland between the living and the dead, and so my father, Ngamathamb, spoke to the child in my womb and commanded it to cloak itself in the whiteness I'd taken from the Englishman. The child was born Xhosa, but such was Ngamathamb's magic that Europeans saw only his stolen skin.

Publicly, I called my son Alexander Gordon, adding an emperor's Christian name to his English father's surname. When I showed the baby to the moon, the tide of his blood swelled within him, and he squalled to show himself as the Englishman's true heir. Privately, his name was Umntu Wehlathi, but not really – names hold power and oughtn't be given freely. Umntu Wehlathi means 'Person of the Forest', or 'Leopard' if you like, and as he grew, spots appeared on his face and arms and legs and all the places the sun touched.

My curiosity urged me to read the blood that stained the birth-sheets and foretold Alexander's destiny; a stupid thing to do, for what mother would willingly witness the death of her child? He would spill his own essence, blood within blood, a hall of mirrors. But my mouth runs ahead of the story.

After a fixed number of days, I buried Alexander's umbilical cord beneath a thorny bush tree, chewed euphorbia root and spat it over him, made a soup from the placenta to help me with my milk, chanted his birth-poem. *Wush, wush, wush!* Listen carefully on this! I can't repeat it. Poems come when they want to and go once they've been spoken:

*Hide your secret! Say nothing from this day*
*of your birth.*
*Hide your secret! We have lost all our*
*precious things from the age of abundance.*
*Hide your secret! The cattle are gone.*
*Hide your secret! We have fallen beneath the*
*grinding stone.*
*Hide your secret! The gloaming spreads over*
*us.*
*Hide your secret! Deny the things you know!*
*Hide your secret! Don't even tell your woman!*

Who can say from where these words come? It's as if I dreamed them.

This next part is true. There was once a peckish boy who cried always, a child of the spleen. Wherever I carried my son, the forceful Cape winds shifted against us, no matter the direction. It took four years before Alexander grew strong enough to walk outside by himself, and his childhood mates quickly tired of fighting those winds and took different paths.

Now following the birth, a fellow came to tell the Englishman that he was no longer the first-born son and we must remove ourselves from the great house. Thus it came about that we went to live in a *dikki* house of daub and wattle with a thatched roof and dung floor, one that had been closed up and left to fall down after its owner died. I didn't miss the great house, only the toast. The Englishman rubbed clay into his skin and wrapped himself in the red blanket of my people, and he soughed for the whiteness I'd stolen from him. All those lost years, punishment enough for allowing myself to become distracted with the Englishman and his great house and all the choice things inside it. Who can stare too long at another's wealth without blindness?

Then came the second child as foretold – a female – whom I birthed on the dung floor of that house which belonged to the dead. One needn't look into the blood that covered such a baby to see her destiny; I already knew the shape and heft of every stone that would be heaped upon her. I called my daughter Mahulda Jane Braxton because it sounded to my ear like a servant's name. No words came to me for her birth-poem and I threw her umbilical cord out into the bush for the rats to fight over.

A moment.

I apologize. It's the details that trouble me.

Mahulda grew well, surpassing her secret brother, and she walked in front of Alexander to break the ceaseless cape winds that blew against him. I resumed my blood reading until Alexander reached his seventeenth year. At this time I straightened my son's ginger hair, and we left my Englishman on the dung floor of that house which belonged to the dead. Therein hangs his part in this tale. I confess that I'd accustomed myself to his touch, the first and only man to do so. Even here in this fleshless place, my spirit still aches for it.

Listen to how a house rose up and quit the country in which it was built.

With the money from my blood reading, I purchased the house on Anne Street in my son's name, and we sent the bargirls away. There Mahulda and I and The-Body-that-Once-Belonged-to-My-Father's-Third-Wife would wait as servants upon my son. A deed of ownership is a magical thing, and when we returned with it to the house on Anne Street an electricity pulsed through that place and animated my hands and feet. I raced through all its doors, ran my itching fingers over the worn planks that covered the floor, pulled down the dried lavender that hung on the flesh-coloured beadboard. Alexander paced against the wind that swept the verandah, his face fixed with distaste, while Mahulda delighted in the canaries that lighted in her hair and on her shoulders. The-Body-that-Once-Belonged-to-My-Father's-Third-Wife immediately fell to scrubbing the floor.

At my insistence, Alexander was baptised into the English church and passed into his manhood uncircumcised. His sister continued to watch over his every movement, and she brushed and straightened his ginger hair and cut the nails on his fingers and toes, and he followed close in her steps as she carried his books to the university and shielded him from the Cape winds. I forbade her to learn to read or to calculate figures though she beseeched me.

'Things will go easier for you this way,' I told my child.

But the Xhosa groundskeeper sometimes allowed Mahulda to stare into the windows while she waited for Alexander to come out of the university, and in this way she gained her education against my will.

We settled into life inside the house on Anne Street and the years flew out to sea with the pelicans. I placed a kitchen chair in the attic where I set out meat and poured beer for Ngamathamb. Ancestors don't require affection from the living, only remembrance.

Once Mahulda found a starving pelican that had torn its bill-pouch on a fishing hook. No matter how many fish it caught, they would all slip away before they reached its gullet. Mahulda sewed the hole shut and fed the bird mashed fish morning to night, but it remained unsated, its belly pinched by a never-slaking hunger. Like Alexander, the bird dogged her footsteps, its open bill trying to swallow the sky, and they waited together for her on the verandah, the bird and its hunger, the brother and the winds. Mahulda began to stay indoors, only leaving the house on market day, and then she carried a shovel to chase them both away from her.

* * *

I could wave my arms at you and use my storytelling voice for this next part, but I've almost emptied this story of every drop and I'm truly spent.

Now it happened that Mahulda became pregnant, a mystery, and she developed a tooth for cream mixed with port, and she grew stout on her love for her unborn baby. But the sun cannot set in the east, and she birthed a still child. Alexander looked at its lifeless face, as white as my Englishman's, and he grew distant and proper in his relations with his sister.

Mahulda believed the child's death was my doing, which of course was true, and she fell into a deep grief. When she regained her strength, she climbed up in the eaves of the house on Anne Street and upset all the canaries' nests and trod upon the eggs. *Shee shee*, settle a little, my heart. I bathed her forehead in lavender water to prevent insanity, but Mahulda's eyes became empty, like those of The-Body-that-Once-Belonged-to-My-Father's-Third-Wife, and to look into them made my heart grow old and worn like my teeth, until finally it ceased to beat, which is a death from which no one returns. Before Alexander and Mahulda could finish digging my grave in the lavender bed, I'd gone on. So ends my journey.

Let me tell you how death comes to you – a person does not go all at once. First, Breath leaves, because it must circle the earth seven times before it can depart. This is the draught you sometimes feel on your neck on a windless day, that swirls the leaves round your feet. Next away is Heart. Some people think the essence of the dead person accompanies the Heart, but they're mistaken; Blood remains with the body, though it ceases its flow. Then departs He-Who-Grips-Bowels-Shut-with-His-Right-Hand-and-Bladder-with-His-Left, followed by Thoughts, which leave like a swarm of bees. If you return to life at this point, you'll have no more understanding than a stone. He-Who-Dwells-in-the-Muscles waits with your corpse to ensure it's treated properly. Sometimes this one becomes restless and makes fists, or sits up and whispers to the women as they prepare your body for burial. Your spiritual essence, Blood, goes last, then the light is parted, and – *ewe!* – you've hopped the twig!

Alexander and Mahulda shaved their skulls after my death, and wrapped my body in a blanket and placed me in the bottom of my grave. That hole was three days in the digging and still not deep enough to suit my children. Mahulda bestrew me with thorns so animals wouldn't dig me up and eat me, nor witches tamper with my remains, and the wind whipped at Alexander as he shovelled in the dirt and tamped the ground until it was level.

I'd instructed my children not to burn the house on Anne Street to ashes, as custom dictates. Instead they sold the parrots and used smoke to chase the canaries from the eaves, and they hired carpenters to disassemble the house, which they moved away on the backs of lorries that left deep ruts in the lavender bed over my grave. The canaries died on the tree branches in an August freeze and the jackass penguins swam away, never to return. Even the pelicans avoided flying over my burial ground. Stay well in life if you want to do so in death.

Ancestral spirits converse only with the living, and so we don't require our own language. But if such speech existed, I might tell you that the word *mahulda* means 'secret well kept' in the tongue of the dead.

In the year of their lord 1926, Mahulda and Alexander shifted our house far north and reassembled it in a forgotten glen in the highlands of Rhodesia where no one knew its history. In this never-never country, with only howling bobyjohns for neighbours, my son hoped he might find relief from the Cape winds that had blown so hard against him.

Mahulda continued to serve Alexander and, in time, his fair wife, a German woman, and their fair son – your father. Have you ever seen so many generations crowded into one story? The past and the future spread out before me like a feast!

Now let me tell you something else that appeared to me long ago in Alexander's birthblood. I saw my son bringing beer and tuck to this place inside the attic where my essence abides in this familiar house amid these foreign mountains, an offering to honour the Bones, the Flight, the Destitute Wandering, the Secret Well Kept, an unbroken bloodline that stretches to you. Perhaps this is tragical after all.

Wait! I might find for you a new ending to this old story. Perhaps God will send me the words for a poem in praise of Mahulda.

*Ow*, only silence and hunger and the attic's cold, and soon the waking-up-song of the morning birds.

## *Ropa Rimwe*

The Waiting, 1965

*The Umtali Post,* Monday, October 12, 1966:

TERRORIST KILLED

An officer of the Southern Rhodesia Constabulary was wounded on Sunday evening when a Shona man violently resisted arrest. Responding to reports of terrorist activity, officers shot and killed a man known only as Timothy when he returned to create mischief at an isolated mountain estate where he had formerly been employed as a gardener. No other arrests were made.

IN THE YEAR THAT I LEARNED TO READ BLOOD, THE rains failed to move across the mountains, and drought struck the glen.

The flame trees in our garden grew pallid, and brilliant blue panicles wilted and dropped from the jacaranda trees in slimy clots of yellow-grey. Timothy the gardener looked at the straw-coloured blades that peppered the carpetgrass like the strands of white in his beard, and he came to the realisation all men eventually face, that his life's work was nothing.

It was 1965, a time of growth and enterprise among the white men of our nation, and Mr Gordon devoted his every moment and thought to his furniture store in Umtali. Mrs Gordon had long ago retreated to her darkened bedroom. I was left in the charge of our groundsman, Timothy, and our housekeeper, Mahulda Jane Braxton, a Cape Town coloured who watched over me like I was the son she had lost at birth. The Shona have a word for this arrangement, *kurera*, which means to bring up a child for pay.

Mahulda was not a young woman. Dr N'gono once listened to her chest with his stethoscope and found she had a hole in her heart. Yet no one thought to hire another servant to help with the housekeeping, cooking and child raising.

Every Thursday, Dr N'gono visited Mahulda in her kitchen to prattle on about the adverse effects of a maize diet on the Shonas' eyesight, or to harrumph over an article in *The Umtali Post* of some failed rebel border crossing into Rhodesia, and to ask Mahulda to accompany him to the dance clubs in Umtali the following evening.

Most Shona distrusted Dr N'gono and his gory surgical rites, and they went instead to the tribal trust land where there lived an old *ngangga* who healed with herb-based nostrums. During Dr N'gono's visits, Timothy remained within earshot outside the kitchen door, throwing his weight behind each axe swing, riving logs into kindling. Timothy couldn't understand dancing without ceremony.

Dr N'gono was blind to the distress these visits caused Mahulda. She believed the loss of her baby was God's punishment for some past transgression, and so she set aside all relations with men. The nature of this offence was a source of speculation among the old trust land women who came each day down the mountain to fetch water from the river of their ancestors.

During the cool mornings I helped Mahulda make a pot of peaberry coffee to revive her spirits, despite Dr N'gono's warning that coffee strained the heart. It was my job to stand on a chair and turn the handle on the coffee grinder while she measured in the dark beans. With a small mortar and pestle she mashed dried coriander seed from Timothy's garden and added it to the peaberry to soften its acidic taste and to serve as a digestive. After the brewing, she stood before the kitchen window with saucer and cup and stared past her rippled reflection into the depths of the black liquid. If I climbed onto my chair beneath the grinder, I could see over her broad shoulders and through the pane of glass to where Timothy stared in at her from his moribund garden.

One morning, as I ground the coffee, I heard a soft cheeping from inside Mahulda. She unbuttoned the neck of her blouse and leaned forward to show me a pair of canary hatchlings Timothy had brought her. 'He said the canaries are too much trouble and noise. He'd have to crush them with a rock if I didn't take them, as they're not old enough to set free.' She smiled at the hatchlings nestled in the warmth of her cleavage and refastened the buttons.

Our well could no longer support the stream of water that passed through the cherub's penis, and in the second month of the drought Timothy shut off the fountain. The child stared into the dry dish where his water once overflowed, and his stone flesh turned scurfy and cracked with dried algae like the sear and yellow skin of an old man. Timothy pruned the honeysuckle around the fountain and fed its dead leaves to Neville, my pet goat, while I played at breaking the ground with my toy hoe, raising clouds of dust from what had once been a rich, black vlei. 'Here we'll plant Lady Bankshia roses for Mahulda's hair,' I declared. 'She grew them in Cape Town.'

Timothy looked up and his eyes brightened for a moment. 'We could plant them against the east wall of the house where they will receive shade from the afternoon sun.' He looked about the ruined garden and his shoulders sagged. '*Shee, shee.* All our talking is dreaming, little man.' He fixed his gaze upon his feet.

Timothy stooped beneath the hump on his back and he only raised his eyes long enough to look skyward at the gathering storm clouds that refused to break over his garden, or to glance over his shoulder to consult with Sojini, his ancestral spirit, a great-uncle who advised and watched over him. To look at the world from such perspectives, I think, must have isolated Timothy from the rest of us. The only time he looked forward was to peer over his hedge clippers into the kitchen window where Mahulda drank her peaberry coffee.

Every Sunday Timothy travelled by bus to Umtali where he purchased the tiny beans from a tuckshop at great expense to himself. He told Mahulda that he received the coffee as a gift from an admirer but he could not drink it, as it burned his heart. It was at his suggestion that Mahulda added coriander to the coffee to promote good digestion. 'Coriander also promotes love,' Timothy confided in me.

Shut away in her dim room, Mrs Gordon's presence dampened any homely comfort the bungalow might have provided, and Mahulda's kitchen was the only place where sunlight was allowed to enter and words were spoken above a whisper. I spent all the moments of my childhood in

Mahulda's kitchen and Timothy's garden, except for the rare occasions when I was given an audience with my mother in her bower, or when I accompanied my father to his furniture store to watch him bark and kick at his Shona employees, though it was no longer acceptable for whites to do so. Once he chased away a boy of mixed race who came to the loading dock looking for work. 'Goddamn *munt*,' he said, looking sideways at me.

In the third month of the drought Timothy procured a jar of pregnant mare's urine from Adam, a Shona stableboy who served as sacristan for the neighbouring mission school. Timothy brought the urine to a boil in a saucepan on Mahulda's stove, over her vigorous protests. He added a cup of molasses, a cup of dish soap and a beer, stirring each into the urine with a wooden spoon. 'Most important,' Timothy said, 'we add the gardener's *ropa*,' and he pricked his fingertip with a needle. He averted his eyes from the stove as his blood dripped into the pot. 'A man never looks into a cooking pot, or his eyes will sink into his skull and his face take on the shape of a baboon's.'

Steam rose from the saucepan and the kitchen became redolent with animal musk and prenatal secretions. The humpbacked gardener emptied the saucepan onto the roots of the flame trees, his favourites, and doused them with water drawn from the river. The well had fallen to an unhealthy level and Mr Gordon forbade its use for gardening.

The following morning I stared, astonished, at the revived trees. Their scarlet flowers had reopened and appeared all the more vibrant amid the surrounding desolation. In my eyes this was grand witchery of the same proportions as the zombification chronicled in my comic books, or lightning, or popcorn making. 'There is no magic in this world, little man,' Timothy said, shaking his head at my amazement, 'only things you cannot yet understand.'

The clouds over Umtali swelled and purpled – 'a painful sky' Mahulda called it – and she hugged her breasts as if they still ached, engorged with milk for her stillborn child. She squeezed a dropper filled with water and crushed butterfly into the gaping beaks of the hatchlings tucked inside her blouse.

Despite the swollen and darkening sky, there was no rain for the garden, and Timothy's cheeks sank and his skin became leathery. In the fourth month of the drought Timothy disappeared into the shed where he lived at the back of the garden. I stood in the goat yard and spied through the shed's single, paneless window to where he stood, shirtless, a network of old and fresh scars covering his back. Timothy whetted the knife he used to butcher the goats, then reached behind his head and drew it deeply across the hump on his back, releasing a flood of blood and serous fluid. His teeth shone wetly, gums exposed.

I must have gasped, because Timothy looked sharply at the window.

'*Ehe!* Little man,' he said, clearly embarrassed. 'Do not be afraid.' He had pulled on his shirt by the time he caught up with me in the garden. The cotton stuck to his hump, wet and dark. Timothy searched my eyes while he struggled to compose an explanation. 'When I cut myself,' he said at length, 'the flowing shows I have spirit within me, that the fountain and I are the same.' Here language failed him and his voice trailed off. Timothy's only book was *The White Fathers' Shona to English Dictionary.* The White Fathers deemed the inclusion of an English-to-Shona section unnecessary, and so Timothy's attempt to speak in metaphors across languages was doomed from the start.

After the neighbour's mare foaled amid a flood of amniotic fluid, the oestrogen left her urine and Timothy's flame trees died. Mahulda ceased to take her peaberry coffee at the window facing the barren garden, and the acidic aroma, tempered with coriander, no longer floated out to the gardener as he busied himself beneath a lifeless canopy of brittle leaves.

* * *

Timothy forbade me to enter the garden after dark. But we had only recently weaned Neville from his nanny and the little goat was frantic and bleating, so for the first time in my life I disobeyed him and slipped out to calm my pet.

I went to the goat yard where we kept him tethered and saw Neville, glassy-eyed and slack in the jaws of a leopard. The kid's chest heaved but he made no struggle as he was dragged away from me. I was eight years old and without fear, the hero of every story told to me over a cooking pot, and so I seized my toy hoe and ran towards the leopard, yelling like Mwari, the god-king, singing and swinging the little garden tool as if it were a battle axe, calling out the beast's name, *Mbada! Mbada!* until she dropped Neville and turned her attention towards me.

The leopard braced for the charge, tail twitching, snarling, head low, outstretched forepaws, hindquarters arched. There is a moment, just before a leopard springs, when its eyes swell. Spear hunters push bones through the sockets of slain leopards as a safeguard against that glassy stare.

The impact knocked me from my feet and the air rushed from my lungs as I fell beneath the animal's weight. I smelled the rank flesh of earlier kills lodged in the claws that searched for my eyes, her breath still hot with Neville's blood. Her jaws closed around my shoulder to hold me in place and give her back claws purchase to rake my thighs.

I tell all this in a detached manner only to mirror my frame of mind as I lay limp in the jaws of the leopard and breathed in the carrion reek that jetted from her nostrils.

A weaker creature falls into shock when it finds itself helpless in a predator's embrace, and the rent flesh and blood and pain are no longer its own; nature is merciful after all.

I was only distantly aware of Timothy's hunched figure standing over us, and the blur of the woodcutting axe as he brought it down on my attacker. His other hand gripped a rake before his face to protect his eyes, for these are the leopard's choice target. The wounded creature snarled and sprang away, leaving me to lie and pule in my ruined body.

I managed to lift my head and turn it towards Neville. Through the blood that filled my eye sockets, I saw his life running from his jugular to form a puddle on the ground. The moon cast a dull sheen across the surface of the goat's blood, and I looked past the reflection to see a long procession of beasts that stretched back to the age of iron, each waiting its turn at the butcher's block. Neville was my pet only until he gained sufficient flesh to warrant his slaughter, and whether the fatling nourished the leopard or our household made little difference. The dry soil sucked Neville's blood into the earth and the image disappeared, leaving only an inscrutable stain.

A gauzy light surrounded the periphery of my blood vision. My gaze followed the trail of inky spots left by the wounded leopard. In each drop of blood I could see the gash in her shoulder worsen until she could no longer hunt, her slow death from starvation, her relief as the hyenas finally closed in on her, and then only blackness as Timothy gathered me into his arms and carried me towards the house.

* * *

In Shona lore a union of love produces beautiful offspring. I was an ugly enough child, even before the leopard mauled me. One of her dewclaws had slashed diagonally across my forehead, eyebrow, nose and cheek. Although Mahulda applied a fresh astringent of sanicle when she changed my bandages, the carrion trapped in the dewclaw infected the wound and it healed badly.

'It is unfortunate,' Timothy told me. The hump on his back rose and fell with his shrug. 'Such marks do not go away. One must learn to wear them.'

I felt very small inside my body as a result of the attack. The leopard's fangs had met in my shoulder and deep furrows ran down my thighs where her hindquarters had ploughed my flesh. Miraculously, both my eyes were untouched, but though Mahulda rinsed them with boric acid, I could not rid my vision of a faint roseate tint.

Mahulda prepared raspberry leaf tea to ease the soreness in my shoulder and leg muscles. She fed millet to her canaries and sang into her blouse while she steeped the raspberry leaves in scalding water and added grated bark from one of Timothy's dead cinnamon trees. The young birds looked hungrily to her, their eyes black and empty. I took the raspberry leaf tea with milk from Neville's nanny, but no sugar as it made me restless.

'*Aiwa!* I swear by my great-uncle who died in 1896, it is a miracle you still live, little man,' Timothy said to me each morning by way of a greeting. When I told him of the things I read in Neville's lifeblood and in the blood trail of the leopard, he seemed to sink into his hump. 'Now there is real trouble for you. Even so, such things would be impossible without a diviner in your sib. It is a birthgift you must master.'

The next morning he brought a trap splattered with gobbets of vlei rat, its blood filled with panic. The day after I stared at the menstrual blood that soaked the rags of a *fambi*, a prostitute who lived in a house Timothy frequented, and from these stains I learned that, for Shona women, this was a new profession.

Timothy made a doss for me on the verandah where I could lie during the day and stare into the dead garden. Bush babies no longer licked nectar from blossoms, their faces dusted yellow with pollen, and the fruit bats had flown away to the river where the effects of the drought were less severe. Empty weavers' nests dangled from lifeless tree branches and flea beetles and cotton stainer bugs provided the only movement in that empty place. There was little for Timothy to do in the garden now, and he spent his time collecting new blood for me to read. 'What do you see, little man?' he'd ask. Blood from a goat in heat, surging, demanding. Startled blood from a fatal highway accident. Blood from the downy feathers of a hornbill chick, frantic as it was pecked to death by its father. Timothy brought me the rhinoceros-hide whip that decorated the otherwise bare walls of his shed. In the long-dried stains at its tip, I read the *daka*, the grudge hatred, that welled inside Timothy's father as his previous employer *sjamboked* him before his own son. Timothy nodded absently, lost in memory, while I recounted the bloodlore contained in the whip, and he quit bringing me these sanguine texts.

After the leopard attack, Mahulda became afraid that I might die in a state of sin, for my parents hadn't baptised me. Once I'd recovered sufficiently, she dressed me in a gown sewn from a bolt of white cotton – she'd bought the material long ago in Cape Town to make such a garment for her own child – and Timothy carried me to the river where Adam, robed in his sacristan's vestment, waited in the failing light.

There were only four present at the christening, including myself, the baptismal candidate. The low wood-notes of a roller served as a substitute for *Gloria in Excelsis* following our final response to Adam's versicles. A large gathering would invite arrest and detention in Constable Teasdale's jail.

Constable Teasdale had always treated the Shona with respect, and for the first twenty-three years of his tenure he carried no weapon. But small acts of rebellion against the white government had begun to disrupt the peace of the glen. Saboteurs stole dynamite from a granite quarry and used it to knock down power lines. Monkey-wrenchers broke into the lumber works where they beat the watchman and poured oil and sand into the gang mill. An arsonist set fire to a shed on the grounds of a convent. Trees were felled across the highway. Agitators appeared at the trust land market.

A contingent of armed policemen now accompanied the constable, a dozen red-faced Boers on loan from the South African government. Constable Teasdale's holstered pistol beat against his round bottom as he struggled to stay with the South Africans while they combed the district in search of suspicious activity, and he listened without understanding when they called out to one another in their harsh, guttural Afrikaans.

'Do you desire to be baptised?' Adam whispered. Adam was the only person at the mission Mahulda could approach to serve as celebrant for a baptism in which a Cape Town coloured and a Shona gardener would be named my godparents in the absence of blood family. If we were caught, the teenager would be finished as sacristan.

'I do,' I said. Water bugs skittered across the surface of the river.

'Will you be responsible for seeing that the child you present is brought up in the Christian faith and life?'

Timothy cradled me in his arms as the low river swirled around his waist. Because so many people believed in the Christian Gods and because there were only three of them, Timothy thought the Trinity would be stretched too thin to be of any real use to a man. Still, Mahulda Jane Braxton had asked him to do this, and he knew the importance of ceremony. 'I will,' he glanced over his shoulder at Sojini, 'with God's help.'

Sunset filtered through silhouettes of branches and leaves, throwing a stained-glass pattern of muted colour over us. The current of my life would soon carry me away from the Anglican faith, and this cathedral of forest and river would be the only church I'd ever enter. Adam made a cross over my scarred face and murmured, 'I baptise you in the name of the Father and of the Son and of the Holy Spirit,' and we answered, 'Amen.'

Mahulda met Timothy's eyes. Perhaps, if they had met when they were young, I might have been born to them. With such parents, I began to think, I might not be so ugly after all. The roller's mournful notes fell from the trees.

Timothy immersed me in the river and the water loosened the sutures in my legs, opening the wounds so that my blood commingled with the water and I almost believed I was the river's source. I thought of Timothy drawing the butcher's knife across the hump of his back to release his essence.

A crimson cloud spread across the christening gown over my legs, wavering beneath the river's surface, and in it I read through two generations of lies and secrets to see my Xhosa great-grandmother casting bones across her kitchen table to divine a future which already had taken place. Here was the source of my father's discomfort with me and with his place in the world, my ancestry manifest in the darkening cloud.

The river's gentle current lifted me slightly, and I floated in a reality that moments ago had felt like solid ground. Above us a rataplan of thunder sounded in a swollen sky that still stubbornly refused to yield its rain. Adam's eyes widened as my blood clouded the water around him. The young sacristan backed away onto the riverbank and disappeared into the forest, and so ended my initiation into Christendom.

* * *

In the fifth month of the drought, Mr Gordon emerged from his study to inspect the grounds. Such visits were rare when the garden still pulsed with life. He tugged at a tendril of rose that climbed the verandah and it gave way with a dry rustle.

'Christ,' he said, examining his hand where a thorn

had pricked him. From where I lay on my doss, I could see into the oval of blood on his fingertip. In its wetness I read his secret relief that the garden had been extinguished. The spot of blood disappeared as Mr Gordon wrapped his thin lips around the injured finger and sucked his essence back into himself. He looked out over the gnarled roots of trees and shrubs that clawed the dust in death. There was a beauty in that place, even then. Mr Gordon was a businessman above all else and could find no reason to employ a gardener to tend lifeless grounds, so he discharged Timothy without notice. Mr Gordon removed the damaged finger from his mouth long enough to mutter his regret. 'Can't be helped, sorry.' The saliva-thinned blood filled his fingerprint, but I could read no sorrow in it.

'Yes, baas,' Timothy said softly to his feet when my father dismissed him. Like his father before him, Timothy lived under a feudatory arrangement with his employer. In return for keeping the grounds, the hump-backed Shona was allowed a shed in which to sleep, a small kraal for goats, and a plot of ground to grow rukweza grain for brewing beer. The land on which the bungalow stood once served as Timothy's ancestral homestead until his grandfather lost it through the magic of His Majesty's courts. Timothy had no other place to go, and since his shed was hidden from sight, he remained on the grounds after his dismissal. He reasoned that only a *nggarara* would deny him occupancy of land not in use.

Each morning the gardener returned from the river with clay pots suspended from each side of a yoke that rested across his hump, stepping carefully to avoid slopping the water that would keep his rukweza crop alive. Normally it would fall upon his wife to fetch water, but Timothy had not seen the woman since he left for the war more than twenty years ago.

Rukweza is a difficult crop and requires many workers to thresh the small grain from the chaff. Timothy recruited help by providing spirits distilled from the rotted deadfall of his loquat trees. A dozen Shona crowded into his little shack, threshing and drinking and singing. As the moon rose above the naked branches of the flame trees and the millet filled the baskets and the spirits disappeared, the normally puritanical Shona began to flush and make obscene references to each other's sexual organs, and their laughter sounded like the troat of wild animals. Mahulda indulged in neither the spirits nor the conversation, but continued to work steadily at her threshing. Apart from this gathering I seldom heard Shona men swear, and never in front of women. Even Adam the sacristan joined in, declaring Timothy's penis to be the ugliest in the village and claiming its location to be somewhat above the gardener's navel. I looked to see how Mahulda received this information and saw her chuckling softly in her corner.

As with everything important to Timothy, brewing involved ceremony. 'Now the Shona drink Fanta and Coca-Cola,' he told me, 'and bits of their spirit leave them in great belches.' After the threshing, Timothy filled a basket with rukweza millet and prayed over it to Sojini. To say he prayed is misleading, but that is the closest the White Fathers could come to defining the Shona notion of *kupira*, in which ancestral spirits are addressed with a sort of easy familiarity absent in church worship. The Shona's relationship with their ancestors is one of mutual benefit: the ancestors watch over the living, and the living attend the dead to keep them from becoming forgotten and lonely.

Timothy spread the millet in the depression of a large rock and soaked it in river water overnight. The next morning he spread the sodden millet over a flat rock and covered it with leaves until, two days later, it sprouted and became *chimera.* On the fourth day he removed the leaves, dried the *chimera*, and ground it into meal. For two days Timothy chopped wood and stoked the fire, bringing the enormous pot to a boil, adding meal, bringing the sweet beer to a boil again, and finally straining it into smaller pots until only the *masese* remained at the bottom to be thrown away. On the seventh day, Timothy rested and watched his creation cool.

He grumbled to himself as he covered the pots with plates to keep debris from falling into the beer while it fermented. Like cooking and water fetching, Timothy considered brewing a woman's duty. For six days, while the beer stood, the Shona came to Timothy's shed to oil and tune drums of all sorts, and to stamp sorghum for porridge, and to roast Neville's nanny.

At the sunset of the last day of fermentation, a barrage of percussion electrified the air and shook the pictures of dour Scottish ancestors on the walls of my mother's bedroom and coaxed me away from the bungalow, through the garden, towards the source of the booming drums, until I stood beside Timothy's shed, at the edge of the goat yard where men clapped and women trilled in intricate harmony and varied pitch and rhythm, first sharp and staccato, then sonorous and rolling. To call the *bira* a rain dance would conjure images of blood sacrifices and pagans prostrated before terrible gods. This ceremony was simply part of a larger dance that included the sky and the land and the spirit.

Timothy raised a calabash of beer above his head to his ancestor Sojini and declared, 'Everything is complete,' and the drinking commenced. The night gathered around the fire and dancers toped uncounted calabashes of rukweza beer, the youngest drawing first because the surface was covered with drowned flies and cockroaches and dusty foam.

Properly brewed rukweza beer is as strong as brandy. Soon the Shona opened themselves up to the *mashave*, ancestral spirits who commandeered their hosts' sweating flesh and made it dance and drink as they experienced once again the sensory world of the living. Adam, the sacristan, rose with a jerk and looked about with the eyes of someone long dead, and a woman began speaking in a guttural tongue, and others danced in powerful motions, like strong men who have not used their muscles for ages beyond reckoning. Their eyes shone lifelessly in the fire. Timothy's flailing dance was all the more odd for his hump, and for the old assegai he brandished. Perhaps the spear had belonged to his great-uncle Sojini, for the tip was tarnished and the wood grey with age. Others were seized by the spirits of animals and strutted birdlike, or leaped like baboons or paced like leopards, or capered like eland.

I never discovered which of my parents ordered Timothy's arrest. Perhaps the drums stirred something in Mr Gordon that he wished to remain still, or their booming intruded into the dark room that served as Mrs Gordon's sanctuary, breaking the illusion that she was still in Scotland.

Ammunition clips rattled in equipment belts and strap fasteners tinked against rifles as the South African policemen moved into position. The fire was dying and the wood glowed on the ground, highlighting features that would normally fall in shadow: the underneath of the South Africans' chins and noses, the hollows of cheeks and eye sockets, turning the faces into negatives of how they appeared in daylight. Constable Teasdale followed, panting. 'Stop at once!' he yelled, and I wasn't sure if he was addressing the dancing Shona or the policemen. The drums rolled over Constable Teasdale's voice and it went unheard, except by me from where I stood frozen on the periphery of the ceremony. One of the South African policemen discharged his rifle into the starless sky, silencing the feverish din of the *bira*.

Timothy awoke from his trance and blinked at the policemen who had come to take him away from his ancestral home. The other dancers disappeared into the surrounding darkness. I heard the slide and click of oiled gunmetal as the South Africans locked back their bolts and thumbed the releases on their safety catches. One of the policemen spoke in clipped English, 'Lie down on the ground and place your hands behind your head.' Timothy seemed not to understand. He ran his hands over the throwing spear as if to reassure himself that he was back again in the material world.

The leopard had taught me fear, but still I forced myself to stand before Timothy. Confusion crossed the faces of the policemen as they looked at me over their gun sights.

'Please,' Constable Teasdale pleaded, as he moved in front of the South Africans' picket, pushing their rifle barrels groundward.

Timothy paused to glance over his shoulder at Sojini,

listened a moment, then turned to me and sighed. His garden was dead and the *bira* ruined. 'Here, little man,' he said, 'let me show you something.' Timothy gave me a shove which propelled me facedown into the dirt, and he drew back the assegai, his weight on one heel. Perhaps it was Sojini who guided Timothy's spear straight and level through both cheeks of Constable Teasdale, severing his tongue, before it came to rest in the shoulder of a South African policeman. Timothy reeled back from the force of their return volley, which sounded in my ears like the magic maize he popped for me over the fire.

Blood from a small cut on an extremity, say a finger, is bright red and it reflects surrounding light. It's difficult to read too deeply into it. But aortic blood, lifeblood that is pumped out of the body directly from the heart, is a deep, unreflecting burgundy, and in its depths one can look back across millennia. I watched Timothy gasp as the arterial blood sprayed rhythmically from a hole in his neck. In the darkness that soaked through his shirt collar, I saw him standing at attention, back straight, in the khaki of the Southern Rhodesian African Rifles, before he was sent to North Africa for a shilling a day and no allowances for dependants, where a 40mm shell from an Italian tank shattered his back and left him writhing on the Saharan sands of Abyssinia. Beneath that image was Timothy in his childhood, learning to stare at his feet while the *sjambok* bit into his father's back. I saw Sojini, Timothy's great-uncle and ancestral spirit, charge into a British picket during the Rebellion of 1896, armed only with a spear, perhaps the very one that passed through Constable Teasdale's face. I witnessed the *mfecane*, the time of troubles, when Shona dynasties crumbled before waves of invaders and Timothy's distant kin were left to knock out their front teeth to decrease their value to Arab slave traders. I watched the stone ruins of Great Zimbabwe spring up from the ground to their original magnificence, and there I followed Timothy's line to a Zanj slave who worked the furnace to separate the copper from the slag. And still deeper into the *ropa* that Timothy's sluggish heart pumped from his neck, past the fire-bringers, beyond the cave-painters, image giving way to image, death to birth, fall to rise. By the time the fountain of blood ceased to flow from the severed carotid artery, I could clearly see my own ancestors and I no longer felt as though I were a *mutorwa*, a foreigner on this continent.

Mahulda led me away from where Timothy lay dead in his blood and took me into the house to undress me. As she ran my bath I examined the dried blood on my hands, impenetrable as black diamond. On its cracking surface I could read only the anguish Timothy felt for his dead garden, and the ache of his love for Mahulda Jane Braxton, and his sorrow that I would no longer have a father.

* * *

Here is where Timothy's story ends abruptly and, for want of a better one, mine resumes. Since Mahulda was refused permission to bury Timothy in the mission chapel cemetery, we interred him secretly in his garden with neither light nor ululation nor any mourners apart from Mahulda, myself, and Adam, who officiated. The sky finally broke, and driving rain turned Adam's bible to pulp, and water swamped the grave before we could fill it.

Sojini left his place at Timothy's shoulder for wherever forgotten ancestors congregate. I took to glancing over my own shoulder, half expecting to see Timothy there, until I grew old enough to learn that such things are not on foot with my reality.

The following morning, Timothy's kin came down from the trust land to beat the grave, their patriarch driving a stick into the mud until it touched my godfather's chest. They would return after the rains to remove the stick, and Timothy's spirit-butterfly would escape through the hole to wander homeless, until the harvest *bira* when he would be welcomed back to the clan.

I set fire to the blood-spattered clothes, making sure not to look into the dark smoke. My birthgift was now awakened, heavy and sluggish in my veins, and I knew I'd take it up again someday, sure as fate.

On the Thursday after the grave beating, Mahulda Jane Braxton stared into a cup filled with the last of the peaberry coffee, and I watched it slip through her fingers and shatter on the floorboards as her heart stopped. When Dr N'gono arrived minutes later and tore open her blouse, two canaries flew up from between her breasts and circled the kitchen before flying through the open door and into the rain. Dr N'gono fell back from Mahulda's prone body, crossed himself, and ceased his efforts to revive her, and I became an orphan in my eighth year.

I tried to close her drying eyes but they refused my touch, and I succeeded only in giving her a dreamy, heavy-lidded expression she never wore in life. There was no dark stain on the corpse for me to read, nor did I need it to know we were *ropa rimwe*, Timothy, Mahulda and myself, one blood.

A flame tree sapling rose out of Timothy's grave. Feathery shoots appeared where the coriander had reseeded. Raspberries spread beneath the gutters of the bungalow, and rukweza spread into the beds. Thousands of empty cocoons hung from the new growth, the garden alive with butterflies, a landscape of wandering spirits. Mahulda's canaries and their hatchlings nested in the branches of a lifeless flame tree that towered like an ancient ruin over the tangle and creep of new growth. I listened to their portamenti each morning as I collected the wild coriander and placed it beneath my tongue, the seeds softening, pungent in my mouth.

Sometimes, in dreams, I see myself again cradled in Timothy's arms as he stands beside Mahulda in the river of my baptism, our reflections broken by the motion of the current, my wounded cheek, a tress of my godmother's hair, a bit of plaid shirt that covered my godfather's broken back, an eye, fingers, the splinters scattered together across a surface as black as peaberry coffee in the gloaming, the coriander floating on my breath.

# *Half-beast*

October, 2011

THE TWELVE INTERIOR DOORS IN MY HOUSE SWELL and stick in their jambs, the dead leaves blow southward, and the pain in my leg worsens, all signs that the rains are coming.

A half-a-century since the death of Gordon's godparents, and still they're dying before my eyes. This is how it is when you are taken by a story-ghost, no memories of your own, no voice but Gordon's.

My own past comes to me in images that fade upon awakening. Last night, on the roof of my house, I dreamed myself beneath the surface of a river, and God streamed through the hippo grass like sunlight through a canopy of trees.

Here are Gordon's beginning years. They unfold in a spiral of seasons. Timothy covers the flowerbeds with bark to help with the drainage, the sky opens, dousing the glen, and the leopards cease their prowl and take sanctuary in the forest.

It's a season of stories. While the storm rattles the kitchen window in its frame and the cat cowers in the laundry bin, Timothy sharpens his shears at the kitchen table in anticipation of the surge of growth.

Gordon listens to the whetstone sing: *sheeer, sheeer!*

'Hear this!' Timothy announces. 'It begins in an unformed world where Mwari, Wonderful God! stirs the river into a mist that masks the spirit world from the world of the living.' Here he switches to song. 'See Him pile granite rocks into a mountain,' the notes falling in odd-numbered beats, thunder imparting portent to the words, 'hear Him call forth the sacred places – trees and rivers and kopjes.' Timothy's voice takes on qualities of the various animals with which Mwari populated the land, each shaping the existence of the other, and for a moment the world becomes clear to Gordon, and he is no longer a frightened child on the kitchen floor beneath a window that faces out on an endless universe of wind and lightning and pelting rain. Each story ends abruptly, with Timothy staring into Gordon's eyes, and then just as abruptly, another begins.

'*This is the story of the baboon who flattered himself that he was a man . . .*

'*Listen to how a barren woman took a guinea fowl as her son . . .*

'*Here is a story of how the diviner died and became a leopard . . .*'

Because they lived in trees, Timothy considered leopards to be mediators between this world and the other.

Mahulda tells stories of her childhood in Cape Town beside the faraway sea, and Gordon lies at her feet on floorboards that smell of kelp, lavender and birds. Once she spoke of her lost child, and Gordon imagined himself stillborn in the hospital room while Mahulda rocked him in her arms, and he became lost in the soft voice, the quiet of hands that reached down and stroked his forehead.

The thunder ceases, green shoots unfurl, and shafts of light pierce the clouds, 'a God sky,' Mahulda calls it. Timothy plants rukweza seed in the muck beside his shed. While he works, he tells Gordon about the lisping half-beasts who roam the garden each midnight.

Gordon searches for spoor left by these unformed creatures who, like him, exist in the margins between this world and the next. He places his bare foot inside one of the half-beast's pugmarks.

'You have the same footprint,' Timothy says, laughing. He picks the husk of an empty cocoon from a leaf, stoops, tastes the soil. 'The rukweza has germinated.'

'Who taught you to be a gardener?' the boy asks.

'It is a birthgift.'

Then comes a day when a band of landless Shona sweep through the glen, sowing thorn seed in the English country gardens and lawns where once grew brewing grains and cattle grasses. The men are remnants of a broken clan relocated to the trust land after their ancestral homestead was taken away. They beat Timothy when he tries to stop them.

'Why do these men want to ruin your garden?' Gordon asks when the gardener comes bleeding into the kitchen.

Timothy winces as Mahulda straightens his broken nose, and the damaged cartilage crunches like ground glass. 'These men need no reasons,' he says, his voice adenoidal. 'They do it only.' During the weeks that follow, Timothy tries to uproot the sprouting thorns sowed by the trust land Shona, but their tendrils snake across the flowerbeds, choking the cosmos.

Fresh produce begins to appear in the trust land market stalls. Mahulda hands the boy a woven basket and leads him up the mountain, only to be turned away at the entrance. 'Filthy place to bring a white child,' Constable Teasdale tells Mahulda. A vendor stares at them over the spectrum of cucumber, melon, tomatoes and miracle fruit arranged on his table in bands of colour. Mahulda enfolds Gordon's hand in hers, both acutely aware of the contrast in their skin, and they carry their empty baskets back down the mountain in silence.

Butterflies cease their forage and bees swarm to form new hives, a sign for Timothy to reap the rukweza and brew the harvest beer. The winds shift, peeling back the mountain mists, caterpillars wrap themselves in silk, and stems bow with the weight of their fruit.

Gordon had been born in the waiting: a cold, arid time. Such children are said to come into the world reluctantly, with good reason.

Near the end of the season, a blind diviner wanders the glen, guided by her son. In the days before the trust land, Shona farmers paid her to predict the next rains and the destinies of their children. Timothy holds Gordon before her foamy eyes.

'Let us see what God has woven into his future,' the doorstep diviner says. She gathers the bones in her beautiful hands and casts them into a tray.

Her fingers pass lightly over the yellowed surfaces. 'What's this?' The blind woman seems perplexed. 'This child is also a seer, but of a different sort.' She rises to leave. 'Bad luck for one diviner to read the destiny of another.'

Timothy hands her a dollar and the woman sighs. Her hand finds Gordon's face, tracing its contours. 'A diviner's future always comes as a riddle,' she says. Gordon bites down on the slender fingers and shakes his head viciously. Timothy pinches the child's nostrils as the woman struggles and still Gordon clenches his teeth, refusing to open his mouth even to breathe.

‘Hah!’ the diviner says when she finally pulls free. She waves her hand like it’s on fire, and the boy twists in the gardener’s grasp.

‘Before this child’s story ends,’ she cants, ‘he will be twice born and twice orphaned, twice baptised and twice buried!’ Such is the nature of diviners. It takes a good bite for them to speak one’s true destiny.

The earth dries and shrinks beneath an empty sky, snakes emerge from the long grass to warm themselves in the sun, and the glen shudders atop the earthworks of the universe, the terrible worm at its work below.

* * *

At the other end of his life, three miles beneath the dark, hot earth, Gordon would recite these words, turning over each storified memory. The rains. The harvest. The waiting. For as long as they lived, Mahulda and Timothy would keep Gordon safe inside this cocoon of seasons, and in his child’s mind, they would live forever.

# *Backmilk*

Commencement Day, 1957

*I WAS BORN FACING HEAVEN, AND MY NOSE CAUGHT ON my mother's cervix, arresting my progress into a larger world and turning what promised to be an easy labour into thirteen hours of unmedicated suffering for the woman.* She moaned with each contraction, low at first, then rising in an excruciating glissando.

Blood soaked through the blankets and cushions, filling the cracks in the floorboards. The servant had insisted on a kitchen birth, citing its access to hot water, proximity to the linen closet, and cleanable surfaces.

Mrs Gordon's husband stood by, and her housekeeper gently spoke advice between contractions, and the gardener looked in through the kitchen window as he pruned the bougainvilleas. But at the height of her pain, it seemed to Mrs Gordon that she was alone in Africa, and she stared without recognition at the faces surrounding her.

* * *

Mahulda Jane Braxton, who passed a sleepless night attending the home birth, would spend much of the next day scrubbing her mistress's blood from the walls and ceiling of the kitchen. She had immigrated to Rhodesia thirty-one years earlier to keep the house and cook for its inhabitants. Mr Gordon engaged her services when he acquired the bungalow through an inheritance. He liked to say the woman came with the house.

*I was delivered beneath the bungalow's corrugated iron roof in an isolated glen on the eastern frontier of Rhodesia, an unmade place where ancestors and diviners overruled the laws of physics.* It was a large bungalow with many doors, but Mahulda Jane Braxton attended to all the housekeeping, save for the setting and winding of clocks. She never thought to look at them, and the duty was given over to the gardener. She worked without complaint, even when called upon to sacrifice her free Sunday afternoon to assist in the home birth. The only requirement she placed upon her employers was that they address her by her full name. *It was she who sank her hands to the wrists between Mrs Gordon's legs and turned me in the womb, enabling me to be born alive.*

Mahulda Jane Braxton began lactating spontaneously at the sound of the baby's cry, a surprise as she was approaching her fiftieth year.

'It is a boy,' she said, absently. *Mahulda Jane Braxton*

*clamped a clothespin on the base of my umbilical cord and, with twice sharpened and twice boiled pruning shears, she cut the cord above the pin, severing me from my birth mother. She gave the appendage to the gardener to bury beneath a thorn bush tree for luck.*

'Push, Madam,' the servant told her employer. 'You must still expel the afterbirth.'

Mahulda Jane Braxton would later make this into a soup to help with the milk production. She'd been pregnant long ago, in Cape Town, but lost the baby during a parturition that scarred her uterus and left her barren. She asked to hold her stillborn child, rocking it in the dark labour room until she fell asleep and woke alone. Thereafter, Mahulda Jane Braxton carried a wisp of the baby's reddish hair in a sealed, heart-shaped locket. The matter had left her unable to distinguish one moment of her life from the next, and clock winding became a neglected duty.

Mahulda Jane Braxton's heart heaved as she placed the baby in Mrs Gordon's lap, and the ground quaked softly beneath the soles of her shoes, as if in sympathy. These tremors were a common occurrence, the residue of ancient, cataclysmic forces that had shaped the glen. The infant's screams hung in the disturbed air.

'He'll quiet when he's fed,' the housekeeper said,

unbuttoning her employer's blouse. 'A baby knows its mother through her milk.'

Mrs Gordon had laboured with all her strength to be rid of the child. Already more was expected of her. She drew out a breast, but the infant pursed its lips and turned away.

'Babies don't know how to nurse, Madam. He'll need to be taught.' Mahulda Jane Braxton gently squeezed the newborn's cheeks until his lips curved outward to form a seal around her employer's nipple.

Mrs Gordon chucked him under his chin, but still the child refused to suckle. She handed her son back to the housekeeper, and the gardener came into the kitchen and gathered the broken woman into his arms. She looked small and childlike as he carried her past the bloody table where Mahulda Jane Braxton was stripped to the waist, holding the baby. *If I'd been capable of focusing my filmy eyes, I might have seen the melancholy in my birth-mother's tight smile as I, still slick with serous fluid, latched onto her servant's nipple.*

Mahulda Jane Braxton looked down at the nursing child. His eyes were almond-shaped and they slanted downward at the corners, as did her own, and they shared the same broad, flat nose. *She broke the seal on the locket and matched the ginger wisp of her dead child's hair to mine. It was identical. Her milk was sweetish and tasted faintly like nutmeg, thin and tepid at first. But the backmilk was rich and hot, and I drank greedily.*

* * *

Mr Gordon was a successful furniture merchant who, for nine months, had closeted himself in his study, keeping his accounts and avoiding his gravid wife. As Mrs Gordon bore down on her final contraction, he turned his back on the spectacle of his son's birth. Proximity to nature discomfited him.

Following the child's refusal of its mother's milk, Mr Gordon directed the gardener to remove his wife to the master bedroom. He drew the curtains, put out the light, and closed the door on her. She would remain in that darkened room until her death nineteen years later.

Mr Gordon stood over his servant, waiting for the infant to complete its suckle so that he could bring it to his study for a careful inspection and, if necessary, smother it with the leather arm pillow from his reading chair.

The child seemed pink enough, and its eyes were navy. But that proved nothing, as all humans are born with blue eyes. He craned his neck to see if the infant had Negroid features. Its nose was broad and flat above Mahulda Jane Braxton's nipple.

His sharp intake of breath was audible.

'All babies have such noses,' the servant woman told him, 'so they can breathe while they nurse.' She unnerved Mr Gordon with her ability to read his thoughts. Though he considered public nursing unseemly, he couldn't resist angling for a better view to see if the child possessed any atavistic traits.

Mahulda Jane Braxton covered breast and baby with a receiving blanket and gave him a reproachful look. She wasn't embarrassed, but there was something menacing in Mr Gordon's stare. For three decades she'd witnessed her nephew's attempts to slough off all traces of his ancestry. Every other Wednesday he would disappear into town to have the kink removed from his brownish-red hair, though there remained at the base of his neck the telltale curl no chemical could straighten.

When the child finished nursing, Mr Gordon reached to take it. Muhulda Jane Braxton was uneasy with the way he grasped at the infant, the glint in his eye. She instinctively drew the baby closer to her chest.

'I'll take it now,' he said.

Mahulda Jane Braxton held the child fast.

'Leave off, woman!' Mr Gordon said, snatching the baby away. Although the child carried no outward traces of its African ancestry, Mr Gordon saw his Xhosa grandmother staring back at him through slit eyes. He decided that his son would be a chrisom child. Two generations of Gordons had enjoyed the rewards of passing for white, guarding their lineage against even their own wives, until fear overshadowed the secret itself. Mr Gordon looked upon the infant as he would a bush pig that was raiding his garden.

'That'll be all, Mahulda Jane Braxton,' he told his servant when she tried to follow him into his study.

Mahulda Jane Braxton nodded doubtfully. She was forbidden to enter the study, except when her employer went into Umtali to tend his furniture business, and she would dust the shelved books – *Specimens of American Poetry With Critical and Biographical Notices, The Life and Virtuous Deeds of Saint Augustus of Hippo, Historae Romanae Brevarivm, Readings for the Railways, Primitive Copper Mining, Death of a Hero* – volumes chosen more for their crushed gilt edges, polished calf bindings and engraved frontispieces, than for their content. After tidying the study, she'd open a book at random and read until she heard footsteps.

Mahulda Jane Braxton could guess why her employer had insisted on a home birth. *She paced the hallway for almost a full minute before entering the study, thereby saving my life twice in as many hours.*

*The following night, while the Shona celebrated my birth outside the bungalow, Mr Gordon dragged his bed into the study so he could work late without disturbing his wife's recovery, a sleeping arrangement that would persist for the duration of their life together.* He closed the study window against the incessant singing, the heat of the bonfire, the stink of roasting goat, and he opened a ledger, its cover embossed '*Third Quarter, Fiscal Calendar Year 1957*'. Therein he pencilled the expenses related to his son's birth: a receiving blanket; a nursing brassiere; booties, onesies and nappies; a mobile of carved leopards. A line is drawn through the cost of a dozen roses budgeted for Mrs Gordon but never purchased. *These entries would provide the only written record of my early existence.*

* * *

For three decades Mahulda Jane Braxton had ignored the young Shona men who waited for her at the trust land market on Thursdays when she came to buy produce for the house. She refused to respond unless addressed by her full name, and so kept herself at a distance.

Timothy, the humpback Shona who kept the garden and wound the clocks, thought her haughty and intimidating and beautiful. On the rare moments when she wasn't bustling around the house, he observed her staring into another time, her hand at the locket that hung around her neck. He spoke to her only on Fridays when he asked permission to clean his cages in her laundry sink.

The gardener supplemented his income by stealing bush babies away from their mothers during the day while they slept in the trees. Despite his hump, Timothy could scale an acacia swiftly and silently. The garden shed where he lived was piled with cages filled with bush babies waiting to be smuggled to England where they would grace country gardens. The animal was popular for its enormous eyes and its cry that resembled a human baby weeping. 'There now,' he'd say, staring into a bush baby's wet eyes while it wrapped its tail around his wrist and nursed from a bottle of goat's milk. Timothy fed half his bush babies ground glass before shipment to maintain a keen demand for the little creatures and to keep their prices high.

As he worked in his garden, Timothy often watched Mahulda Jane Braxton through the kitchen window. Something had halted the flow of life inside the woman.

'Why are you so hard, Mahulda Jane Braxton?' he asked one Friday as he scrubbed his cages.

Mahulda Jane Braxton stiffened. She did not look at him as she lighted the paraffin stove. 'It is not my intention to be so, Timothy.'

The Shona gardener nodded. He said nothing more, but on the following Tuesday, he began washing his cages in the laundry sink twice weekly, watching the beautiful Cape Town coloured with sidelong looks as she stared out into his garden.

Timothy had arranged the garden in such a way that at no time of the year would a stroller be out of sight or scent of a newly unfolded blossom. Canopies of flame trees, copper and burgundy msasa leaves, shocks of golden shower, pungent honeysuckle and the loud keening of insects assaulted visitors in violent waves of colour and smell and sound. Mr Gordon found the garden unbearable.

*In the second hour of my birth, the gardener heard loud voices coming from the study.* He began trimming along the bougainvillea toward the window. Mr Gordon's words floated out between the slats of the closed blinds. 'Nonsense! I was only arranging the cushion beneath the child's head.' Timothy detected fear in the voice.

'I know what I saw,' Mahulda Jane Braxton stated flatly.

'Don't get your head up, woman. I'll not have you slandering me, d'you hear?'

The voices moved out of the study, and Mahulda Jane Braxton appeared on the verandah, followed closely by Mr Gordon. Timothy's head retreated deeper into his hump as he cut at the bougainvillea. He could see her in his peripheral vision as she settled into the rocking chair with the baby.

Mahulda Jane Braxton was thankful for Timothy's presence. 'I have no interest in speaking of this matter further,' she told Mr Gordon. 'The baby needs milk and quiet now. I'll care for him until Mrs Gordon is herself again, no worries.' The housekeeper unbuttoned her blouse, fully aware of the discomfort it caused her employer.

Mr Gordon turned away as his servant nursed his child. A stick bug crawled up his trouser leg and he slapped at it. The gardener stopped shearing the bougainvillea and stared openly at him. Mr Gordon's gaze travelled over the throbbing aberrance of the grounds, a Christmas beetle's high-pitched sawing in his ears, and he retreated to his study to rework his accounts

Timothy bustled in the flowerbed closest to the kitchen while Mahulda Jane Braxton made a soup from the placenta to help with her milk.

*Between the two of them I was never left alone, and thus the matter of my upbringing was settled. The day after my birth Timothy slaughtered a goat, and Shona servants from the neighbouring mission came to the garden to drink whip beer under a galaxy of pulsing stars. They sang as they drank, weaving ever-changing patterns around a simple chant in spontaneous six-part harmony, welcoming me into this world.*

* * *

*On the evening of my birth, Mahulda stared at the curve of my cheek against the larger curve of her breast as she rocked on the verandah. She gently nudged me beneath my chin each time I fell asleep at the nipple.* In the darkness of the garden, a mother bush baby wailed for her stolen child locked away in one of Timothy's cages. Milk leaked from Mahulda's free breast at the sound of it. Her breasts had begun forming early, even before she menstruated, and yet it wasn't until that moment, nearly forty years later, that she fully appreciated their function.

She sang a nonsense song from her childhood: *What would you do if the kettle boiled over? What would I do but to fill it again?*

She heard the tick of the grandmother clock in the parlour.

*And what would you do if the cows ate the clover?* A roller lighted in the branches of a flame tree.

*What would I do but to set it again?* Mahulda's finger traced a fine vein on her baby's cheek.

*A rout the da doubt the da diddly da dum.*

A cat ambled onto the verandah, its tail curling around Mahulda's ankle. Moths made shifting patterns in the aura of the pressure lamp. *A rout the da doubt the da diddly da dum.*

Her baby's face fell away from her nipple, glassy-eyed and sated. *Da diddly da dee da dee da dum.*

Milk dripped from Mahulda's breast as she paced the verandah. Each drop struck the floorboards with the regularity of a timepiece.

*Da diddly da dee da diddly da dum.* Mahulda stepped slowly, savouring each new moment. The cat followed in her steps, lapping.

A tremor rippled through the glen, startling the roller out of the flame tree. The child released a milky belch. *These memories flowed into my blood with the backmilk. Or perhaps it's only me, storytelling. I lay in my mother's arms, suspended between the corporeal and spirit worlds, and we remained that way until sleep came upon us.*

# *Acknowledgements*

My deepest appreciation to Neil Connelly, the savviest reader on the planet; to Rikki Clark, my sounding board; and to Rorrie Clark, my ginger-haired muse. Also many thanks to Tom Avery, Isobel Dixon, Ben George and Michael Vasquez for their edits, advice and support. Without their help, this book would be a shadow of itself.